DERANGED

**Edited by David Owain Hughes &
Jonathan Edward Ondrashek**

ISBN 978-0-578-62161-6

Contents

DOGFACED EVE

BY ANTONIO SIMON, JR.

Everyone wants to be the alpha male
until it's time to do alpha male shit.

The moment he'd perfected the angles he was falling headlong through the sigil he'd drawn. Where once there had been a floor there had opened a yawning gulf into blackness. Gravity had done the rest. Before he could react, he was hurtling through time, space, and God knew what else, crashing into a sand dune. This was all very wrong for several reasons, not least of which was that up until then he had been sitting in his twelfth-floor apartment in the midst of a Colorado snowstorm. The last place he had expected to find himself shunted to was a sunny beach. But magick was a fickle thing, and however grudgingly it did one's bidding, it always sought creative ways to fuck people over.

That was a year ago—correction: a year from when he'd started counting, assuming time here passed similarly to how it did on Earth. In that time, he'd built a thatch shelter where the rainforest ended and the beach sand began.

He'd also discovered he wasn't alone.

When he'd first arrived, he'd ventured from the beach to seek help. He found none, but his trek across the island allowed him to get his bearings. The beach where he'd made his home was on the island's east side. Traveling west put him in the woods. The ground rose steeply beyond that into a plateau of balmy grassland that stretched to the cliffs ringing the island's far end.

It was in the fields that he saw her.

The sun had already begun to dip behind the western crags, its burnished bronze glow giving the illusion that the expanse of swaying tall grass was ablaze. Off in the distance he'd seen a human silhouette shimmering like a heat mirage. He'd cupped his eyes against the glare for a better look into the horizon. It *was* another person, her pair of trim thighs slightly apart as she stood rigidly at attention, surveying the prairie.

"Hey!" he'd shouted, waving his arms over his head.

He knew he'd been heard when her silhouette shifted in his direction; but what he didn't expect was that she'd drop to all fours and begin sprinting toward him so fast that great dust clouds started billowing up in her wake. He'd turned and run like hell into the safety of the thicket. When he'd heard the thrashing of undergrowth in the wake of her pursuit, he shimmied up a tree and sat on a bough, curled up in fetal position to get as much of him away from her as possible.

The thrashing had slowed, then stopped as his pursuer halted in her tracks. Then there had come a wet snuffling sound as she sniffed the air.

Crunch—branches snapped under her tread.

Crunch—another cautious step.

Pause.

Sniff.

Crunch.

A leg clad in brown fur boots cleared the branches obstructing his view below. She advanced a step. He could only see her from the waist up, but more of her came into view as she stalked closer to his tree. The fur boots stretched up her calves, her thighs, her flanks, across her belly, onto her pair of bare breasts—

He drew an alarmed gasp when he saw her for what she was. Down below was a naked woman, except a hyena's coarse brown pelt had sprouted all over her body. She stood erect without difficulty despite her legs being decidedly canine, with her knees bending backward as a dog's might if it stood on its hind legs. Dewclaws sprouted from just above the major joints in her limbs. Her fingers were short and clubbed—rudimentary

2

hands but effective nonetheless, as evidenced by the crude spear in her grip. The rough-hewn flint that served as a spear tip was caked with dried blood.

She plodded forward and raised her chin, searching him out. Her wet, black nose was squashed into a shaggy face that was part dog, part bear, and all teeth. Her predatory eyes darted about—wherever she turned her head to sniff the air her eyes followed soon after.

And then she spotted him.

Her flashing eyes locked on him for a heartbeat, and then she threw back her head and let out a rapid-fire yipping. He shimmied in his tree, pressing his back to the trunk in an effort to put more space between him and her, it—whatever that was down on the forest floor.

She yipped again, true to her hyena nature, high-pitched and ululating, sounding almost like human laugher. Almost. There was no mirth in her cackle, and her snapping jaws spoke of her intent. She wanted him for dinner, and that wasn't a euphemism.

He dug his heels into the bough, pushing backward, creeping up the trunk until he stood. Once on his feet, he was at a loss for what to do next.

She decided for him. The hyena woman hurled her spear like a javelin. The pointed stick split the air, whistling before crashing into the trunk just beneath him. She'd undershot her mark, but it served her purposes all the same. He jerked instinctively when the spear went airborne, lost his balance and spilled out of the tree.

He tumbled fifteen feet to the forest floor, breaking the fall with his arms. The soft ground accepted his weight, dampening the blow, leaving him more dazed than hurt but still too stunned to move. His senses focused to razor clarity when he felt searching paws clutch at his body. She turned him over onto his back. Out of reflex he shielded his face with his arms. She batted them away and squatted atop his hips, upper torso primed to catapult her jaws in a parabolic arc for his throat.

She hooked her stumpy fingers into his waistband and tugged at his pants. He took a wild swipe at her but she caught his wrist in one paw and rammed his forearm into his screaming mouth. Her other paw yanked furiously at his pants until the button popped free of its eyelet. The zipper drew apart under her repeated assault. In moments, his pants were halfway down his thighs, exposing his crotch. The prospect of imminent death and the friction of all this excitement had given him an inadvertent erection.

She paused, head lowered, eyes locked on his member, and gave a sigh that bowed her shoulders. It sounded like the anticipatory breath from an exhausted marathon runner who had spied the finish line ahead. Then she snapped her eyes back into position with his and bared her fangs, lips pulled back beyond her gum line.

He bumped his hips up to pitch her off him but she sat down hard, crushing his pelvis into the ground. He wheezed, feeling like a fresh tube of toothpaste that had been crumpled in a person's fist. That knocked the fight out of him—he could do little else but watch with glassy eyes as she readied her jaws for a pass at his jugular.

She raised her haunches off him. What looked like a dead black python drooped between her legs—a tail?—and swung in metronomic rhythm like a grandfather clock's pendulum.

Oh my God! his panicked mind quailed on noticing it was her penis, but the follow-up to that thought was what actually tore the scream from his lips: she had a penis, and she meant to use it *on him*.

Before he could react, she rammed her appendage into his crotch. The black length of hose between her legs accepted his member into itself and then cinched, forming a tight seal around the base of his root and at all points in between. She threw herself into him, hooking her elbows beneath his armpits and her forearms around the back of his head, smashing his face into her perky pair of furry breasts, each only a small handful in size. Her coarse pelt felt like a copper scouring pad against his exposed flesh as she rutted like a bitch in heat, her pelvis jackhammering a fast staccato rhythm against him. She lifted him off the ground each time she pulled back; he plowed a little deeper into the dirt

4

with each thrust. His arms flailed under her, groping blindly for purchase and finding none, fingers threading though fur too short to latch onto.

His hand closed around her ear and he tugged on it hard, yoking her head aside. She snaked an arm free and socked him in the ribs. His eyes bulged from their sockets. She was taller than he was by a head and deceptively stronger than her trim body had let on. And the stink—dear Lord! Her body reeked of wet dog and sun-dried carrion. He was certain that if he survived this, he could never scrub that reek from his pores.

An involuntary shudder racked his frame. His biology reacted in the manner that could be expected of it—instinct would not be denied. Her body tensed in anticipation as he blew his load. He hardly realized he'd come until his body slackened, drooping into an exhausted, bloodied heap. It hurt to move. It hurt to even *think* of moving.

She rose off him and walked away, returning a moment later with her spear in hand.

This is it, he thought. She'd had her fun and was going to have him as her after-sex snack.

Bitch, make me a sandwich, he thought.

He supplied her response: *Bitch, you* are *the sandwich.*

He lacked the energy to scream as she drove her spear point into the side of his belly; what left his mouth was more akin to an exhausted groan. It was a shallow poke, a half-inch into the skin, but what she did next left him flummoxed. She raised the spear point to her mouth and lapped at it until it was clean of his blood. She took her time with it, savoring it, in no apparent hurry (not that he could do anything to stop her if she tried that again). Her tongue flicked at the oozing blood on her weapon like a kid eating ice cream in summer, or—he shoved this next thought aside, but it trickled into his conscious mind regardless—like those girls in softcore porn who eat bananas far more enthusiastically than necessary.

She yipped three times in rapid succession, paused a beat, then did it again.

Yip-yip-yip.

Yip-yip-yip.

She was laughing at him—laughing!—at her latest conquest, and he, he . . .

A subconscious part of him refused to admit the truth.

He'd been raped.

The thought sifted through his reeling mind like pudding through a sieve. Understanding crashed down onto him a heartbeat later.

She'd *raped* him!

Hate surged in his breast, first at the outrage, then at the consequences. His mind went flying through possibilities of how very sick he might be now. That bitch, that cunt, that . . . that *whore*! Bad as she stank, she could have had any number of venereal diseases, which said nothing of what he might have contracted when she jabbed him with that filthy spear.

He rocked his head forward in a half-assed attempt to sit up but couldn't manage it. His chest was on fire with angry red chafe marks, feeling like someone had taken fine-grit sandpaper to his torso and looking every bit the part. Changing tack, he flung an arm across his trunk and used its momentum to roll onto his front. Noticing this, she took a hesitant step back, then scampered away into the safety of the brush.

That'd been a year ago. Since then, he'd burned for revenge. That dog-faced bitch needed to die.

She was cunning. Grudgingly, he'd give her that. She knew how to ambush, as she reminded him each time she got horny— their initial rendezvous hadn't been their only one. There were times she'd hunt him down two or three times a week, each time ending the same as the first. Each time he came away with her stink on his body. It felt like no sooner had he washed her musk off him, she'd find him again and give him an extra helping.

He wondered if she was part skunk—given what he'd experienced thus far, he was in no position to shut out possibilities, no matter how outlandish. Her musk was heady and persistent. It'd ruined his clothes, which he'd long since forgone as a lost cause, opting to go naked.

When it came to cleaning his body, her stink withstood multiple seawater baths and would only somewhat dissipate when he scoured himself with beach sand and lay out to dry under the sun. Her aroma hung in his nostrils even after he was certain he was clean. That part was all in his head, he knew—scents persisted in the mind even after the things that caused them were long gone, as he'd learned as a boy that summer he'd come upon a nest of rotten duck eggs their mother had abandoned.

This was perhaps what most infuriated him: it was bad enough she'd made him her bitch, but her stink reminded him of this when she wasn't around. Worse, he was half-certain she used that scent to guide her back to him.

His first order of business was to arm himself. He gathered supple branches and fashioned a bow and arrows out of them. The bow shot true within five feet—disappointing by any stretch, and effectively useless. He discarded that idea. If she could make a spear, so could he, and he'd make a better one.

He located a bamboo thicket growing beside a brook in the woods and snapped off a piece as big around as his thumb. Within the stream he found black stones—obsidian, he guessed—and whittled away at a largish piece until what was left was a steep isosceles triangle with honed edges. He collected the brown fiber that fell from the coconut trees and tore it into strips of thread which he used to tie the obsidian onto the haft of his spear. By the time he was done, his weapon stood taller than he.

Mine's bigger than yours, he could not help but think. It was a point of pride for him.

While his new weapon helped his odds, it did not even the playing field. She possessed the advantages of superior senses, strength, and speed. The spear was a weapon of last resort, as he still would have little chance against her if they went toe-to-toe. If he really wanted her dead, he would have to catch her unawares, get at her before she had a chance to fight back, ambush her like she'd done to him countless times. This was poetic justice in its rawest form.

He grinned at the prospect.

He observed her clandestinely for the better part of half a year, making sure to keep downwind of her so she would not detect his presence. The island wasn't terribly large, but pinpointing her den proved slow-going. He knew her burrow lay in the prairie, but the land there offered no natural markers. Simply getting around without losing his sense of place was difficult.

After weeks of tracking, he was fairly certain he'd found her home. Hidden behind a tuft of tall grass was a natural burrow. It was little more than a geological freak of nature that spoke of the island's volcanic origins. At the center of a patch of rocky ground was a cave mouth that rose about thirty degrees from horizontal. The opening was tight; it gave her trouble shimmying inside. She had to crouch and go headfirst through it, then work her shoulders past before disappearing within.

This much he observed from ten yards away; he dared not come closer. He was ill-prepared, and to charge in now would be taking a needless risk with no chance of success. Cautiously, he made his retreat, confident he could find the burrow again going on memory alone.

He'd learned other things about her too—she hunted day and night, but was least active in the late afternoon, just before sunset. That played in his favor, as he'd be approaching from the east, the dark side of the island, and the sun would have sunk behind the western cliffs.

The day finally came when he'd strike her when she'd be most vulnerable. He sat in his thatch shelter, waiting for the sun to dip below the horizon, all the while envisioning his plan of attack. What if things went badly? She'd kill him. Animals were most dangerous when cornered, and ambushing her where she bedded down would surely result in her killing him if he didn't kill her first. He accepted this, along with the prospect that even if he did succeed, he might come out of it maimed. Eventual infection would take him, but he didn't care—he was too single-minded in his purpose to let such thoughts deter him.

He took a breath, eased it out his nostrils—do or die time—then stood and headed for the prairie.

Spear at the ready, he snuck through the forest, minding his footfalls. All around him, insects called from places unseen. With his ears perked for the slightest sign of her approach, the forest's noises seemed louder. Crickets and cicadas chirped a bleating call and response that sounded like a distant fire alarm.

Alarm was the word—*danger, danger*, the insects chirped. The hair on his body stood on end in anticipation.

He slipped through the woods without incident and stopped short of the prairie. He'd arrived right on time—the western sky was ablaze in maroons and wine purples. It offered him enough light to see by, but not for much longer. He'd have to hurry to catch her still in her burrow.

Stooped over to keep a low profile in the grass, he stalked across the flatlands. Before him was the cave mouth at the center of the rocky clearing. Braced against his spear, he crouched onto his haunches, keeping a lookout for her from the grass at the clearing's fringe. He held his breath and shut his eyes, listening closely for sounds of activity. Faint shuffling noises rose from within the burrow.

A grin stole across his face. She had to come out sometime. He'd be ready for her when she did.

He retreated a step at the sound of raspy breathing. The noises coming from the cave sounded like a dog panting at the end of a vigorous walk. Her head popped out of the hole as though the ground itself were giving birth to her. Struggling, she thrashed her body one way, then the other, freeing her shoulders. Then came her waist and finally her hips, and she was clear of the hole, scrabbling for purchase on the rocky soil. With all the trouble it gave her, he figured the cave mouth sloped in such a way that made it harder to exit than to enter.

She stood and stretched her limbs, looking all too human as she did so, and this gave him pause. What he was about to do was tantamount to murder. He shook these notions from his head. It was only murder if you killed another human being and—more importantly—if you were caught. Circumstances on the island gave him carte blanche to act as he pleased.

Her ears stood straight up like sails. She angled her face skyward to sniff at the air. He took another step back then sidled crabwise, shifting out of her line of sight. She sensed someone was near, but by her expression she looked unsure of who it might be and where they might be hiding. He smiled inwardly at this; those hours scrubbing his skin to rid himself of her funk had paid off.

She took a cautious step forward, sniffed, looked back toward her burrow and set her eyes forward again. He read her like a book—she sensed danger but was unsure of whether to face it or go back into her den.

He aimed his spear for the small of her back, took a deep breath, and charged out of the bush, screaming his throat raw. She wheeled in place but froze on seeing him, only darting aside at the last minute. The spear missed its target, plunging instead into the back of her shoulder. He let his momentum carry him past her. His weapon spilled out of his hands as she tumbled sideways. He lost his balance and face-planted to the ground, did a quick push-up to stand.

She, too, was back on her feet, her torso slumped toward her injured side. The spear had impaled her from back to front, its point jutting out of her shoulder blade. Its length prevented her from standing erect—the shaft's blunt end lay on the ground and this wrenched her upper body lopsided.

Before she could react, he took a running leap and plowed his foot into her midsection. She crumpled in on herself as she hurtled backward, landing on her ass, the force of his kick casting her onto her back with her legs in the air. She came to rest lying supine, one shoulder on the ground and the other propped up by the spear, looking like a lean-to shelter. She kicked at the ground, attempting to turn over, but the spear's haft was anchored in the dirt and kept her from shifting her weight.

While she was by no means helpless, she was no longer a threat. In the position she was in, he could subdue her without much effort.

As she lay on the ground snarling at him with canines bared, the thought crossed his mind that he could revenge-rape her. This time, he'd be the one in control, not her! He'd get her back for all the times she abused him, pin her down and grind his hips into her until he fucked her so brain-dead she'd forget how to even walk, assuming he didn't dislocate her hips in the process. And if he did, too fucking bad, that was her problem. And afterward he'd cut off her hyena girl dick or whatever the fuck that thing was—he hated that goddamn thing—and toss it to the sharks. That'd show her! The thought of all the awful things he'd do to her made his dick rock hard.

He plodded toward her, sneering, cracking his knuckles in anticipation. He was a foot shy of her when she whipped her neck around to face the cave mouth and let up a wavering trill. The urgency in her voice stopped him cold; this was not a cry of fear or despair but—and the thought of it got his blood up—one of warning. He leapt back, eyes flying to all corners in search of hidden dangers but just as quickly setting back on the cave mouth. A head popped out of the burrow's entrance—a young hyena hybrid, its face covered in patchy tan fur. It wriggled its lithe body out of the hole with ease and stood beside its mother.

This was another female, young but well along in coming into her own. Her smallish pair of breasts—B-cups, if he had to wager—were tight, mostly lean muscle but unmistakably feminine. She watched him with flashing yellow irises that were too big for her face.

He returned her gaze, his body tensed for action. Movement from out of the corner of his eye snagged his attention. From the burrow came another hyena girl, and yet another, streaming out of the cave mouth one at a time like children on a particularly busy playground slide. They all looked the same age, as though momma hyena had birthed them in the same litter.

Arrayed in a half-moon with their backs to the cave, the daughters stood mute, their faces expressionless. He took a tentative step back. He was outnumbered six to one. Even if he were still armed, he'd have no chance against all of them at once.

Yip-yip-*groan*-yip.

11

The mother's laughter sounded too human to be denied now, and it went too well with the knowing sneer playing on her face for it to be dismissed as a mere animal cry. The message was clear: just who had ambushed who?

The first daughter advanced a step. There was something about the look she gave him, a bizarre glimmer in her eyes that wasn't there when first he'd seen her. It looked terribly out of place on her canine face and yet it was universally recognizable. That look, those *bedroom eyes*, spoke of animalistic rutting that would leave them both covered in scrapes, bruises, and stink. It was the same expression on her mother's face the first time she'd attacked him.

The next thought hit him like a sledgehammer: could these be *his* daughters? He had no idea what a hyena's gestation period was—let alone a hyena woman's—and nary an inkling of how long they took to mature, but by the looks of the young one, she was ready for him and she knew it.

"No," he choked out as the weight of all these realizations crashed onto him.

His hesitation bought the daughters all the opportunity they needed. The lead girl sprang on the balls of her feet, legs spread and arms extended, looking to snare him like a living net. He put out his hand and stiff-armed her in the snout, turning her aside as he spun away. Another daughter pounced on him from behind and he rolled with the impact, reaching up to grab her by the scruff of her neck and flinging her off him as her momentum carried her forward.

No sooner had he tossed her aside than a third grabbed his arm and tugged, setting him off balance. He pulled against her but lost his footing on the stony ground, his legs sliding out beneath him, pitching him onto his side. He broke the fall with his opposite hand and got up, but he wasn't yet steady on his feet when another daughter yanked his leg out from under him, dropping him onto the flat of his back.

The daughters grabbed him by his limbs and lifted him off the ground like a roast pig tied to a barbeque spit. Screaming, he thrashed against them but could not break free of their grasp.

12

They rotated him so that his head was in the lead as they angled his body down into the cave mouth. His shoulders were too wide to fit. They drew back and charged in, plowing the tops of his shoulders into the lip of the cave as though he were a medieval battering ram bashing down a reinforced door.

Pain spiked across his back and along his spine with each impact, until at last he felt something in his left shoulder pop. There was a wet ripping sound from within his chest as the tendons anchoring his arm in place strained, then tore. His shoulder broke free of its moorings and dislocated, flopping uselessly at his side, the ball of its joint floating down by his ribcage. With it out of the way, his body slid further into the den.

He howled as fresh hurt flooded his nerves; his cries of pain echoed within the tight confines of the burrow. He was in up to his waist now, and he knew that if they got him in all the way there would never be any getting back out.

He jerked his legs up, breaking free of the daughters' grasp, and plowed his heels into the turf. Pulling with his legs and shimmying on his ass, he inched backward out of the hole. A hammerblow of explosive hurt stopped him cold. Something like an anvil had descended onto his knee, crushing the kneecap, stretching his tendons until they snapped like over-tightened guitar strings. His right leg had been snapped in two at the joint; the tip of his big toe scraped the top of his thigh.

He clenched his eyes shut and screamed, hardly noticing as the rest of him was shoved through the hole into the den. There was barely enough room to lie flat. His back hooked like a parenthesis as the ground beneath him demanded, and his legs were partway bent, his thighs short of vertical. He rocked forward to sit up but scraped his forehead against the den's ceiling—there were at best two feet of airspace between his head and its top.

He strained his eyes to open and saw the cave mouth above him, beyond his feet. The aperture let in just enough waning daylight to see outlines within the burrow. Then this too was snuffed as a body squeezed through the hole and wriggled up

13

next to him, followed by another, and yet another, until all light was drowned out by the press of furry, reeking bodies.

Each draw of hot, stale air filled his lungs with the scent of flyblown carcasses. He gagged, then threw up a little but managed to swallow his spew. He felt like a shirt at the bottom of a laundry basket piled high with used jockstraps after spring training.

Their bodies writhed against his, undulating like the waves, throbbing, pulsing, humping every inch of him with orgiastic fervor, their coarse fur scouring his naked flesh raw until it was slippery with his blood. One of them caught hold of his erect member and shuffled to position herself atop his hips. In the next instant she was thrusting into his pelvis with her inside-out hyena parts, impaling herself on his shaft as much as jabbing him with hers.

Mustering what little strength he had left, he tightened the muscles in his lower torso to clamp shut the pipes before instinct did what it did best. It was a losing tactic—he held out for a few seconds before his body stiffened and his hips rocketed upward into her, pressing her against the den's ceiling. She yelped in surprise when her back smacked into the cave's top, then yip-yipped in triumph when she'd gotten what she'd come for.

She either slid free of him or was wrestled off his body when another slung herself onto him, pincering his flanks with her knees like a cowboy breaking a stallion. Her female parts cinched around his abused member with the suction of a fire hose on an open hydrant.

He groaned, breathless from the stench, his penis ultrasensitive from the non-stop sex. Then he crushed his eyes shut and sobbed, bawling openly and screaming for help. His shouts died in his throat, forced back down in a space filled to the last cubic inch with rutting hyenas.

This was the culmination of his existence: to be buried alive in this womb in the earth, relegated to filling hyena girls' bellies with babies, spawning them in litters of six at a time and breeding generations of them until they fucked him sterile or he died of exhaustion.

And yet part of him knew he would not be so lucky as to die prematurely. That part of him went flying up and away from him, across time, to envision the fruits of his coerced labors— the island stripped clean of anything remotely edible and packed to bristling with the heaving, stinking bodies of his hyena hybrid daughters. There'd be too many of them and not enough of him to go around. The combination of heavy inbreeding and their constant state of heat would drive them to fornicate with anything that moved in a mindless, fruitless effort to satisfy the biological imperative.

They'd breed themselves mentally defective, well past the point of being capable of caring for themselves, and they'd keep him alive long enough to see it happen. It'd take time, but he'd have his revenge, eventually.

And yet, he never did.

With each passing day, the hope for his eventual escape and vengeance waned along with his physical senses. The literal fuck-hole his body had been stashed inside of became the sum of his reality.

It was always pitch dark in the burrow, and thus his eyes stopped working. It made no difference if he kept them open or shut, and so he shut them so an errant tuft of fur or prodding finger wouldn't jab him in a socket.

In time, his ears became so accustomed to the drone of ragged breaths and messy sex sounds that he shut them out. As they were all he ever heard, his mind ignored them altogether.

Overstimulation caused the constantly firing nerves in his skin to quit. Numbness overtook sensation. How tough his skin had become from the constant chafing of fur on flesh practically foreclosed any chance he'd feel anything ever again. His body was a giant scab that had crusted over into a quarter-inch thick carapace of dried blood as knobby as an elephant's hide.

His sense of taste was shot from the pervasive reek of hyena bodies. The girls brought him food often enough, though he could never see what it was, let alone savor it as they rammed it into his mouth and massaged his throat to work the food into his gullet—sometimes even while they used him for the only function where he could still perform.

Smell went next. He regretted its departure, because it was the last thing that anchored him to any sort of existence. Once his nose had had enough of the ever-present stench, he was alone in a vacuum of nothingness.

His mind was the last thing to go, shattering with a resounding crack as shards of it went skittering off to all points on the compass.

His last conscious thought—when he was still capable of forming them—was on how he could no longer smell the hyena stink.

This had brought a wan smile to his face, not because he was at last free of their stench, but because now, after however many generations of hyena girls he had been with down in that hole, he smelled just like them. They had at last become like him, and he like them, and in this exchange, both sides had achieved whatever esoteric purposes the universe had laid out for them.

From somewhere deep within the most primal, reptilian part of his atrophied brainstem, he thought he felt something that faintly resembled pride, then his mind snuffed out like a guttering candle and he knew no more.

ABOUT THE AUTHOR
ANTONIO SIMON, JR.

Antonio Simon, Jr. is an award-winning multi-genre author, with several books and over thirty short stories published. His debut novel, *The Gullwing Odyssey*, was an instant hit, attaining the number five spot on Amazon's Kindle Bestsellers of 2014. He is one of the founders of Darkwater Syndicate, an independent publisher in Miami, Florida, and has been involved in the company's operations since its inception in 2008.

Twitter: @DrkWtrSyndicate

Facebook: https://www.facebook.com/DarkwaterSyndicate

Webpage: http://www.DarkwaterSyndicate.com

RIPPINGS

BY SARAH CANNAVO

The first time it happened she was thirteen, tagging along with her older sister Lisa and a few of Lisa's friends on a Friday-night trip to the movies. Allison Lambe knew her sister was tolerating her presence mostly so their mom wouldn't bitch at her, and she herself had little interest in the movie—*House of Wax*—one way or another, especially since all Lisa & Co. would be doing was squealing at all the gross parts and groping each other when the girls pretended to be too freaked out to look anymore. But it beat hanging out around the house and Mom'd given her money for popcorn and soda, so Allison got her ticket ripped and plopped down in the squeaky theater seat (which'd been crimson once but had been darkened to a cheap wine color by years of asses and spilled drinks), ready to kill ninety minutes.

But as the cadre of dumbfuck teens wandered deeper into the psycho brothers' wax museum, Allison noticed something coming over her that had little to do with the movie and everything to do with the wax itself: a strange flush that shortened her breath and found an epicenter between her legs, startling and sharp but also somehow pleasant. And when the cute guy from *Gilmore Girls* got it, stripped naked, strapped down, and covered in hot melted wax, the feeling flooded her so strongly she gasped, but the friction only sent a new wave of sensation through her, crawling from her crotch up her spine, the nipples of her budding breasts stiffening beneath her tank top. Despite the cranked A/C she felt feverish, but not sick—thrilled with a flustering excitement each glimpse of bubbling wax stirred higher.

She knew what sex was; her mother had left a book about all that stuff, along with a maxi pad and a training bra, on her bed the day she got her first period. And an awakening part of her brain told her, in less than words, that was what this new pulse was connected to. However, this was different than reading the footnotes of a cartoonishly illustrated diagram, or even the flutters of feeling she got looking at Bryce Dillahey on the soccer field or Jake Gyllenhaal on her sister's posters. This was a rush, a power, a tingling ache, a sweet agony—completely and utterly baffling.

That night, alone in her bedroom, she masturbated for the first time, fumbling in the dark, feeling clumsy, unsure. But even so it felt too good for her to care, tongue between her teeth, recalling the thought of wax on skin, exorcising the ache that'd been trapped in her since the theater. Her eyes flew open, breath bursting from her lips like a moth escaping into her bedroom's blackness, strangling a cry in her throat lest she wake the household.

As she grew, Allison learned she wasn't alone: there was a flourishing subculture of waxplay enthusiasts. She didn't bring her interests up to the first few boyfriends she slept with but kept cultivating them within herself. She didn't need her kink to have fun or get off, even once she started finding guys who were willing to indulge in it with her, but there was no denying that the splash of wax on skin, whether physical or in her fantasies, really got her going.

Which made for some interesting moments while she was finding her way, figuring out her edges, the intricacies of this wax-splattered web being woven around her. Like when the power went out one weekend while she was visiting her college roommate and she accidentally splashed herself with wax while moving a lit candle, only to be swarmed by her concerned roommate, who'd mistaken the dazed look on her face for pain. Or the first time she'd gotten a bikini wax and found herself getting wet when the technician spread the wax on her skin; embarrassment hadn't done much to dampen her arousal, and when she'd jerked on the table and cried out it hadn't all been in

19

pain, though the technician, thank God, hadn't seemed to notice. After that, Allison took to waxing her legs and bikini area at home—even looking forward to it, as she usually masturbated afterwards.

She knew other people would feel ashamed if they had something like this running beneath their skin, that they would expect her to be ashamed of it, too. But at this point in her life—twenty-six years old—she was comfortable with it, with herself and what she liked. "Some girls shop at Adam and Eve," she'd said once to her friend Vanessa with a shrug and smile. "I shop at Yankee Candle."

* * *

At least there was something in her life she was comfortable with, Allison thought, slumping over and drumming her fingers on her checkout counter, blowing a loose lock of brown hair out of her eyes with a huff of breath. Certainly her job left something to be desired. The pay was decent, which was why she hadn't quit, but slaving away eight hours a day in the Quik-Buy Superstore wasn't her idea of a dream job, just long stretches of routine boredom broken up by arguments with belligerent customers clutching expired coupons and possessing an odd sense of superiority. Topping it off, she had to face it all in a uniform management had apparently concocted from pieces of the worst uniforms available: navy blue polo shirt, red vest, khaki pants.

And her love life wasn't going much better. She and Shawn had broken up long enough ago that the relief of being single was again starting to wear thin, that the empty space beside her in bed she'd been stretching out in wasn't worth the chill. She missed having someone to bitch to after a long day, to laugh with over carryout pizza, to kiss awake on Sunday mornings. She missed having someone, pure and simple.

She sighed and shifted her weight from one aching foot to the other. She could feel her thoughts spiralling, what Vanessa, with her psychobabble shit, would call a cycle of negativity she'd

20

have to break if she ever wanted to attract positivity into her life. Allison wasn't sure if she believed that crap, no matter how many chattering daytime talk show hosts blathered it at her, but she knew dwelling on her life's current low points during the slow hell of a long shift only made her feel worse, as if someone had pulled her brain out and filled the gap with a pound of cotton wool. She sighed again but straightened when her eyes fell on a familiar customer turning into a nearby aisle.

Maybe today won't be such a shitshow after all.

Josephine, who worked in customer service, had said his name was Connor. The extent of Allison's interactions with him was announcing his totals, but no matter the day she was having, a sighting of him always brightened it. He was handsome in a solid, Jeremy Renner kind of way: brown hair, blue eyes, and an easy style Allison liked. Whenever she saw him, he usually wore jeans, boots, a T-shirt or plaid shirt, and a leather jacket, looking like someone she'd have fun with but could also bring home to her mother without getting looks shot at her across the dinner table—not that she based her love life on that, but it was always nice to avoid unnecessary conflict.

She supposed there was something of the creeper in drooling over a customer like she did Connor, but at least she didn't do it as obviously as Wendy the stocker did, or Arnold down at register nine. And anyway, what was the harm in looking? And daydreaming? At night, in bed, with her vibrator in hand?

She was also curious about him, admittedly, because of what he bought. She'd been seeing him for a few months now, and every few weeks or so, among his other purchases, he always loaded up on candles of various colors, shapes, sizes. There were a million reasons he might use so many, but that didn't keep the wheels in Allison's head from turning steadily in one direction. She sighed for the third time today as she lost sight of Connor. *A girl can dream, anyway.*

And at first she thought she was when, a few minutes later, she looked over and saw him heading toward her register; thought boredom had knocked her out at last and this was the start of one of those porn-movie dreams that would go in mere moments from banter to she and Connor painting each other with wax and fucking on the checkout conveyor in full sight of God and manager. But a glance down at herself dispelled that notion: she was still trapped in the terrible Quik-Buy uniform, not the skanktacular version she'd be wearing in a porn. She straightened up and prepared the usual banal chitchat that passed between clerk and customer.

"Find everything all right?"

"Yeah, thanks." He loaded his groceries on the belt and— yep, there they were: two packs of white taper candles, the kind normal people would use on a dinner table or during a power outage.

Allison would never be able to say what possessed her, but when she opened her mouth to comment on the rain that'd recently let up, what came out instead was, "Give a lot of candlelight dinners?"

He blinked. "Huh?"

She gestured at the items on the belt. "I couldn't help but notice you're always buying candles and figured you either lived somewhere the power's always going out or you have a lot of candlelight dinners." Before she could stop herself, she added, "Unless you *really* know how to show a girl a good time."

Oh, fuck. She could hear it already: the indignation, the outrage, the complaint to management if he was especially sensitive. *Congratulations, Allison. Have fun explaining this one at the next job interview.*

But Connor smiled, and her chest loosened. "The right kind of girl, maybe," he said, and Allison straightened up from her cringe, sculpted eyebrows arching. Connor chuckled, adding, "I'd make some sort of terrible 'if-you-can't-stand-the-heat' pun, but I don't know if that'd help or hurt my chances right now."

Allison laughed. "You're doing fine."

"Oh, good. I don't always do so well with this part of things."

His self-deprecation was endearing rather than the practiced bait several guys she'd known fished for compliments with, and

Allison's smile grew, along with her sense of dreamy incredulity. "Your talents lie elsewhere?"

"Some have told me so. You should see me juggle," he deadpanned.

"Maybe I will." She'd been ringing up his items as they talked—Quik-Buy training/brainwashing ran deep—and after the register churned out his receipt, she scribbled her name and number on the back of it.

He smiled again. "Does Friday work for you?"

"It does."

"Friday, then. My name's Connor, by the way. Connor Grant."

She handed him his last bag, the one containing the candles, accompanying it with a catlike curl of her lips. "Good thing you stocked up, huh, Connor Grant?"

"Isn't it, though?" He raised the candle bag to her as if in a toast as he walked away, and Allison's smile lingered as she watched him go, the automated doors parting to let him through. This time her sigh was of anticipation and not a little amazement. *What are the goddamn odds . . . ?*

Wendy the stocker sidled up, her hiss bringing Allison back to earth. "Did you just . . ."

"Yep."

Wendy gave her what passed for a playful shove. "Bitch."

Allison smirked. "I know."

* * *

Friday couldn't come fast enough. Neither, it seemed, could she, once she and Connor got back to her place, an apartment she'd fixed up to look charmingly vintage rather than rundown and old. They'd started kissing outside her door, and as she fumbled it open they stumbled inside, mouths locked and hands roving. Beneath her tight black dress she was wet already, aching, and as Allison cupped his crotch through his jeans she felt him hardening. Connor groaned into her mouth at her touch.

23

Somehow they made it to her room. Allison kicked her skinny black heels off and tossed her long hair out of her face as she climbed into bed, looking up with unabashed lust at Connor as he ripped his jacket off, his shirt following. Her fingers drifted beneath her panties, trailed over her clit, between her lips, and as she tipped her head back and moaned, Connor came to her, muscles striped by the amber light slipping through the slats of her blinds. His mouth moved between her lips and her neck, his hands kneading her breasts, sliding down her thighs; she arched and clutched his ass. "God, Connor, *yes . . .*"

He broke his mouth from hers and panted, "D' you have anything . . . ?"

She grinned and rolled over, rooting around her bedside drawer and coming up candle in hand, cherry-red and barely used. "You?"

Connor grinned back, pulling a lighter and a condom from his pocket. "Let's do it, then."

The bedroom bathed in the wavering liquid-gold light of several other candles, the couple's safewords firmly entrenched in each other's minds, both of them stripped to their skins. Allison lay back and loosed a throaty moan, running her hands through her hair as Connor started dripping wax from the red candle onto her bare body. Droplets peppered her breasts, spotted and streaked her stomach; her pussy throbbed, and Connor stroked and teased her between drippings, always slowing before she climaxed.

"Oh, baby, that's good," she gasped, hands kneading the rumpled sheets. "More . . ."

He obliged, wax pooling on her smooth stomach, crackling as she arched in pleasure. "So is red your favorite?" he asked, gesturing around the room. "I noticed you have a few."

Something she'd learned early was that candles with colored dyes had different melting points, which could make the temperature hotter and was extremely fun to experiment with. "It's up there," she said, not resisting as Connor guided her onto her hip, kissing her neck before pouring more onto her side, scarlet tendrils trickling down her ribs. "You?"

"Blue's always good. Navy, you know? Always been something about it. Don't know what, though."

Allison gestured for the candle. "My turn."

He passed it over without argument, and with a few deft flicks she marked his smooth chest. Connor laughed breathlessly, looking down at the *A* she'd sketched between his nipples. "A scarlet letter. Nice."

Grinning with an artist's satisfaction, Allison added a capital *L* on his stomach, candle in her left hand, her right squeezing his stiff—impressive—cock, thumb tracing his tip in teasing circles. He jolted, twitched in her hand, and groaned, and her climax rippled closer.

By the time he entered her, both they and the sheets were wax-splattered, the crimson giving it a crime-scene element Allison chose to ignore. They fucked hard, feeling every inch of each other, and Connor proved apt at reading her cues, finding her every sensitive spot, getting her off twice before he came. As he collapsed beside her, she curled up against him, draped her leg between his and felt his cock softening.

"Well, that was fun," he said.

She laughed, still saturated with afterglow. "Yeah, it was." She traced his chest with her fingertips, using the edge of her nail to chip off a clinging droplet. "It's been a while since I had this much fun, actually."

"What? No." He looked at her; his short hair was rumpled, and something about that bit of disorder touched Allison, put a small soft smile on her face as she reached up and ran her fingers through it. "You're telling me a beautiful girl like you has trouble finding someone to get freaky with on a Friday night?"

Allison shrugged. "It'd probably be easier if I was just cruising for hookups, but on the whole I prefer actual relationships. I know that probably sounds old-fashioned as hell, but . . ."

"No, I get it." Connor nodded, gaze reflective. "I'm a bit old-fashioned that way, too." He caught the way she was looking at him. "What?"

"I'm just wishing I hadn't waited so damn long to come onto you."

"That's all right." Connor wrapped an arm around her. "It just means we've got lost time to make up for."

Allison cupped his face, pulling him close for a fierce kiss, and they made up for a little more.

They were too engaged to notice a gob of wax that hadn't dried as it should've, glistening bloodily in a spot on the sheet soaked with their respective juices.

As Allison and Connor continued, it pulled itself free from the sheet and rolled around the writhing limbs until it dropped off the edge of the bed with a small wet pop and disappeared into the darkness beneath.

* * *

Things were going so well with Connor after a few weeks that Allison told Lisa about him during one of their infrequent calls, leaving out their shared proclivity and sticking to safer things like his office job, the books he recommended to her, how comfortable she felt with him—had felt with him immediately. The dirtier details she saved for conversations with Vanessa, who with her typical enthusiasm ascribed the relationship to fate and already had them heading down the aisle.

Allison wasn't scanning *Brides Monthly* yet, but she and Connor *were* seeing a lot of each other, enjoying it, and, in a pleasant surprise, connecting on a level beyond their shared kink. She liked the confused expression he wore when he woke up, like he couldn't remember where he was or why, even if they were in his apartment. She liked the way he so earnestly tried to convince her football was interesting, and how excited he got during games. She liked the discussions they had about everything from *Lethal Weapon* to Pink Floyd, even when those discussions devolved into arguments that as of yet had no bite to them. When something funny or irritating happened, Connor was the first person she wanted to tell, and whenever she fantasized his was the first face she saw.

26

It would've all been perfect if not for the disturbances.

Small things, they were, but they sunk their teeth into Allison and clung to her like her aunt's Pekinese had when she was twelve. They'd started a few days after her and Connor's first date, when she'd opened her kitchen cabinet and found a few streaks of scarlet on the inside of the wooden door, which, as she'd looked closer, she'd realized were dried wax.

What the fuck . . . ?

She'd noticed a few more dots on the door handle, as if something'd gripped it, and looking in deeper, pushing dishes aside, she'd found further streaks, all dried, all scarlet. She'd tried to think up a reason for it but couldn't, unease pooling in her stomach, and finally just cleaned it up, as if doing so could also scrub the questions from her mind.

If that'd been the only time she might've managed to bury it, but a few days later it happened again: scarlet splatters on the rim of her tub, this time mixed with lilac, the same color she'd used on her last romp with Connor. They hadn't done anything in the tub except shower, though, and she'd cleaned the bathroom up after—at least, she could've sworn she had. And she didn't think she or Connor had made the odd, tiny tears near the bottom of her shower curtain, the patterned plastic shredded with ragged, inch-high gaps.

Please, God, don't let it be rats. She could handle a lot of shit, but the thought of rats having free run of the place while she was gone or sleeping made her skin crawl. But rats wouldn't explain the wax streaks she kept finding, or the moving objects—not just knocked over or broken, but sometimes moved to another room as if by a curious someone who set them down when they got bored again, always dotted or stained with various waxy shades. So if not rats, then what?

She hadn't mentioned it to anyone, much less Connor; she wasn't about to spoil things by raving about random wax spills and misplaced knickknacks, at least until she figured out what the hell was behind them. She hadn't managed yet, though, and those nagging teeth wouldn't let go.

27

It was another Friday, early evening. Allison had taken a rare day off, the afternoon spent with Vanessa, and returned home with an hour or so left before Connor was due to come over. They'd planned to stay in, and they'd apparently made the right choice: thunder rumbled as she reached her door, and she grinned in triumph at beating the storm.

Her grin promptly vanished when she flicked her light on and stepped inside. "Oh my *God*!"

The end table and vase she kept by the door were smashed, blue and green glass glinting around her black leather boots. The shoes she'd left in the front hall were scattered to the kitchen, where she could see tipped chairs and broken dishes warning her the rest of the place was no better.

And overlaying it all were slashes and small pools of wax in a muddle of colors: peach and cream, pink and lilac, deep blue and bright red—*that* most of all, so much that at first Allison thought feverishly it was blood until she took an unconscious step forward and some crackled beneath her boot's spiky heel, the unmistakable sound of dried wax breaking. She flashed back briefly to her first fuck with Connor, but her heart was pounding triple-time for a different reason now, her head spinning, sick heat flushing her skin.

Jesus Christ, was I robbed?

But the wax—and the door was still locked when I came home . . .

Shaking, Allison pulled her phone from the pocket of her long gray coat, fumbling with her other hand for the closest possible weapon. Her fingers closed on the handle of her umbrella and she hefted it, moving cautiously forward. Wax and glass crumbled under her shoes. Her blood roared in her ears. The disarray had reached every room she saw, but as far as she could tell nothing had actually been taken. Stereo, TV, laptop— all still there.

None of this makes any fucking sense.

A sound of movement jolted her. A cry shot from her sandpaper-dry throat and she whirled, umbrella raised, phone clattering to the ground. She saw nothing, though, and in the

28

silence broken only by her sudden pulse, her ears strained, her muscles tensing.

A moment later it came again, and she realized both that, while weighty, it sounded too small and quick to be human, and it was coming from her bedroom. An animal, maybe? Her neighbor, Mrs. Okami, had a cat that was always getting out, or maybe a squirrel had come through a vent—

Allison Lambe, that's so fucking thin . . .

"Chester?" she called, moving to her bedroom. The skittering came again, but away from her. *Please be the cat, please be the cat . . .*

She eased her bedroom door open further with the tip of her umbrella and found a similar colorful scene of chaos: her comforter shredded and stained, books knocked from shelves, her clothes ripped from their hangers and piled corpselike on the floor. She peeked in just in time to see a small hunched shadow, roughly cat-sized, darting under her bed, and her legs buckled, weak with relief. "*Chester,*" Allison said, flipping the hall light on because her bedroom lamp was on the floor. "How the hell did you even get in here, you—"

She lifted the edge of the bedspread. Two eyes glowed beneath her bed, hot, yellow, slitted.

Not cat eyes.

As Allison screamed and stumbled back, it leapt at her, gibbering and shrieking. It was a naked little *thing,* somehow unfinished and wizened at once. It had long pointed ears, twiglike limbs and clutching claw-like hands, all molded from glossy, glistening . . .

Wax?

It was, somehow ridged and furrowed into this leering goblin shape—mostly scarlet, but running with several other colors, the ones also strewn through her apartment—all the colors she and Connor had used so far, she realized through her shock. Even as her mind was screaming this couldn't happen, it wasn't fucking *possible,* the wax-creature lunged for her leg and locked around it. She wasn't sure if the creature or her jeans hissed as wax soaked the denim, heating her skin. Allison screamed, kicked

29

again, managed to dislodge it and scrambled for the umbrella she'd dropped, taking a wide, clumsy swing as the thing scrabbled for her again.

She connected, and droplets sluiced from the creature as it flew across the room. A piece of it—finger? toe? ear-tip?—broke off at the blow, and by the time it hit the floor it was already dry. *Or dead?* Allison wondered. It cracked apart beneath her boot as she rushed after the dripping goblin, but it was already crawling up the wall, leaving bony, glistening handprints in its wake, and as she watched it vanished into the vent with a horrid, thick sucking sound, a few last rivulets of crimson wax running down the metal covering after it.

For good measure, Allison screamed again.

* * *

The good news was Connor seemed to believe her, once he got past the panic of finding her apartment wrecked and further cluttered with cops. The bad news was the cops weren't quite as open-minded. After their walkthrough, examining the mess and marks, they returned to where Allison sat shaking on the couch beside Connor, and the stockier of the two said, "It looks like some kind of animal, ma'am. You mentioned a cat—"

Allison's gaze snapped up. "It wasn't a cat. Cats don't look like that; cats don't fucking do what this thing did. I know what I saw!" *Good, show them what a calm, rational woman you are. Keep it up, Lambe.*

Connor squeezed her hand and she subsided, seething but silent as the scrawny cop explained how her emotional state could've affected what she thought she'd seen.

"Uh-huh," she ground out, hearing only the wax-goblin's gibbering as it capered through her skull. "Thanks for coming out, officers. I'll keep an eye out for that cat."

When they left, she glanced around her ruined living room and groaned, dropping her head into her hands.

"You all right?" Connor asked, rubbing her back.

"Yes. No. I don't know."

"Want me to help clean this place up?"

"Yes. No. I don't know." Allison looked up just as lightning licked the window, white-blue flashes in the dark. "Connor, I know what I saw. I mean, I don't know what the fuck it was, but I know I saw something."

"Yeah, I know. I mean, I know cats are agents of Satan, but I've never met one who could do what you said this thing did."

Unable to help it, she laughed.

Connor grinned, then sobered. "Seriously, though, Allison, whatever I can do to help, I'll do it."

She grabbed his hand. "You can get me the fuck outta here."

* * *

"When did you first realize you were into it? Waxplay, I mean."

Connor looked at her. They were at his place, in his bed, cream-colored sheets beneath an evergreen blanket. The air smelled of fresh sweat and sex. Rain drummed on the windows, thunder rumbling occasionally. "You want to hear that now? After . . ."

Allison's breasts still ached sweetly from his mouth, her cunt from his cock. She nodded, staring up at the ceiling. "Yeah. Distract me." She'd tried to bury herself in the fucking just as she'd let Connor bury himself in her, but for once she'd been unable to lose herself completely in the rhythm, through no fault of his. Maybe this would help instead, at least for a bit.

"All right." Connor propped himself up on his elbow. "My freshman year of college I was visiting my girlfriend's house, and her parents were out. It wasn't my first time, but it was hers, so I was trying to be the good romantic boyfriend—you know, rose petals, candles around the bed, that kinda thing."

Allison grinned, absently stroking his cock. "Aw."

"I know, I'm awesome, right?" He laughed, rocking back at her playful shove. "Anyway, we start going at it, and she's squirming all around and moaning like hell, which is getting me this close to losing it—"

She firmed her grip. "I'll have to remember that."

31

"—and we must've been shaking that bed something good, because it jostled her bedside table and a couple of the candles tipped over. They put themselves out as they fell, but hot wax splashed across my side. Nothing serious, but something about it—that was what made me nut."

Allison was laughing, making this bed shake too. "Oh my *God*, Connor."

"Well, it's no *House of Wax*, but . . ." He shrugged, grinning in the *what-can-you-do* way she loved. "So Britney, my girlfriend—"

"Of course her name was Britney."

"—she starts freaking out, screaming, thinking I'm hurt. Which technically I was, but I didn't know how to explain I'd shot my load because of some fucking Mulberry Delight runoff searing my flesh. This is not what normal people say, and I realized that."

Allison rolled over, laughing into the pillow. "Mulberry Delight. Jesus *Christ*."

"So, I just play along, act like 'oh shit, yeah, that *does* hurt, babe,' and she started fussing over me, and of course I had to let her, right? Plus, when she was done playing Clara Barton we finished what we started, so everybody won." He gestured grandly. "So there you have it, Miss Lambe: the awakening of Connor Grant. I hope it entertained."

"It did. Thank you." She wiped her eyes, caught her breath. "One thing I can say about you, baby, is you always deliver."

"Good. I'm glad." Connor ran his fingers over her breasts, belly, skated swirls around her navel. "You feeling any better?"

Allison exhaled slowly to tame the shake. "Getting there."

But even as the storm subsided and Connor drifted off beside her, Allison lay awake in the dark reliving the bizarre attack and even more bizarre attacker. She hadn't managed to puzzle it out by the time she fell asleep and into nightmares about it.

* * *

32

As she crouched by her tub, watching it fill with steaming water and idly flicking her fingers through it, waiting to drop the bath bomb in, a sharp thud reached Allison over the roar of the faucet. She whipped around, heart pounding and hand clutching her only weapon: the lime-green and lemon-yellow bath bomb. Ready to lob it if the wax-goblin capered into view, she peered around the bathroom door and down the hall to her room. "Connor?"

He appeared, grinning sheepishly and waving something. "Sorry, dropped my phone."

She nodded and withdrew, dropping the bomb. The water fizzed and bubbled, releasing a scent supposedly tropical but in actuality closer to Mountain Dew. As she twisted the faucet off, climbed in, and sank, she cursed herself for shaking.

Two weeks and the creature, whatever it was, hadn't come back. That didn't stop her from still jumping at every sound, or a sick feeling from gripping the pit of her stomach each time she put her key in the lock and opened her front door. Connor, as promised, had helped her clean up the mess the creature'd made, but the marks the encounter had left on her couldn't be erased as easily as wax on a wall. Tonight was the first time she and Connor'd used the wax—white, with dashes of dark blue, to further differentiate from what she'd seen—during sex (at her place, anyway). But she'd've been lying to say there weren't moments as Connor tattooed her and she him that the sight of wax rolling down his shoulder blades, his stomach, or lacing her nipples had brought her back, reawakening those memories.

It's gone, she told herself, sinking lower, steam clinging to her tender skin. *Whatever it was—close encounter, ripple in reality—it was a fluke. Those exterminators didn't find shit. It's done.*

She tipped her head back, closing her eyes, exhaling slowly. She shifted languidly, letting the water lap at her—not as good as a tongue between her legs, but still nice, relaxing. And besides, there was always round two with Connor to look forward to. Allison smiled.

A hot wet droplet hit her forehead. Condensation, she thought. The plaster ceiling tended to drip at the slightest hint of moisture, and when the next drop came she flinched at impact but didn't open her eyes. It was a familiar nuisance, at least.

But water didn't stick to her skin as it dried, like this did.

Allison's eyelids cracked open. Her gaze rolled to the ceiling, where the scarlet goblin clung to the cracking, yellowed plaster, its head cocked back unnaturally. It grinned down at her as its glistening skin dripped, hissing, into the water beneath.

It was bigger now. *Engorged*, her horrified mind whispered, and the word fit. The creature throbbed above her, new length in the limbs, new clarity to its maniacal features. As it opened its needle-toothed maw and cackled, strings of slick wax dangled from its mouth, pattered down on her. Blue and white wax.

Allison's shriek brought Connor bursting in. "Allison? What—" As she scrambled to her feet, water and suds sloshing to the floor, he heard the laughter and looked up, eyes widening. "Holy *shit*!"

It dropped as Allison clambered from the tub, grabbing at her hair. A hand or foot pressed to her left breast, searing a print on her skin. She cried out, grabbing for it as tiny claws bit into her. It clambered monkeylike over her, swinging from the shower-curtain bar and splattering the mirror and walls with wax.

Connor snatched a towel from the rack, ducking and cursing as the dangling thing swept and snarled at him, waxy spittle flecking his cheek. He got one end of the towel over it and grabbed it, yanking hard. The creature screeched and writhed, the impromptu sack snapping from side to side, but Connor strained and held it, teeth gritted.

"Holy fuck, you got it." Allison gaped, hand over her wounded breast.

Before they could celebrate, there was a tearing sound and a slit appeared in the wine-colored towel, widening as the creature forced its head and claws through. More red wax splattered the couple as it burst free, shrieking. Too quickly for them to absorb the sight, much less react, it dove into the tub, dyeing the water a bloody froth. A moment later the drain gurgled, the plug

34

floating free, and the water sank. Allison grabbed the plunger and jabbed it into the tub but felt nothing, and when all the water'd drained, nothing remained but a red silt in the tub bottom.

Allison lurched to the toilet and dry-heaved a few times, knots of wax-clumped hair dangling in her face.

Connor, rooted to the spot, stood staring, stained, shredded towel hanging from his frozen fingers. "I believed you before," he said as she stumbled upright, shuddering, low noises she couldn't control escaping her throat. "I didn't understand, but I believed you. Now . . ." His mouth worked, and dully Allison wondered if he realized nothing was coming out.

"So I'm not insane," she said. "I feel so much better."

* * *

They cleaned up, Allison shuddering as her shirt brushed the burn on her breast, and then sat down to figure out what, exactly, was going on. Again, cleaning up proved easier.

"I mean, what do you even google?" Connor asked as they sat at her kitchen table, her laptop open but untouched. "Crazy wax goblin? You might get some kind of weird anime, but that probably won't help."

Allison absently caressed the keyboard. "We know it has something to do with the wax. At least, that's what it's using to take form. And the colors coming off it—they're all the colors we've used."

"So we . . . made this somehow?" Connor's brow furrowed. "How the fuck does that work? Because I've been doing this for a while now and I've never had my . . . sex-wax come to life before."

"No, me either." Allison drummed her fingers, nails clicking on the tabletop. "It was bigger tonight," she pointed out after a moment. "Pulsing, too, like it had just fed or something. All of this started after we had sex that first night—using the wax . . . And tonight's the first time we used the wax here since it

35

attacked me, and it shows up again? I can't call that coincidence."

"Maybe *goblin*'s the wrong word. What's that thing sorcerers were supposed to be able to make? Little people-creatures, kinda like imps? Homo-something?"

"Homunculus," Allison supplied, straightening up.

Connor snapped his fingers. "Yeah, that."

Excitement bubbled in Allison's blood, dulling the sting of her burn. "Oh, yeah, I've heard of those. One of my ex-boyfriends was into magic—not card tricks and crap, but actual spells, charms, everything. He told me one time that sex is a powerful fuel for magic—the energy, the bodily fluids, stuff like that." She pulled her laptop close, keys clacking and screen flashing as search results popped up.

Connor scanned with her. "All right, say that's true. Our . . . bodily fluids mixed with the wax we used that first night and made that freaky homunculus motherfucker, which feeds on our energy and gets bigger and freakier each time we use the wax and screw. It's a hell of an argument for abstinence, I'll admit that. But why did it happen? We didn't cast a spell or anything. You piss off any wizards recently?"

"A few priests, probably, but no wizards I can think of." Allison sighed and rubbed her forehead. "You?"

"No. I had a girlfriend who said she was Wiccan, but she just liked fucking outdoors. She dumped me, anyway." Connor rubbed his chin. "So how do you deal with an accidental homunculus, if that's what this is?"

"I don't know, but we have to do something, because I don't want to feed this thing each time we fuck, and I like fucking you too much to give it up."

Connor grinned. "Allison Lambe, you're one of the last true romantics."

She hadn't imagined she'd ever smile again after the attack, or at least for the rest of the night, but now she found she could. She reached across the table and took Connor's hand, soaking up the touch, the warmth. He linked his fingers through hers and squeezed, a comfortable closeness and pressure.

36

"Don't worry," he said. "We'll figure it out. I like fucking you too much to give it up, too."

Allison laughed. "Who ever said love is dead?"

* * *

"I feel like goddamn Elmer Fudd," Connor muttered the next day, crouching beside Allison as they peered down the hall from her bedroom door.

Be vewy quiet, we're hunting homunculuses, Allison thought, smothering a half-hysterical giggle. Her legs ached from crouching; her nerves were as frayed as if someone was massaging them with a bandsaw. She checked her phone. She and Connor had been waiting for almost thirty minutes now, though it felt far, far longer. And he was right. The trap they'd set for the little goblin was Looney Tunes-esque in its simplicity: a bunch of new knickknacks, sandstone seashells and ceramic cows, a small glass tray filled with colorful stones, all picked up for cheap at Quik-Buy—to the clear confusion of her coworkers, who knew she'd rather take a hammer to the shelves than spend an extra moment wandering them. They'd been set up together, all surrounded by a large loop of clear fishing line (also a Quik-Buy pickup), the tail of which led down the hall to Allison's hand.

"It likes moving my things around, right?" she'd said during their brainstorming session, their thoughts lubricated and nerves calmed with generous doses of wine. "So maybe some new shiny objects'll get it to show itself." It was either this or she and Connor pull out some candles and start screwing on the living room floor to draw the creature out, but she wasn't *that* desperate yet.

Yet.

"Maybe it's not gonna—" Allison started, line slackening in her grip, but Connor nudged her and pointed. It was back, hunched over, ears quivering as it scuttled around the curios, muttering to itself in that strange wet gibberish that crawled down Allison's spine, lodged into the most primal part of her nerves. It came close, drew back, moved to another vantage point, repeated the process, occasionally pointing a dribbling claw at one thing or another or baring its teeth in a jackal's grin and cackling.

Come on, *dammit*, Allison thought, realizing she was quivering as well, tension tautening every inch of her like a trigger about to be pulled. *Get in.*

It sniffed, scurried around, on two limbs, on four. Veins of colored wax pulsed in its scarlet skin; its fat yellow eyes probed the arrangement greedily, gleefully.

Get in!

It did, and she pulled the line closed, the loop catching its knobby ankles and yanking it off its feet. It screeched, and Allison thought briefly of a bobcat caught in a trap, as seen on a nature documentary during a 2 a.m. channel surf. Then she started pulling, Connor helping when he saw her straining. The goblin was heavier than it looked, and its thrashing didn't help matters. As it slid down the hall it left a fat red streak, and a few of its retaliatory pulls nearly threw Allison and Connor to the floor.

And then with a thick squelching sound the wax-goblin was free, two red lumps falling from the noose—its feet, Allison realized, nausea rising. She and Connor tumbled forward as the pull on the other end of the line vanished abruptly. Pain exploded through Allison as she collided with the hardwood.

"*Fuck*!" she snarled, rubbing her throbbing elbow. She and Connor hurried to disentangle themselves, but the creature was already scrambling forward on its clawed hands, trailing wax from its stumps. As they rushed forward, it pulled itself up to the vent in the living room and squirmed through it—fitting somehow despite its new girth, another snaillike track glistening down the white paint.

"God *dammit*!" Allison howled, half-hearing through her roaring blood as Connor strung together a series of profanities she would've applauded under other circumstances. "I want this thing outta my house, *now*! *Fuck*!"

She brought her foot down hard and something splintered beneath her boot: shards of one of the two wax-lumps, dried, probably punted inadvertently down the hall by her or Connor in their mad, fruitless rush. With a cry of frustration, she kicked, scattering the pieces, but felt no better.

"Well, that accomplished shit," Connor said hoarsely, flushed, chest unevenly rising and falling. "Aside from giving my nightmares even more ideas, anyway."

As Allison's temper cooled, heartbeat slowing, she looked down again, sifting with the tip of her boot through the cracked wax, and another memory stirred in her: the first attack, when a piece of the creature had broken off and gone inert, lifeless, just like today. "I don't know," she said, picking up a hard piece of wax, rolling it between her fingers as another idea bloomed. "Maybe something useful came out of this after all."

* * *

Connor's mouth moved against hers as they lay in her bed, intoxicating her with slow, deep kisses. His fingers moved between her legs, massaging her clit, circling her opening before slipping inside and stroking as slowly and knowingly as he kissed her. Allison gasped into his mouth, groaning as she arched. The candlelight cast a wavering silhouette of the scene onto the wall as it colored the couple in golden shadows, and she raked her hand down Connor's back, kneaded his ass and pulled him closer, urging him on.

"I want you inside me," she said, feeling his swollen cock bob against her, aching for it to fill her. "*Now.*"

He chuckled, running a finger over her lips. She sucked hard, tasting herself on his skin, and his cock twitched. "Well, I'd hate to disappoint both of you."

Allison loved the noise Connor made whenever he entered her, as though he was doing it for the first time and couldn't believe how it felt. She contracted and released her pussy around him, massaging him from within, and drank in the throb of their entanglement. Her climax whirled closer as he started thrusting, bedsprings keeping time beneath them.

"God, babe, you feel amazing." Connor tipped his head back as he rode her, a sheen of sweat shimmering on his skin. "You're so *wet* . . ."

She grasped and released him again, tweaking his nipples as she did so, listening to him hiss and smiling up at him. "I'm so close, baby," she panted, legs wrapping tight around him. "So fucking close . . ."

Connor was right: she couldn't remember being this wet before, even with him. She squirmed, slick and aching, so aroused it was almost painful. And then it *was* painful, a sharp hot burning that split her crotch to navel, and she jerked, gasping, clutching her stomach. Searing fluid oozed down her thighs, pulsing from her core in agonizing waves, and in the low light she saw it was red. "Connor, shit—I think something's wrong," she said, panic dizzying her. Blood—was she bleeding?

But Connor was already reeling back, face contorting in pain as he pulled out—or tried to, because he only got so far before he stuck fast, still inside her, wounded penis wilting but her fluid clinging to his skin, trapping him. His howl was of agony and horror knotted close as he and Allison were, and she propped herself up and watched with shallow heaves of breath and a scream lodged in her throat as more red fluid, growing thicker and hotter with each wave, poured from her pussy, hissing as it steamed and sealed Connor tighter to her. It crawled over their thighs, stomachs, hardening into a heavy shell as it burnt their flesh beneath its implacable progress, and her scream finally burst forth because it wasn't blood, had never *been* blood, because of course it was—

Allison bolted upright in bed, the darkness smothering her senses, her scream breaking in her throat and emerging only as a hoarse gasp. She fumbled among the blankets, which clung to her skin, sweat-dampened, but her shaking hands found only skin unmarred. She collapsed into a half-moon curve, breathing raggedly into her hands while she waited for the realization it

40

was just a dream to reach her nerves, her lungs, her trembling body.

"Hey." Connor, heavy-lidded, rolled over, touched her arm. "Another nightmare?"

Allison nodded, wiping away tears she hated herself for but couldn't fight. She didn't have these nightmares every night, but even the nights she didn't were blighted by the fear she might. They were all variants on the same pattern: her mouth bobbing up and down on Connor's cock as he perched on the edge of the bed, giving him head while he moaned and clutched at her hair until he spurted hot and thick in her mouth, and she thought she'd swallow to make him happy though she knew he'd never ask her to, only to realize as her throat flooded and mouth blistered that it wasn't come but wax, clogging her throat and mouth and scorching as it solidified; the reverse happening as Connor went down on her—anything and everything her dreaming brain could pervert, it did, showing creativity she'd give it credit for it if didn't feel so violating.

Connor tugged gently on her wrist. "Come here."

She went, burrowing back under the covers, cocooning herself in his arms.

"It's going to work, you know," he said, smoothing damp hair back from her forehead, kissing it. "We can do this."

"You really believe that?" Allison murmured against his chest.

"I have to." Connor shrugged. "Otherwise, what's the point?"

She couldn't find a way to follow that, so she lay curled with him until sleep swallowed her again.

* * *

Despite wanting to get this whole fucking thing over with, they waited to enact Allison's second plan. She wasn't sure how smart the creature was. So far it'd shown only a crude, animal-like instinct for survival—and love of shiny things—but she didn't want to risk spooking it by laying the second trap too soon after the botched first attempt. She also hoped waiting would

41

starve or shrink it a bit, and on that front she seemed to be right: the few times she went home to grab some of her things and found the bastard's handprints, they were smaller, and the skittering coming from the walls or ceiling sounded lighter, missing some of the heft they'd gained over the past weeks.

Allison and Connor set the date for the second attempt, and as it approached Allison was wrung with nervousness about the actual act and relief that it could finally be over soon.

* * *

Sunday dawned gray, a chill wind buffeting litter and dead leaves down the city streets. Allison huddled deep into her coat as she and Connor walked up her building's chipped steps, a kaleidoscope of butterflies wheeling in her stomach. After she slipped her key into her lock, before she turned it, Connor grasped her hand and squeezed. "It'll work," he said, and she managed a smile, squeezing back before pushing her door open.

She strode past the clothes strewn petulantly over the hall floor into the kitchen, where Connor leaned against the counter and she stepped over crumbs of food and broken dishes to the stove.

"So where do you want to go tonight, babe?" Connor asked.

Allison marveled at how casual he managed to sound. She pulled out a sizeable pot she rarely used and set it on the burner. Out of a drawer came several packs of wax melts, which she broke from their bars and dropped into the pot. "Why go out at all?"

Connor eyed the multicolored soup she was stirring, lips curling. "Sold."

Allison heard a skittering overhead and struggled not to look up at the nearby vent and give away the game. If the thing didn't realize or care that this wasn't how she and Connor normally played, so much the better. "Oh, shit," she said, glancing at the empty counter beside her. "I forgot to grab the mail when we were downstairs. Come with?"

"Of course. I've had a pretty boring day so far. This oughta liven things up."

Allison punched his arm playfully. As they walked away, the wax continued to bubble and hiss, the low flame still licking the pot. *Just don't let us burn the apartment down*, she prayed as she shut the door. That would be something to explain to the co-op board.

"How long, you think?" Connor asked under his breath.

"I heard it above me when we were in there, so probably not long." Allison's heart hammered her ribs hard enough to drive steel, and an eternal minute later her fingers felt cold and slick on the doorknob. She and Connor exchanged a nod and crept back in.

She heard the gurgling just before she saw the goblin perched on the rim of the pot, reaching down into the wax she'd left melting. Two things struck her at once: the creature *was* smaller, back to the size it'd been during the first attack, and its arm wasn't just reaching into the wax but was a part of it, pulsing as it connected creature and sustenance. It was distracted *and* vulnerable.

Allison's blood surged and she followed suit, slipping up behind it, knocking it into the pot, slamming the lid down and bracing herself against it while Connor snapped the burner off. The creature screamed and battered back, shaking the pot and almost managing to push free, but the couple held on until all sound and movement stopped.

"Think it's a trick?" Allison asked hoarsely.

Connor gave a grim shrug. "One way to find out."

Allison inched the lid off and they peered in. The creature's silence wasn't a trick; now it was a mass vaguely reminiscent of its former shape, like an unfinished or avant-garde sculpture, molded to the shallow skin of wax Allison had baited it with. The heat had softened it enough to distort it, and the loss of that heat had rendered it inert and powerless, just like every piece that'd broken off it before.

What hadn't changed were the eyes, yellow orbs glaring up at them from the cool mask of its ruined face, still alive with

43

malevolent light. Allison reached in and snapped off a malformed ear, a hot burst of pleasure surging in her at the muffled squeal this occasioned. "You can feel? Good." She crushed the ear in her fist. "This is for everything, you little bastard."

She drew the butcher knife from the cutting board and plunged it into the pot.

For a moment afterwards, as she and Connor collected the chunks and shards in separate bags, Allison almost felt sorry for the thing—after all, it hadn't asked to be created, however the hell it'd actually happened. But then she remembered the pain and fear it'd caused, the glee it'd seemed to take in it; her breast burned with memory, and the droplet of pity melted away.

She'd been unsure where to dispose of it to ensure it never reformed and returned until Connor suggested the river. Jackets zipped against the wind, the couple walked to the promenade, each carrying a bag that weighed more than it should've, to the small gray-stone bridge that spanned it. In grim, distant silence they tossed the wax pieces by handfuls into the slow-sweeping water below until the current carried them all away. In the same silence they watched white-tipped ripples pass along for a few minutes, then turned and walked off the bridge.

"I understand if you never want to see me again," Allison said, hands shoved in her pockets, kicking at a small pebble.

"Why?" Connor looked at her. "Do you not want to see me?"

"No, I do. But if you couldn't handle it after all this"—she waved a hand in general circles—"then I get it."

Connor's brow furrowed in thought. "It's not like it was one person's fault or the other's—if anything, it's both. But that doesn't mean we can't get past it if we want to. If we try. And I'm sure as hell ready to try."

Warmth suffused Allison, shielding her from the chill. "How about we swing by the liquor store on the way back to my place, then? We can get a bottle of cheap-ass champagne and start celebrating."

Connor grinned. "A candlelit celebration, maybe?"

Allison blanched. "Um, maybe not yet."

"Yeah, that's probably for the best."

Smiling, Allison took his hand, and they walked back to her place.

ABOUT THE AUTHOR
SARAH CANNAVO

Sarah Cannavo is a writer of prose and poetry living in southern New Jersey, a short trip from the Pine Barrens. Her poems and short stories have appeared in anthologies and magazines such as *Carrying On, Untimely Frost, Parody, Poetry Quarterly, Postcards From the Void, Schlock! Horror!, Darkling's Beasts and Brews*, and *The Literary Hatchet*, and her poem "The 5 Stages of Being on Hold" won third place in the 2018 Wergle Flomp Humor Poetry Contest. Upcoming short stories will appear in Darkwater Syndicate's anthology *It Came From the Garage!* and HellBound Books's *The Devil's Hour*.

Author Website - The Moody Muse:
www.moodilymusing.blogspot.com

Twitter: @moodilymusing

FILTHY SECRETS

BY JONATHAN BUTCHER

Helena had cooked her husband Simon his favourite—smoked haddock and leek risotto—but this time she'd topped it with two stems of asparagus, hoping to tap into its aphrodisiac qualities. She'd brushed her teeth and used extra mouthwash, because once or twice Simon had used her breath as a reason to avoid intimacy. She'd applied the faintest layer of what she thought of as "bed make-up" and she'd dabbed candy-sweet perfume between her breasts. It's also Saturday night and there are no funerals due tomorrow, so he can't use work as an excuse.

Sitting up in bed, Helena wears a pine-green nightdress that complements her sand-coloured hair and shows off her curves. It fits tighter than when she'd bought it a few years back, but she's always loved it. She wants to look alluring but not intimidating, as she's learnt how easily Simon's once-proud manhood deflates these days.

When Simon comes into the bedroom, Helena is on top of the bedclothes reading a paperback, showing a glimpse of thigh through the slit in her nightdress. She looks up as Simon tugs off his socks and lets his trousers fall to his ankles, like a slapstick punchline.

"Thought any more about that gym membership, Helly?" he asks, circling the bed. "We could have you fitting that nightie again in no time." He lies down on his side, facing away from her, and yawns. "I'm so sleepy. Don't stay up too long. Nighty-night."

And within a minute or two, the only man Helena has ever loved starts to snore.

Alone in the restroom, mesmerised, Helena locks the cubicle door.

Simon is outside in the men's section of the department store, shopping for a new shirt. He's been buying new clothes more often since the funeral home has been struggling; generally colourful, wildly patterned items, contrasting with the conservative outfits he wears when dealing with grieving families and bereaved spouses.

But in the bathroom stall, away from her husband and the other shoppers, Helena has become transfixed by something rubber dangling from the toilet seat.

A hasty knot seals the condom's contents and anchors it in place. It hangs into the bowl, plump with pale fluid. A faint smear, either scabbed red or soil-brown, runs from the knot down to the bulging teat.

Helena's throat constricts, her breath held like a promise ready to be broken. She's picturing the sordid act that led to the stained prophylactic being draped here. Was it left by a couple suddenly overcome by lust? By strangers after a one-off act of public copulation? Is it the calling card of a sex offender, too squeamish to risk disease but aroused by leaving his evidence in plain view? Then there's the question of that dark streak . . .

Helena remembers to breathe and leans against the door, rattling the lock. Her knees shake and when she reaches down, the thrill is so great that her vision blurs.

After six celibate months, Helena lifts the contraceptive with one hand and slips her other below her jeans into her underwear. Tentative, she raises the condom to her face. She sniffs, extends her tongue. There's no revulsion; only heart-hammering anticipation. Then she bites down, rips, and swallows the sluggish fluid.

She cums before the cum leaves her throat. Her body convulses and she slides down the door, legs giving way as something raw and vital floods her system.

The moment passes and Helena pulls herself to her feet, still not disgusted by her behaviour but keen to start moving, telling herself that this strange blip in character is best ignored. She hurries out of the cubicle and splashes cold water onto her blushing cheeks.

Back on the shop floor, Simon models the turquoise checked shirt he wants to buy. "What do you think, honey?" He gives a twirl, his gangly arms outstretched like a child spinning in the playground. His thin moustache bristles and his eyes gleam. "Pretty neat, huh?"

Helena is lightheaded but manages a supportive thumbs-up. Simon practically skips to the till, leaving her bewildered by what had just taken place in the bathroom.

* * *

In the evening, following a day of trying to dismiss her actions and rewriting those restroom moments in her mind, Helena melts butter in a saucepan and fries some red onion. She hopes the delicious aroma of a homemade curry will settle her stomach, which has been rocking and sloshing all afternoon. She crushes garlic in a grinder and sprinkles it into the pan, then goes to the fridge for the paste she had prepared the day before.

Helena and Simon have an open-plan kitchen/lounge, and as she prepares their meal Simon leans forward from the couch to pore over the business accounts laid out on the coffee table. Helena can feel tension radiating from him like a sick heat.

He huffs over the sound of the sizzling pan. "Tori worked out that, by next summer, we'll need six extra clients a month just to keep afloat."

Tori has been working for them for just over a year, and her admin duties have expanded to include business strategy. With larger funeral homes competing for the corpses that Simon's family company should, by right, be preparing for their final farewells, Sloane-Martin and Son needs all the creative thinking it can get. It's a struggling, century-old business that's steeped in tradition and old-school thinking, and the rise of corporate funeral care has hit profits hard. So far, Sloane-Martin and Son has survived on reputation alone, but Simon and Helena both know they'll reach a point when it will no longer be enough.

Helena is as bothered by the way the stress has affected Simon's libido as she is by the threat of bankruptcy. They used to be so close.

The frying pan steams on the hob, wafting delicious aromas into the kitchen air.

Helena's stomach lurches and, barely making a sound, she vomits white foam over the onions, the garlic, and the curry paste. She doesn't cough or retch; the creamy froth simply shoots from her mouth and splatters the ingredients. The mixture bubbles and pops. Helena raises a hand to her mouth.

In the lounge area, Simon smacks his lips. "That smells a-*maze*-ing, Helly!" he exclaims.

That same pleasure Helena had felt in the department store is suddenly back: the glee of private, degenerate knowledge. She watches the creamy concoction simmer in the pan and considers pouring it into the sink, but she hasn't felt anticipation like this since before meeting Simon. And what's the harm? She'll keep cooking, all the while imagining serving up her Spicy Stomach Acid Surprise to her spouse, then at the last minute she'll pour it away, announcing that she'd curdled the cream. They'll order a takeaway and watch another movie on the couch, with her head resting in the bony crook of Simon's neck. Yes, that will be nice.

"Can I try it yet?" Simon asks, suddenly behind her. "I don't know what you've done, but you really are a chef extraordinaire."

Helena stirs the pot, her body tingling.

She doesn't stop Simon when he dips a teaspoon into the curry and takes a noisy slurp.

"Oh . . . my . . . *God*. Why haven't you made this before, you delightful woman?" he asks, leaning in to peck her damp lips. "That recipe's a keeper!"

* * *

That night, with Simon snoring beside her, a tasty meal of chicken, pulses, and regurgitated semen digesting in his belly, Helena considers her day.

Something that has been absent from her life has returned: excitement.

As long as the stranger's sperm wasn't infected, her actions had been harmless. First, hyper-aroused, she'd committed an act of private transgression with the condom. Then, second, she'd cooked a meal which had *accidentally* contained an unconventional ingredient.

Even if the contents of the rubber sheath had been diseased, Helena doubts any parasites or damaging cells could have survived her partial digestion, so she would not have spread them to her husband yet. Simon hadn't even suffered while eating her vomit; in fact, as Helena had sipped water, complaining about her upset tummy, he had gone back for a second helping.

Helena's thrill is in knowing she has done something other people would be appalled by, *and yet no one else will ever know about*.

A special, sordid, harmless secret.

With the failing funeral home draining Simon of his once-enthusiastic sexual appetite, Helena realises how bored she's become. Perhaps it's time to change that.

* * *

While Simon is at work dealing with a problematic client—something he often calls "Only Fools and Corpses"—Helena strolls to the supermarket to pick up some kitchen essentials. She's dressed in a shabby blouse and a long grey skirt that she hopes looks hippy chic. Like Simon's garish clothing choices, Helena prefers a relaxed style when she isn't bound by the expectations of the business.

Helena isn't sure what attracts her eyes to the bar. It's nothing like the family-friendly places she usually visits for those once-a-month meals out with Simon, or the wholesome pubs she, the funeral directors, and the rest of the chapel team sometimes drink at. Chart music thuds from the open door and spills onto the street, sounding like roadworks played through an auto-tuner.

A bulimic-thin woman stands outside, sucking on a long cigarette. Her cheeks are dragged between her teeth, skin ruddy, eyes squinting pits. She's chatting with a plump guy in an electric wheelchair who wheezes like he has emphysema whenever he speaks.

The dingy dive is a long, narrow room containing no more than a dozen drinkers. She sits on a stool at the bar and orders a lime and soda. The barman seems to measure her up before he serves her.

Helena takes in the other drinkers, wearing their low-cut tops, tight jeans, and pectoral-hugging shirts. The average age is probably early 50s, 20 years her senior, and although it's only 2 p.m., several of the punters already seem tipsy. Helena drinks slowly, hoping she will soon feel that secret excitement warming the private place between her legs, which she thinks of as her "foof".

She doesn't have to wait long.

After a few minutes, she catches the eyes of a lone thin man in a leather jacket sipping a black beer. When he smiles, the skin cloaking his skull becomes a mask of white folds and deep shadows. He gestures with his head for her to come and sit with him, and that first touch of desire shivers through Helena. She slides onto the cheap wooden bench across the table from him.

"Looking for someone?" he asks, raising his eyebrows.

Helena thinks he's trying to flirt and almost smirks. "Like whom?"

"Most customers who look like you want Charlie."

Helena had been wrong: he wants customers. "Oh, um," she stammers, as an idea occurs to her. "Actually, no. I'm looking for Molly. Is she here?"

He laughs. "As a matter of fact, she is."

* * *

52

"Splendid chow mein, wasn't it?" Simon says, patting Helena's thigh companionably before returning his hand to his lap.

"Lovely," Helena agrees, hiding her excitement. "I wonder what their secret is."

It's not long before Simon's legs are vibrating as if he's sat at a drum kit playing a rapid double-bass beat. Helena glances his way, noticing the sheen on his forehead. He runs a hand through his hair, raising it to a centre-peak. "Phew, is it getting hot or is it just me?"

"No honey, it's rather cool in here," Helena replies, and pecks his flushed face.

"I don't know. I feel hot."

He leaves the room and returns guzzling a glass of water.

Before they had married, bought the house, and taken the reins of the business from Simon's parents, he had always refused the occasional ecstasy tabs or baggies of MDMA Helena enjoyed with friends. All the warning signs of Simon's blandness had been there from the start, but she'd come to love him, and that had meant more than partying ever could. Helena wants that shared love back more than anything, and she had always known how much he would enjoy himself if he'd just let go.

She isn't sure if a spectator would understand why she's done what she's done, but she knows she isn't doing anything wrong. Once the MDMA kicks in properly, Simon will have a fantastic evening—he just won't know why. With any luck it might even get him in the mood for sex, if he can still get it up.

Simon sits beside her again, clutching his glass with both hands. His legs judder and he rolls his neck. "I feel weird," he says, taking deep breaths. He sounds on the brink of panic, but then makes a cooing noise. He closes his eyes and groans.

Helena wishes she was enjoying those fluttery rushes too, but she'd abstained to make sure he stays safe. Besides, as with the condom incident the other day, the thrill is in the secrecy, and she isn't harming him—she's giving him a gift.

It isn't long before the powder's pleasant effects take hold. Unlike some people Helena had seen on the drug, who needed to move and dance and thrust their bodies to enjoy the rush, Simon goes straight to euphoria. He wraps his arms around himself languorously, eyes lidded as he strokes his triceps through the thin fabric of his pale blue top. Helena hasn't seen him looking so relaxed and attractive in months.

"Everything feels lovely," he says, his voice as gentle as falling feathers.

Helena watches him, embracing the power of her knowledge, the thrill of secrecy, but also the rare pleasure of seeing Simon truly enjoy something. She strokes herself in turn, tracing lines across the front of her blouse. Her hands form mirrored motions as she runs her palms over each breast. She watches Simon writhe, relieved that he isn't flustered or questioning the experience. She'd purchased some high-grade tranquillisers to calm him down (well, knock him out) if it became necessary, but it seems her uptight husband is finally going with the flow.

Simon opens his eyes and his pupils are perfect round beetles. "What's going on?" he asks dreamily.

Helena feels an unexpected surge of emotion. "We're just safe and happy."

When she reaches over to stroke his face, he leans into her hand like an affectionate cat. They stay like that for several minutes: her right hand feeling the heat between her legs, her left pressed against her husband's warm skin.

This is how life could be, she thinks. *We could smile, and laugh, and make love, and feel close again.*

Then Simon says, "We should ask Tori round." His eyes roll back in his head. "I like it when she touches me like that."

Ice fills Helena's chest.

The honesty that MDMA encourages—the draining of inhibitions and the melting of soft barriers—often feels irresistible, particularly to the inexperienced. It can convince you you're "one" with those around you, and that your own heartbeat thrums in the chests of the whole population. Helena remembers a time when she'd danced to repetitive music she usually hated, pumping her limbs to the same rhythm to which the sweat-soaked forms around her had marched and gyrated. They'd felt like a single organism, and she had wished she could kiss the lips of every person there.

Had Helena known, somewhere deep in her sex-starved being, that there was more to Simon having offered Tori a greater responsibility in the business? She believes she had.

It seems that Helena isn't the only one who keeps secrets.

"You want Tori here, too?" Helena whispers, keeping the distaste from her tone. "You want us both to touch you like that?"

Simon moans, rubbing his meagre chest with both hands and trailing his fingers down to his crotch. "Would you . . . ?"

Helena hasn't seen him act so brazenly in years, but now he's practically masturbating for her. "Does she use her mouth on you?" she asks, pulling her long shabby skirt up to her knees. She's almost shocked by her own frankness when she says, "We could both do that, one after the other. Or both at the same time."

Simon shakes his head, as if coming to his senses. "I didn't mean . . ."

"Shh, it's all right," she says.

When she feeds him a glass of water containing two of the downers she had bought at the bar earlier, Simon drinks gratefully, with one hand on the glass and the other still massaging his groin.

* * *

With the man she loves unconscious, Helena hurries to the ATM at the end of her road, feeling like a teenager who has sneaked out of home to attend a party she isn't supposed to. It's an enthralling sensation steeped in nostalgia and queasy anticipation, and it helps her ignore the pain of Simon's betrayal. She withdraws the maximum amount of cash from the hole in the wall and then dashes back to her apartment building.

Dark, haggard shapes congregate in a nearby alleyway. Down here, society's outcasts sleep, drink, fight, and exchange stories, which Helena imagines to be tales of woe and romance, desperation and beatnik wonder. Not used to meeting the lowest echelons of society face-to-face, she steps into the dark and braces herself for confrontation. She had always assumed these people despised her for how she ignores them, and for how she rushes past or pretends to check her phone when one of them asks for money. It's time to redress the balance a little.

"Hi," she says, approaching a group of three sat in a row against the apartment block wall, dappled by the strained rays of the streetlamps.

"Evening," the hairiest says from behind a huge beard. "Any change for the homeless, love?"

"Better than that," she says, beaming. "Who wants to make some real money?"

* * *

The two vagrants carry Helena's love from his snoring position on the couch into the bedroom, where they lay him on his front at Helena's instruction.

The sour stench of their clothes and skin is atrocious. When the taller hairy man, whose beard is like a vast nest but whose scalp is cropped short, strips off his trench coat and rancid shirt, a reeking, invisible cloud disperses through the room. He apologises when Helena coughs, seeming overcome by shame.

The scruffy pair stand at the edge of the bed above Simon. Helena leans back into a cushioned wicker chair, stroking herself through her skirt. She's insisted the pair wear condoms, but that's their only limitation—aside from protection, Simon is theirs for the next hour. She's almost jealous.

The hairy, topless guy sounds uncertain. "You never mentioned he'd be out cold."

"This is how we like it," Helena says. "He'll cum so hard when I show him the footage. This really is the only thing saving our marriage."

Her other guest—a shorter, older man with jagged cheekbones and a black eye—says, "Shotgun, I get his arse."

While both strangers had been hesitant at first, they agreed after she had slipped them each a fifty and told them they'll get a hundred more when they are done.

Beardy clambers onto the pillows, tugs his penis out from his stained jeans, and waggles it in front of Simon's sleeping face. The thought of the smell the organ must be exuding makes Helena slip her hand into the front of her skirt.

Black Eye takes Simon by the ankles and drags him down the bed to give Beardy more room. Beardy strokes his member but it refuses to rise from its snarl of greasy-looking pubes. He keeps glancing up at Helena, unsure, uncomfortable, but the call of the extra hundred keeps him trying.

Black Eye is more enthusiastic. "He's not gonna wake up, is he?" He reaches under Simon's prostrate, facedown body and fiddles with his zipper before pulling his jeans down to his calves.

While the sight of the two tramps and her unconscious husband would normally seem disturbing, Helena feels delirious. She's besmirching their marriage bed—as perhaps he has already done with Tori—and Simon is completely unaware. While she wishes she was still sat with him on the couch, ignorant of his affair, there is a certain intimacy at play here too. Helena uses her fingers to toy her skin through her underwear, but the material soon becomes an irritation. She pushes her briefs aside, wets her fingers, and circles the fleshy crown above her vulva.

Beardy still can't get hard, so Helena lifts her skirt to her waist and spreads her thighs to show him how she's touching herself. He watches, clearly heterosexual, but when he accidentally rubs the tip of his penis against Simon's cheek he recoils. His eyes meet Helena's and his look of apologetic helplessness almost makes her chuckle.

"If you manage to ejaculate, I'll add another fifty," she says.

Black Eye glares. "Well, that ain't fair! Just coz he's got no fuel in his rocket, he gets extra?"

Helena shrugs. "It's my money."

Black Eye grumbles as he yanks Simon's red boxer shorts down and gives his buttocks a playful slap. "You've been a bad girl," he says and pulls out his own tool, which is already erect.

It's been over five years since Helena has seen another man's erection in the flesh, and the sight makes her feel filthy. A change takes place in her as she watches.

It's not a penis, or a rod, or a tool, she thinks. *It's a fucking cock.*

Beardy tries again to provoke a rise from his reluctant genitals but it's no good, and when Helena slides two fingers between her labia—no, *pussy lips*—in a last-ditch attempt to give the poor man a show, he shakes his head, defeated. "I won't do it. It's wrong, and I can't get it to work anyway."

Black Eye looks up from Simon's rear. "Come on, Nigel. Shut your eyes and think of England. We've got money riding on this."

"You shouldn't be up for it, either. What's your Maggie going to say, eh?"

"She isn't gonna say anything, coz she isn't gonna know! And *you* aren't gonna tell her anything either!"

"I'm off," Beardy says. "You coming?"

Black Eye sneers. "I want the rest. I'll still do it."

Helena drops her skirt back down over her legs. Their argument is sluicing away the moment's stimulation, reminding her of the mundane life she actually leads and the bond she'd once had with Simon, away from this bizarre fetish for secrecy she has developed and all the possibilities it presents.

She loves this man, and she always will.

But then she thinks of Tori, and how careful Simon must have been to deceive her, and how delightful it is to know something foul and corrupt that those around her are clueless to. She thinks of the sex she'd had before and after she met her husband, and how none of it compares to the nectar of just one filthy secret.

"Leave, then," she tells Beardy, and turns to Black Eye. "I'll give you his share of the cash if you manage to cum twice."

* * *

58

Lying with his pasty face poking out from the blanket, Simon looks cadaverous when his alarm goes off the next morning.

Helena has been up for an hour already, despite having had such a late night.

"What happened yesterday?" Simon asks. His eyes are bruised-looking slits.

"Oh, honey," Helena consoles. She pictures the unexpected squirt she'd speckled the carpet with when Black Eye had shot his load the first time. "We were watching TV and you told me you felt funny. Then you got drowsy and almost passed out. I had to help you to bed! I don't know what came over you." *Apart from Black Eye.*

"My head's pounding," he says, and his throat sounds parched. "I'm sick."

"Oh no!" Helena says. "I was hoping a good night's sleep would have you back to one hundred percent. Should I call someone?"

"There's the Westerner funeral tomorrow. They're viewing at 2 p.m. and they're being quite particular." He groans, clutching his head. "I can't think straight."

"We'll handle it," Helena says. "You need water, paracetamol, and rest."

Although taking time off from work is a rarity for Simon, he doesn't argue. Helena brings him water and painkillers, takes his temperature, and reassures him that he just needs to sleep. She watches him close his eyes, thinking that last night's punishment was a one-off. He's paid for his mistake, even if he doesn't know it.

* * *

Sloane-Martin and Son consists of a reception area, a quiet room for grievers, a private chapel in which relatives can view the deceased, a couple of offices, and the mortuary towards the rear. When Helena arrives, the widowed matriarch of the Westerner family is already there, waiting in her car at the front, five hours before the planned viewing. After inviting her in for a hot drink and sitting her down in the reception area, Helena heads out back.

"Good morning, Tori," she says, standing in the doorway to her office.

Tori sits behind her desk, five years younger and far more svelte than Helena, wearing a pencil skirt and tight blouse. Helena understands what her husband sees in Tori, but not what Tori sees in Simon. He hardly fits the dominant boss archetype; his weak jaw and average build are unimpressive, and he's about as authoritative as a pigeon.

"Morning, Helly," Tori says. She's picked up using the annoying nickname from Simon and is the only other staff member who does so. "Is Simon in yet?"

Helena pictures her husband's scrawny frame beneath this woman, lying flat on her office desk. She thinks of the times they might have made love . . . no, *fucked*. The secret glances they must have shared, the hidden flirtations, the stolen moments of lust—all at Helena's expense. "Simon is unwell, I'm afraid. He looked awfully peaky this morning."

"Oh, dear," Tori says. "Is there anything I can do?"

Helena pins her with her eyes. If it had been anyone else asking she may have been grateful, but this leg-spreading little harlot has no business offering Simon anything. Helena considers telling Tori she suspects her husband has caught something terrible—perhaps even drop the vaguest hint of AIDS, contracted through an affair—but doing so would create the risk of too many questions. It would also lack what she has begun to crave, like an addict with a taste for a new and potent drug: secrecy.

* * *

The siren rips through the night.

Helena dashes away from Tori's car, the brick having opened a diagonal crack across the driver's front window. But instead of running away from the house she runs *towards* it, ducking

60

behind a bush and waiting, panting, her mind racing, blood pumping. She knows the uncalculated risk she is taking, but somehow the knowledge arouses her more.

Helena had gone home after a busy day, spiked Simon's light meal with another tranquilliser, and slipped from the house after midnight. In some ways she's doing this for him, too, so she can bear the weight of his dishonesty and one day make love to him again.

The front door opens and out comes Tori, immediately spotting her car's broken window. "Bastards!" she hollers into the night, clicking off the alarm with her key fob. She marches down the path from her house towards the road, leaving her front door wide open, just as Helena had hoped.

Helena creeps out with her heart in her mouth and enters the house. She's fast, her footfalls light as she climbs the brightly lit stairs, senses wild and alert for signs of any other living thing inside. Her initial plan is straightforward—find somewhere to hide—but the time she has is miniscule. And will Tori call the police following the apparent attempted break-in, or will she wait until the morning?

Upstairs, the wide landing branches off in two directions, one of which leads towards a bedroom and the other towards a dim hall. The silence reassures Helena there is no one else here, but as she paces into the lesser-lit hallway she hears Tori return to the house and shut the front door. Helena's pulse quickens and her rage at the house's owner almost convinces her to stand and fight. But that would be a simple act of revenge, and Helena wants that alluring veil of deceit, too.

She'd hoped to find a closet or bed, but there's no time. She creeps into a dark office on the left side of the corridor and crouches against the wall, listening.

"Fucking kids," Tori hisses as her footsteps pad the stairs, oblivious to her intruder.

Helena smiles in the blackness but remains still, not even willing to risk leaning against the sturdy desk in case it makes a sound.

Out on the landing, Tori coughs and clears her throat with the rattly sound of a smoker. There are more footfalls, the closing of a door, and the echoey clatter of a bathroom light-pull. Helena defines the sounds of urination punctuated by a couple of high-pitched farts, a tap being turned on and off, the door re-opening, and then more footfalls as Tori returns to her bedroom.

Helena waits, considering masturbation as the minutes tick by. An agitation such as the breaking of her car window will surely have left Tori tossing and turning, so Helena waits a full hour before she risks moving again.

Then the house is hers.

She removes her trainers to reveal her softest, most padded socks. The carpet is thick, but Helena doesn't want to take any more risks as she moves around.

Tori hadn't shut the bathroom door, so Helena is able to get inside without making a sound. There's a narrow, frosted glass window that allows in some light, and the first thing she notices is the lone toothbrush in a cup on the sink. She considers for a moment pushing it into her vagina or anus and then replacing it as she'd found it, but the thought is juvenile and cliché. Intriguing nonetheless: the image of Tori scraping bristles against her pearl-white teeth and flecking them with microscopic dots of faeces.

The fear of being caught adds to Helena's excitement, and she feels sticky with juices. She could simply masturbate there in the hallway, frenziedly frigging in secret, but it wouldn't be enough. She needs to take further liberties, to claim the building as her own without the knowledge of its owner.

The heavy breathing of a deep slumber comes from Tori's bed, and Helena thinks she could do almost anything and still avoid detection. Standing in the bedroom doorway, for the hell of it, she lifts her skirt and pulls her panties down around her thighs to feel her wet warmth. She almost giggles, but no matter how soundly Tori is asleep, Helena shouldn't make a noise. She edges closer to the bed, thrilling in the deception.

Looming above the shadowed shape on the pillow, Helena teases herself with two fingers. Would Tori wake if Helena managed to squirt? It usually only happens during full sex when she has fingers or a toy massaging expert circles against her clit, but then again she *had* produced a rush of viscous fluid the night before while she'd watched Black Eye fucking her husband, so who knows?

It isn't worth the danger, even though her fingers feel like paradise.

She inches from the bedroom and pulls on the door so it is ajar, imagining Tori and Simon having rampant sex, Tori on top and commanding her husband to speed up, slow down, and to touch her this way and that. Helena is suddenly shaking with rage, her arms tight against her body, fists clenched like the limbs of dead spiders.

Helena hikes up her underwear and heads downstairs to the dark kitchen. In the well-stocked refrigerator she finds apple juice, orange juice, tomato ketchup, and barbecue sauce.

When she removes the cap of the apple juice bottle, the neck is wide enough to piss into without spilling a drop.

The barbecue sauce is much narrower. She takes a square of kitchen towel from the roll, holds it beneath her ass, and squeezes out a turd into the centre of the sheet. She scrapes the chunk into the bottle, gives it a nice sloppy shake, and replaces it.

There's bleach under the sink, so she squeezes some into the OJ.

She pauses at the tomato sauce, not considering whether she can fulfil the task, but whether it will arouse her. Picturing Tori squirt out a portion of ketchup containing fragments of Helena's body, she decides that it will—her tensing Kegels tell her so.

She takes a vegetable knife drying beside the sink and runs her finger over the blade. Sharp enough. She uncaps the bottle in preparation and then thrusts out her tongue, wincing as she slices into the side of the pink muscle and lets the blood flow from her lips into the red sauce. It runs down the bottle and puddles on the damp metal surface, a sight both distressing yet oddly appealing. She cleans up using a kitchen towel before she leaves, tasting the iron tang of her blood.

Back upstairs, she sprinkles the remaining powdered MDMA into some sleeping tablets she finds in the bathroom cabinet.

Still in total darkness, she returns to Tori's bedroom and pulls open her lowest bedside drawer, thrilled to find exactly what she was hoping for: a realistic silicon dildo, shaped like an erection.

Standing above the sleeping woman, Helena masturbates. She doesn't dare turn on the toy's vibrating function, but it isn't necessary: the stimulation of the bulging veins is exquisite as she slides the shaft against her pussy, not penetrating herself but using its textures to tease sensations from her clit. She bites her lip, determined not to cry out as she approaches climax, and when it happens it comes in delicious waves that rush across her skin and through her veins like insects, weakening her arms and jellying her legs. She almost collapses, almost screams, almost beats the sleeping whore to death with a vibrator slick with her white discharge.

As the sensations fade she imagines making love to Simon, enjoying his body while he enjoys hers.

Soon. It will happen again soon.

Tori sleeps like the dead.

* * *

The desire for further transgression has Helena in its grip as she returns to her car, parked up a couple roads away. She drives with one hand on the wheel and the other in her underwear.

Adrenaline and endorphins have her feeling high, and the frantic pace of her fingering works in perfect contrast to the crawl of the car as she slips from Tori's neighbourhood and onto a six-lane road that takes her towards the city. The traffic is thin and she picks up speed, returning her slick hand to the wheel. The idea of driving undetected occurs to her as important, so she flicks off her headlamps and cuts through the dark.

What would it feel like to be there when Tori drinks her fruit-flavoured bleach? How would it have been to have placed a pillow across her pretty face, sat down onto it, and dry-humped her to suffocation? And if a woman such as Tori can destroy a marriage, if people from the streets can be paid barely a week's wage to rape a sleeping man, and if public restrooms are breeding holes for indecency and perversion, what remains sacred?

The world is a place of corruption and lies, and Helena wishes she could expose them all, lay them bare, but she can't. That's why she needs her own, and why she'll continue to embrace the exotic, toxic power of her fetish for deceit.

A shrill dance beat fills the car, and she pulls over to the side of the road. Catching her breath, she takes her phone from her jacket pocket, which she'd left on the passenger seat while exploring Tori's home, and answers. "Simon."

"Helena." Her husband's fragile voice trembles as he speaks. "Where are you?"

A car pulling a trailer sweeps by. It blasts its horn, so she flicks on her hazards.

"What have you done?" Simon asks weakly.

"What do you mean?"

"You've given me something, haven't you? You've doped me."

A tremor rises from Helena's calves up to her neck.

"I didn't want to believe it," says Simon. "I don't even understand why. But I checked your drawer and found pills. They're tranquillisers of some sort, aren't they?"

Helena tries to answer but instead slumps forward in her seat, bumping her head against the wheel and keeping it there.

"Where are you?" Simon asks.

"Driving . . ." she whimpers.

"Will you come home, please? We need to talk. I'm hurting *everywhere*."

Helena fights back a sob and watches the red brake lights of a moped buzz by.

"Helly . . ." Simon whines.

The word is a trigger: "Don't call me that!"

"What do you—"

"I mean exactly that. You bastard. You lying, cheating bastard." Breath whistles from her nose. "I know about Tori."

There is a pause before Simon asks, "Tori?"

"How long has it been going on? How many times? Can you count them?" And then, as bitter as bile, she spits, "Ever fuck her in our bed?"

The accusation seems to startle Simon. "Helena, I've never gone behind your back. I'd never do that."

"When you were delirious the other night, you told me you like how she touches your face."

Simon sighs. "You're right. I didn't want to tell you, but I suppose I should have. Tori . . . approached me last week. You know the night I had to work late for the Springer function? Well, she rubbed my shoulders. I should have told her to stop straight away but I didn't, and then she touched my face and it felt good. I told her to stop and she apologised. Then the next day I suggested she start looking for another job. I swear to you, that's all that happened."

In a pathetic, Simon-ish way, it made sense. "Why didn't you tell me?"

"Because I felt bad. For liking it, even for a moment. You and I haven't made love in so long. You get hot and you get cold, and then you'll try to spring sex on me. My body doesn't work that way. I actually think there might be something wrong with you."

"*Me*?" Helena says. "You always turn me down, no matter *when* I try to be intimate! I . . ." Her voice fades, and she suddenly becomes aware of how alone she feels.

"Come home, Helena. Please."

She wants to, but she imagines sitting on the couch where she'd poisoned him, or in the bedroom where she'd invited two men to assault him. "I can't yet."

"Then come and pick me up. I'll get dressed and we can drive somewhere and talk."

"It's almost three a.m."

"Yes, it is. Now come and get me."

"Okay. Meet me at the end of our road."

* * *

As she drives, a heavy sadness weighs down on her shoulders.

She might be wrong about Tori.

She might be wrong about Simon.

But whether she is or isn't, how will she ever know for sure?

Simon is the only man she has ever loved, and *she still loves him*. But having started down her own path of deceit, she now knows how easy it is to be drawn into living a secretive life.

She doesn't want to feel such melancholy, but the closeness she'd once had with Simon feels like it took place generations ago.

When Simon's silly, clownish frame comes into view at the end of their road, she places her left hand between her legs, manipulating her heat, her sex, her *cunt*. She slows the car. Simon wears his new shirt, the one he might have bought to impress Tori. It's irrelevant now, because he has started unravelling the threads of Helena's lies. Discovering the pills will only be the start, and soon he will know the strange, terrible woman she has become. She can't let him learn her secrets, and she can't lose him.

He steps into the road, no doubt assuming she is slowing down to pick him up. She keeps her secret until the car is a short distance away.

Then she stamps the accelerator.

The car hits him full force. His surprise looks preposterous before he vanishes beneath the front-right tyre. The impact rattles the car, a thudding up-and-down motion that stops as soon as it starts, like the premature orgasm of a virgin's first fuck.

Helena had hoped that ploughing her lover down would evoke the greatest possible climax in her, a shudder of delightful, tightened muscles that would somehow unite them again. Instead, the car simply screeches to a halt, and the engine starts to sigh and tick and cool. Even when she notices the raised angle of the bonnet, suggesting that part of Simon's body is still beneath the vehicle, she remains unsatisfied by the distance between them, and his failure to bring her to peak.

* * *

The engine purrs beneath them.

Simon had always preferred making love in the dark, and as Helena raises her hips and feels him move inside her, keeping her motions exquisitely slow, she imagines him smiling up at her.

"I love you, Simon," she says, kissing his cheek.

He is hers again.

She had told her team they should not expect her attendance today, saying she will be holidaying on the other side of the planet while she recovers from her loss. They had followed her instructions precisely and without question. Helena assumes her staff and family will think her callous for travelling abroad on such a day, but the truth, which they will never know, is far more scandalous.

Last night, hungry for private intimacy, she had locked herself alone with Simon, and she has been with him ever since.

The engine cuts off, and after a few clicks and judders Helena feels movement. She pictures the six men in tasteful suits carrying them in a winding procession across the grass, and imagines their family gathered, solemn and steadfast, metres away from where they now make love.

Helena rises and dips, remembering how Simon would gasp when she did so during their early days together. His body doesn't feel the same as it had back then, not least because of the impact of the car, but the twin joys of feeling Simon inside her again and knowing something that would horrify the hardiest of souls causes her to buck her hips faster in the blackness.

She soon feels a swaying, lowering sensation, and as the casket settles onto the freshly dug earth of their grave she hears the drone of the sermon, now above them.

It's difficult to hold back the exquisite moans, and even when Simon's soft shaft plops out of her she doesn't allow it to ruin the moment.

68

Something that sounds like heavy powder hits the roof of the coffin.

She reaches down and tugs her late husband back inside, stroking his hair, weeping at the beauty of love and the pleasure of their togetherness. That yearned-for climax arrives at last and she clamps her teeth against the cries that threaten to leap from her, and in the end, it's perfect.

Afterwards, before she sleeps, she drapes her body over her late husband like a shroud, rests her head into the bony crook of his neck, and whispers her secrets to him.

ABOUT THE AUTHOR
JONATHAN BUTCHER

Jonathan Butcher is the sick monster responsible for abominations such as *What Good Girls Do*, *The Chocolateman*, and *The Children at the Bottom of the Gardden*. He lives and types in Birmingham, and he's currently working on a nasty political horror novel. He must be stopped.

Send genital pics and photos of your latest victims via www.facebook.com/jonathanbutcherauthor

SIMPLE PLEASURES
BY COLLEEN ANDERSON

The women didn't take long to spread the word. Like ghosts, they spun out of reach, always tantalizing.

When he had finally retired from the navy with a meager pension, he had visited the clubs for seamen and the armed forces. Sitting, drinking beer after beer, he had watched the women glide by like ships at sea, but he never attracted the sleek ones. Other bars, the ones where each person nursed a drink in the shoals of the room, or even the bright islands where the young gathered under flashing lights and rhythmic sound, even they did not warm to Arne for long.

Only the very lonely women accepted a date or two before they sailed their way. Lush, smooth-skinned, lively ones satisfied his needs but there were few who noticed him. The ones he paid for, with their expert mouths and fingers and strange siren-like words, stayed away after a while. No amount of money lured them back so he resorted to imagination.

* * *

Arne watched the young woman walk down the street. Her short skirt crept up her thighs. She used one hand to pull it down. Sighing, he let the curtain fall as she walked out of sight. He scratched at his unkempt grey hair and ran his hand over the shiny plastic that wrapped his arm. She'd never accept his invitation or want him, or play his games.

Arne moved to the tattered, overstuffed chair and sat. He turned on the lamp and let it catch the reflection of the

71

vambraces that he had made several months ago. Here were the perfect companions. Dream beauties. Each plastic cuff went from wrist to just below the elbow, stitched in long strips. Inside each piece of heavy, clear plastic was a picture of a beautiful woman, her naked contours visible. Five women posed in each arm brace, their heads resting at the end nearest Arne's wrist so he could look at them as if they stood or lay before him.

He smiled; these women were his and when he stood, they stood on their heads to please him. They remained uncomplaining and beautiful and he could make up their personalities as he desired.

He turned the plastic on his left arm for a better view of Sally, the milky-skinned redhead with brown eyes. In black indelible pen he had written about her pleasures alongside her figure. She liked to do it on all fours and smoke afterwards. She also liked to wear crotchless panties.

Arne had bought two years' worth of various skin magazines and some black-market ones to find the exact women of his dreams. There were two wilder ones, from the raunchier rags, and three slightly softer types on each arm. He had spent at least a day on each woman, figuring out her history and what she would do for him, making her his reality.

He unzipped his stained pants and let Sally do what he could no longer accomplish without her.

* * *

Arne awoke with a start in the room, dark except for the illumined spot in which he sat. He grabbed a soiled towel, then cleaned the stickiness from his hand and vambrace. He tossed the towel down and stood, not bothering to zip his pants. Hunger and boredom chewed at him; too many nights of boiling the same mush. It was Wednesday—no . . . Thursday.

Changing, he decided to go out but would leave the vambraces on. He had never worn them in public before. They were toys for fantasies at home. *What the hell, I've nothin' to lose and no one will see them if I button down my shirtsleeves.*

72

Arne left the apartment and walked up the street, along the divide between shore and civilization as sea spray dampened his hair. The salty air invigorated him and the thought that he walked with ten beauties, even if invisible, added a swagger long missing to his stride. A sailor all his life, he needed the ocean near at hand. As he reached the Broken Anchor pub, he thought of the days at sea and the evenings when the water seemed to fill with voices calling him. Voices he had talked to as he gazed or swam or masturbated into the churning waters.

Arne entered the smoky darkness and chose a table against a wall, deep in the pub's interior. He ordered and looked around the wood-textured room, taking in all the women, old and young, laughing and talking with girlfriends and boyfriends. He studied their legs, their hips, their breasts, smiles and clothing, and compared them to his girls. Any of these women would do if they just had a little life. But few too many complained about his wants.

It's adventure they fear. They're afraid if they try something really different, they'll like it. He knew what he was; he didn't fool anyone, like women were always doing.

He scratched at the moisture collecting under the plastic around his forearms. Would his girls keep him happy? *My girls.* He liked the thought of ten women hanging on his arms, obeying his every demand.

After several more pints Arne sighed and pushed himself up from the table. Light-headed, he wandered out into the cool night. The wind whipped his sparse hair about as waves crashed into the jagged shoreline.

The ocean talked to him as it had when he was a young boy. It groaned in pain, and at the same time there were the softer whispers of many voices. Urgent voices demanding something, arguing, to which the deeper tones resisted. *The water.* Arne was swept back to his childhood, his father beating him for breaking the chair. "That was my favorite fucking chair," his father had gritted out, the heavy wood arcing down to leave welts on Arne's tender flesh, imparting a gait that earned him the name "Popeye" in the navy.

The water. He had run to the water to escape the screams, to soothe the cuts upon his legs. And later, when he was old enough, Arne had let the sea carry him from his drunken father and weary, timorous mother.

It had been equally long ago, the night he had been masturbating into the water during a storm, too long at sea and horny as hell. Sure that no one would be on deck, a little drunk and too young to know better, Arne stood fantasizing about mermaids. Then a wave had smashed him over the rail. As the inky water closed over his head, Arne had silently cried out, *Not you too. Not the sea. Don't leave me . . . please*!

Down, down water weighted him, sucking life from his skin and lungs. Freezing blackness blanketed him, yet still he thrashed, knowing he was dead. As consciousness faded, he heard the voices of the ocean, as he had always heard them, but they were clearer, bell-like. *We will save you this once, Arne Simms. We will save you and send you back to the land, because you have asked this of us.*

Then he had dreamed, somewhere between drowning and life, of a woman part fish, who wrapped strong arms about him and pulled him onto rock. She watched over him until he fountained the saltwater from his lungs, then she pushed off the stone, the silvery blue scales sliding sinuously in the night air. The sky had quieted but clouds still scudded across it. Arne rolled over and grabbed her arms, pulling her back onto the rock to thank her. She had turned toward him and he saw the soft pearl-white mounds of her breasts. He ran his hand over them and down over her cool scales. She thrust him back, voicing something in a dream language, her large dark eyes showing anger, but Arne held tight. His fantasy took on a new intensity; a mermaid and he had her. He might never have her again. Her strength was great but could not equal a young sailor's. Arne's curiosity moved his hands over her strange body, searching for that secret fold in her scales. Then he pushed in as she mewed beneath him, her tail flipping helplessly. Eventually he slept.

He dreamed of swimming and had awoken, soaked, lying on the deck of the ship, two friends standing over him saying,

"You're lucky we heard you yell." He had never forgotten that dream, how it had made him feel—so alive, an adventurer discovering something new that was his.

Arne realized he stood on the beach but had no recollection of walking there. He whispered, "If you could come back to me," then rubbed his arm and looked away from the water to his door not far from the beach. Turning back to the frothing waves, Arne noticed a dark silhouette standing off to his right.

A split second of fear seized his vitals and he barked, "Who's there?"

The shadow moved in, coalesced into a woman, the wind whipping her long ebony hair into her face. He peered at her in the dark, picking up some detail as the sickle moon shone through the turbulent clouds. She was tall, nearly six feet, and her skin looked like alabaster in the thin light. Her bare feet dug into the sand, and she wore a gown of red that lay low on her shoulders and came to her knees.

She smiled and said, "Are you not Arne Simms?"

Arne, still feeling the pints he had drunk, thought her voice held a strange accent. Why did she ask if he was not Arne Simms? "'Course I am."

"I have come to talk with you." She shivered slightly and looked out to the water.

"Come," he signaled. "Come back to my place. It's just over there."

They walked in silence, the woman following Arne's steps while he wondered how she knew him. Arne stamped the sand from his shoes and crossed the street to his bungalow. He fumbled with the keys, finally unlocking the door. He entered and stared at the woman.

She stood at the threshold and asked, "May I enter?"

"Yeah, come on in." Arne closed the door behind her and flicked on a light.

She flinched, then sat on his gritty looking, faded green sofa. Arne stared at her and realized she looked a lot like Lisa, one of the women on his left vambrace. Her lips were a deep scarlet, her eyes the color of the sea after a storm. Thick brows, a long

75

nose and a wide mouth. Lisa liked it rough. He wondered if this woman did too.

"Who are you?"

She shrugged. "Call me what you will. I am come for you."

His eyes lingered on her deep cleavage. "You look like someone I know called Lisa. How do you know me?"

She looked up at him and said, "It is perhaps someone you once knew. I am here for you." She stood and reached out with one long-nailed hand.

She must be a gift. He remembered Lisa on his arm and how she liked it. Before Lisa's hand could touch his face, he swung out and smacked hers. She fell to the couch rubbing her jaw. Arne smiled and unbuttoned his shirt. "You liked that, didn't you, Lisa? Well, since you're here for me, there's more for you."

He fell on her and crushed his lips against hers, biting them until blood welled. She struggled and he punched her again. While she lay stunned, he pushed up her dress and roughly fondled her. His shirt off, the vambrace gleaming in the light, Arne moaned, "Lisa, Lisa" into her shoulder while unzipping his pants.

She squirmed, trying to pull her hands from his strong grip, but said nothing. Arne knew she was playing along and when he pushed into her, she lay still, silent as death. He released her hands and squeezed her breasts. He felt pinpoints of fire lance down his back, but the feeling, so long, so good, kept him from thinking of anything.

He looked at her as he came, shouting as fire flared through him. Her pupils contracted and she hissed, smiling—almost a grimace—through gleaming teeth. "Lisa," he moaned and fell against her.

Late in the night Arne came to and realized all lights but the nightlight were out. He was stretched naked on the couch, with Lisa's head rising and falling as she worked on him. He watched her, feeling himself respond. She looked up—her eyes seemed to glow, a reflection of the light—and pushed Arne down. When he came again, he was nearly senseless with the pain that shot through him, slicing up his arms, into his heart.

76

When Arne woke it was early morning. His head ached and his body throbbed. He thought perhaps he had drunk far too much to hallucinate last night's events.

He arose wearily and showered, trying to rid himself of the moldy odor that clung to him. He grunted. Perhaps he should clean.

After lunch Arne felt restored and picked up some of the soiled laundry in the living room. He shuffled papers about and puttered through the day. Then he ordered a pizza, and afterwards pulled off his shirt and looked at the vambraces he had replaced after the shower.

A couple of hours after dark, a knock shook his door. He rose, curious, and opened it, forgetting to cover his odd armbands. A short, well-rounded woman with ginger curls falling over her shoulder stood in the porch light.

She smiled and said, "Are you not Arne Simms?"

He raised his brow, remembering murkily someone else saying the same thing. "I am." He paused. "Wanna come in?"

She stepped across and he locked the door behind her. He glanced at the vambrace and yes, she looked almost identical to Eliza, who liked to be spanked with a stout wooden rod. Arne looked at the decorative African cane that stood in the corner and walked over to it. He turned and asked, "So who are you?"

She smiled and shrugged. "I am here for you."

"Just what I thought you'd say." His hand closed on the cane. "You a friend of Lisa's?"

She looked momentarily puzzled, then replied, "If you like."

"Come over here into the light, so I can see you better."

The woman padded over in bare feet to where Arne stood beside the overstuffed chair. He looked at her face and body wrapped in a tight, short dress. "Turn around." She did so and he pushed her forward over the large arm of the chair, pulling up her dress. She struggled silently and Arne held her head down forcefully. He picked up the carved cane and gave her ivory buttocks a hard smack. She jerked.

"Oh, Eliza, you're a bad girl, aren't you? You deserve a spanking."

Panting, Arne raised the cane and struck again. Red weals appeared on her backside. He continued hitting her as she struggled, till droplets of blood covered her butt and thighs.

The crotch of his jeans pulling tight, Arne stopped when Eliza finally wept. He undid his pants and, holding her in the same position, pushed her legs apart and thrust into her from behind. He mindlessly pummeled her, heedless to her movements, and when he came he fell backwards onto the floor.

He woke to her rhythmically moving up and down on him, her lips sucking hungrily at his chest. He came, blacking out instantly. In the morning, she was gone.

Two more days passed with Arne's vambrace beauties showing up after dusk, all barefoot and alluring. Each stayed the night—after a violent struggle he took his pleasure and felt searing pain. They were always gone by dawn. He decided some old navy buddy was repaying a favor. The first woman had probably studied the armbands, and then found other women who looked close enough to the others.

Arne decided to procure instruments for each of the other women's proclivities. He felt pleasantly tired, only natural considering the nocturnal activities. Some clerks regarded him oddly as he bustled into city sex shops, but Arne had rarely cared how other people felt. He was happy; he was getting what he wanted.

Arne's fifth nocturnal visitor was the black-market magazine woman called Arlene, who liked to be tied. She put up a fight and Arne, not up to his usual vigor, was panting by the time he finished. He almost cut her down and let her go, but after a drink and a few enticing wriggles from Arlene, he was ready. The woman never spoke; just the way he liked it.

Spent, in pain, he crawled to bed, leaving Arlene trussed. She watched silently. Deep in a feverish slumber, Arne dreamt that she came to him and sucked him dry of all remaining sexual fluids as searing agony lanced his nerves. He groaned but didn't wake.

Closer to noon, Arne pawed the grit from his eyes. Arlene was gone; he realized he had not released her. He lay in his bed of crumpled sheets and tugged at one of the vambraces. It itched but the clasp wouldn't undo, and yellowish pus trickled from beneath the plastic.

Somehow, he knew he had to keep the braces on for the women to show up. Finally, he got the cuffs off, staggered to the bathroom and cleansed his arms, then bandaged the necrotic, puckered flesh. Afraid to lose the spell, he refastened the vambraces. Splashing water on his face, he looked in the mirror. Years at sea had weathered him to ruddiness that never went away, but even so his skin looked pale.

Still feeling ragged, Arne swallowed a handful of stale vitamins, then opened the windows. The moldy odor permeated everywhere; perhaps a plumber was needed. Arne threw away a pair of mildewed socks in hopes of eliminating the cause. He spent the rest of the day in front of the TV drinking beer.

He'd been staring at the TV for the past hour but couldn't remember what he had watched. The spilled beer can wet his lap and he knocked it onto the floor. Outside had been claimed by darkness; the only light, the TV's pale blue flicker. Arne pushed himself out of the chair, stretched and scratched at his arm. The damn vambraces were itching again, but he couldn't remove them till morning or the women might not show up. Even though it was a bit exhausting, there were only five days left.

Arne smiled and rubbed the hardening member in his pants, thinking of the next woman. He opened the fridge and grabbed another beer, glancing at the array of sex toys and tools he had laid on the table. The cracked wall clock blatantly displayed 8:00. At the window, he peered from darkness into darkness, hoping to catch sight of the next treasure. Shore leave had never been this good, but then this was extended shore leave and it couldn't get any better.

The anticipated knock rattled the door. As he opened it, a diminutive girl with long strawberry blonde hair asked, "Are you not Arne Simms?"

"Yeah," Arne grunted and asked her in. He smiled, already feeling the erection. This was Sarah, who liked to pretend she was an innocent schoolgirl. Arne peered at her as she walked into the shadow-laden living room. She didn't seem to mind the pervasive damp, cloying stench as she gazed at his ornaments from the sea. A large clamshell, a wooden wheel, a nautical compass and several wall-mounted fish adorned his living room.

Sarah wore a short, pleated skirt barely covering her buttocks, and a white blouse with a large bow at the collar. Arne shifted as his erection grew, but knew he had to wait to get the full benefit of this fantasy. The pinup Sarah was a lush nineteen-year-old. In this light, she looked younger; small breasts, long legs, bare feet, creamy complexion. Arne decided she had done an excellent job on makeup to make herself look so young.

The only illumination was the reading lamp above the overstuffed chair. Arne surreptitiously unzipped his fly and sat in the chair. "Sarah, come sit on my lap and I'll tell you a story of the sea."

Smiling, she sat, and Arne began his tale.

"When a sailor has been at sea for many years it's like the water becomes a second home, full of voices that keep him company."

With a few pauses and stutters, he continued telling her of voices from the water that soothed, until Sarah rested her head upon his shoulder. One of his hands stroked her thigh, until he took her. Her struggle was just a put-on, he knew.

Lost in the act, Arne found himself reliving a day decades ago. He had been thirteen and the neighbor's girl, Charlotte, was ten. He had talked to her and given her candy while they threw stones at tin cans. Then, out behind old man Cramer's wood shack, Arne told Charlotte he'd show her a secret and had unzipped his pants. She had been fascinated until he pushed her down and showed her what it was meant for. He had loved it.

Arne came, the orgasm so exhilarating and so painful he felt like acid burned his flesh. Razors sliced his arms and back. Screaming, he passed into cool unconsciousness. When he awoke it was midafternoon and he felt sore all over and horny. Where was Charlotte? He would have her again. He rolled off the gritty carpet, absently scratching at his arms.

Pulling some slightly moldy pizza from the fridge, he chewed

80

it as he shambled to the bathroom. Urinating absentmindedly, splashing the toilet, he thought of the remaining women. Then he tore off the vambraces and greenish pus-soaked bandages, replacing them and reclasping the sex bands. *Gotta make more of these. This is too good*, he thought and laughed aloud. *Maybe it is magic. I don't know or care.* Once this escapade was over, he'd go to the doctor and make new bands that breathed better.

Arne went to a grocery store and bought enough food and beer so that he would not have to go out for the next four days. Aching, he shuffled back as quickly as he could, not wishing to miss the next visitor.

The seventh and eighth women appeared on their respective nights and Arne proceeded to use them for his fantasies. With the ninth woman, he filled every orifice using phallic-shaped objects. He knew she loved it because he had written out her likes.

Each time, Arne blacked out in searing pain from his orgasm. Each time, the pain grew worse. He awoke later and later.

It was already dark when he rose on the tenth night. He hadn't showered in several days and decided to take one before the last woman, Lamia, arrived. She'd get the works; he had a lovely metal-tipped flogger. Swaying dizzily, he moved to the bathroom. The decaying, nauseating smell permeated every room now. Noxious green mold tingeing to black lingered in the corners of the living room, but Arne would deal with it later. Tomorrow was soon enough, after these simple pleasures.

The dizziness persisted. Arne exhaustedly stepped from the shower and vomited, splashing the toilet with bloody chunks. "Damn store-bought pizzas," he growled. He didn't look too closely in the mirror.

He dressed in a loose, wrinkled shirt and faded gray pants, deciding to forego eating, and grabbed a beer. The curtains closed, Arne turned on one table light, preferring the shadows. He had finished his second beer when he heard the rap on the door. With difficulty he dragged himself up from the couch. The can tumbled onto the floor.

Arne opened the door to Lamia, tall, dark auburn hair full of waves tumbling over her shoulders. Her eyes flashed with a life of their own in palest green bordering on gray. Her blood-red lips smiled deeply; her teeth shone bone-white. Her sharp fingernails and toenails had an alabaster sheen to them, and her dress, the same color as her eyes, covered little.

The ocean, angry and foaming, smashed into the shore tonight, as if to batter back the land. Rain pelted down. Arne could not hear what she said but guessed it the same as all her sisters and asked her in, opening wide the door.

Lamia liked to be beaten and tortured near to unconsciousness. Arne reached up to wind his fingers in her hair. Her arm came up lightning fast and locked on Arne's wrist. He cried out from the pain and the plastic edges cut into his rash-swollen wrist. Blackish blood and green ooze trickled out.

Then he noticed that Arlene stood behind Lamia. "How did she—"

He saw movement out of the corner of his eye and there was Lisa, her wide mouth unsmiling. He turned and noticed Sarah, then Eliza and Rachel, raven-haired Mary, buxom Wendy, Coral and Sally. They were all there, standing in the room. He hadn't seen them enter, but then the sea drowned out the noise.

Lamia smiled and looked as if she were hungry. "We are come for you, Arne Simms."

She pushed him back on the couch with one long-nailed hand. When he tried to sit up, Rachel and Wendy held him down. Slowly the women undressed him except for the vambraces, trailing their nails and tongues down his body. Arne relaxed. It was just the grand finale.

They undressed themselves, never speaking. Arne tried to move, now that he was aroused, but their strength was too much. *Shouldn't have drunk the beer.*

Then, one by one, the women teased with hands or lips while he lay pinned. He tried to respond, sometimes to hit them, but they held him tighter. Each time Arne came, the pleasure grew less and the pain seared him, red-hot blades jabbing into his back and lungs. Still he didn't want to stop. Arne thought he'd black out or have a heart attack, but whenever black wings swooped into his vision, Lamia would come over and touch his brow and kiss it, whispering in her deep voice, "Not yet, Arne Simms. There is more for you."

Lamia's voice deepened, took on a timbre that resonated from the walls, echoing in Arne's skull. "Arne Simms, you called us to you. We came at your bidding and you took us and used us. Not once did you ask if we wished your violence upon us. You only took. We have paid in full and you have forfeited your contract."

It sounded as if crashing waves were inside Arne's head. "What are you talking about?" he shouted, feeling the first vague shivers of unease. "I never formed a contract." These were his dreams, weren't they?

"Did you not seed the ocean with your desires?" Lamia pointed at his wrists. "Did you not form those bands that bound you and us to your wishes? Did our mother not save you? Did you not use her? Were we not what you wished for?"

As Arne looked at Lamia and the women behind her, he thought they looked different, less human. All their eyes appeared large, watery, pale gray. Their skin seemed translucent, the thin veins pulsing beneath, and now they smiled with small, pointed shark teeth, lips pulling back.

Dread shriveled his balls and he babbled, "B-but none of you ever complained. I thought you were sent as a gift. I thought you were here for me."

They began to laugh, small tittering laughs, like birds gone mad.

"Oh, we are definitely here for you, Arne Simms," said Lamia as she leaned over him.

He shrank into the cushions as much as he could, though he was still pinned down by very strong arms. Arms that on close inspection seemed to have the smallest, lightest scales covering them.

"Have you ever, in your long life, done other than take, Arne Simms? Was there ever a woman that received what she wanted? Can you name even one who you treated as real? No,

Arne Simms, you have always taken. We are what you give. We are your seed."

With those words, the door crashed open with the howling of wind and sea spray. The squall and ocean surged and moved with monsoon force. Swirling out of the vapor and steam, forms took shape. Water dripped like tears down the walls, and the women licked the moisture with relish from their lips and faces.

Lamia and two others moved to Arne's sex toy table. He screamed above the roaring wind, refusing to see what took shape in the room. "You could have left, or said something. It was you, wasn't it? That smell? That comes from *you* things," he spat.

Lamia moved in close, holding a whip in one hand and a long needle in the other. "That smell is you, Arne Simms. It is what you have brought to yourself."

Arne's eyes widened as the shapes formed behind Lamia. Hulking muscular figures, like body builders overdosed on steroids. They were only vaguely human. Their gray and greenish skin dripped seaweed, covered in scales or boils. The faces bore shark teeth, slits for noses and eyes of an amber intensity that scorched Arne's flesh with hate. But that wasn't the worst. They were a naked indefinable sex with many large lumpy breasts and stallion-sized, distorted penises. They licked their lips and looked at him.

Lamia smiled widely and gestured at the rest of her species. One moved forward as the women turned Arne onto his stomach. "We are what *you give*, Arne Simms. We have taken the seed of your soul and you are ours now."

ABOUT THE AUTHOR
COLLEEN ANDERSON

Colleen Anderson is a three-time Aurora Award finalist, was longlisted for the Stoker Award in fiction and the Rhysling in poetry. She placed in the Balticon, Rannu and Crucible poetry competitions and has performed her work before audiences in the US, UK and Canada. Colleen also co-edited Canadian anthologies *Playground of Lost Toys* (Aurora nominated) and *Tesseracts 17*, and her solo anthology *Alice Unbound: Beyond Wonderland*, was published in 2018. *A Body of Work* was recently published by Black Shuck Books, UK. Some of her work is in *nEvermore!*, *Beauty of Death*, *Shoreline of Infinity*, *Heroic Fantasy Quarterly*, *OnSpec*, *Polu Texni*, *The Future Fire* and *Cemetery Dance*.

Facebook: https://www.facebook.com/colleen.anderson.9699

Webpage: www.colleenanderson.wordpress.com

COVERED IN CRIMSON

BY SIDNEY WILLIAMS

It starts at a party, the usual red cups and Long Island iced teas. Gemma Brand chats in the kitchen with her buddy Connor Ahn and his acquaintance, Erik—her first time meeting him, and at first she isn't sure about his degree path.

Everyone here's in a master's or PhD program and letting off steam, so Erik Hagen's probably working on a thesis with some yard-long title with words like *exploring* or *impact*. She doesn't really care about that. He's more than six feet tall, blond-haired with a Nordic, Viking vibe and Connor's just a friend, so it's open season for her to twirl her hair as he talks. Hers is almost shoulder-length these days though the curls make it look shorter. Ask her tonight if you're, say, Erik, and she'll tell you the color is strawberry blonde.

Gemma listens, taking in the technical jargon. She's letting her drink fuzz the edges on the econ work in the back of her mind—her thesis involves phrases like *micro influences on consumer decisions*, and she's tired of contemplating those at the moment.

She's instead thinking about how even though she's five-eight, Erik's a bit like a mountain to be climbed. Yeah, because it's there and all that, and she's been too busy for any rock climbing lately, no time even to go the artificial route on the wall at the gym.

While he's dropping terms like *trust* and *submission* that are barely sinking in, she's working on body language, cocking a hip—none of her tomboy accusations tonight—as she leans

86

against the counter and makes eye contact as if she's absorbed by his theories.

She waits a while to touch his arm as she agrees with an opinion. After that, he starts to take notice of her lips as she asks about SSC. It's about safe, sane and consensual activities "in the community," as he puts it. She's genuinely intrigued after that, no need to feign it.

"How does that work?" she asks when he gets to knife play.

"One person submits to play with a blade on the part of another," he says. "Usually the blade teases the skin, and it's kept gentle enough. Some people use showy knives, switchblades and the like to generate fear, but it's mostly keeping the flat of the blade against the flesh."

"Usually?" She doesn't slur it, but discovers there are a lot of syllables in that word.

"It can get darker, knife play extremes being just one example, and that's where some of my research is targeted. Sometimes, if the right buttons are pushed, things move beyond the guidelines for the BDSM community, SSC: safe, sane and consensual."

She finds a lock of hair and runs it around an index finger. "That's more exciting than social behavior in globalism, consumerism, consumption."

"The research is not totally different, because the human factor has to be considered, but I wind up in some interesting clubs."

She touches his arm again. Can he feel how soft her flesh is? "You do any knife play of your own?"

He smiles. It's kind of wry. "I might have to demonstrate a bit for the defense of my dissertation."

"Could you do it for me?"

He smiles again. "I know the parameters . . ."

"Sounds exciting. There's gotta be a room here."

"I don't know that this sounds like a good idea," Connor says. He's been silent, just kind of taking all this in, probably doing observation notes of his own in his head. Maybe a tad jealous.

He also knows she can be a little impulsive even without a few Long Island iced teas in her system. She's been that way as long as she can recall. Rock climbing's just one symptom.

"So you can be the safe guy," she says. "Or referee, or whatever."

Even Erik's a little hesitant. "I don't know that—"

"Oh, come on . . ."

They ask around and come up with a pocketknife. The blade's stainless steel and sharp though under three inches. The handle's exotic with a bit of ornamentation.

Erik experiments with the blade edge as they find a den tucked in the back of the house. He opens and closes the knife a few times, tests the sharpness again, generally gets comfortable with it.

"Like a lot of play, it's about trust," he says, as Gemma drops onto a mini-sofa at the edge of the room and unzips her hoodie.

"Not about opening a vein?"

"Not encouraged, no."

She reclines and slides her tee-shirt up over her stomach, abs looking good, smooth and flat—complexion to go with the strawberry blonde hair. "Does this give you some space to work?"

"For a demo." He looks to Connor. "Why don't you go see if there's a first-aid kit around, or at least some cotton and Band-Aids, just in case. That's always a good idea, even if you're being careful."

Connor's slow to react, but finally nods, eyes wide at the concept that first aid's in the picture. Gemma likes the tease of that.

"So you move that on my skin?"

Erik lays the blade flat against her abdomen near the belly button, letting her feel the cold.

"Wow."

"And we move it around a bit," he says.

He slides it across her skin, downward diagonally from her navel, not getting anywhere risqué, not anywhere to check the righteousness of strawberry blonde, just letting the sensation work. She bites her lip and blinks a few times. It is electric, especially when he lets the sharp edge touch—a hint of a touch really, not quite a scrape, but it awakens nerve endings and sends tingling pulses.

She feels a twitch, her back threatening to arch, but she avoids the impulse for fear of surprising Erik and forcing something unintended.

Fear.

There it is. She's scared, alone here with this stranger. He could do anything with the blade while Connor is out of the room.

Carefully she moves a millimeter along the lounge, seeking a slightly deeper touch and even more of a possibility. He presses harder; the blade's flat spine digs into tissue.

More tingles.

Warmth between her legs, a hardening in her nipples.

"This would progress to cutting off clothing in many cases," Erik said.

"Is that edge play?"

"You've heard of some of this. If you consider anything like this edge play. It's still SSC to most practitioners."

"You'd cut my shirt?"

"Yeah."

It's an old tee from a charity fun run when she was an undergrad, soft and comfortable, lettering long faded. "Do it," she says.

"You sure?"

"I'll zip up my hoodie on the walk home."

He's working on the thick fabric at the hem, getting through that tough part when Connor returns. He's found a bandage package and some alcohol. They already sterilized the knife with rum, but that could come in handy.

"It's okay," she says. "Really."

Erik slices through the hem, pauses, looks into her eyes for consent, which she grants, then he proceeds with the blade, parting the soft thin material with ease. He takes it slow, and she lies back, watching her stomach rise and fall as it's exposed again, then her lower ribs, then the pink bra and the curve of her breasts. She's almost panting as the blade reaches the collar line resting on the tip of her jugular notch.

She closes her eyes and wills him: *Go.*

He does, using the blade to flick back both flaps of cloth. She quivers as the steel moves, again not scraping, just stimulating. He slides the point down between her breasts then rests it on the thick connecting fabric between the cups.

She can imagine the blade piercing flesh and that ignites more warmth.

She does arch her back now. The knife point pricks the inside of her left breast.

Connor gasps.

She opens her eyes to a black pearl of blood. Erik's pulled back, frozen.

She touches the bead, flattening it, smearing it. Bringing her fingers to her lips, she moves the tips along the bottom one, flicks her tongue out. She can't quite believe the charge.

She makes eye contact with Erik, locks to his gaze and asks Connor to give them some privacy.

* * *

It's called blood play. Erik provided the name. After.

She thinks about it as Connor walks her toward her residence hall even though his crazy-rich Asian parents fund a nice place for him across campus. He rarely minds detours to her door.

The hoodie is zippered to her throat. Her hair's disheveled, and Connor can't quit talking about the same dangers Erik mentioned. It is blood after all. Not something to take lightly.

She's too caught up in the rush, wouldn't be surprised if she has a glow at the moment.

The risks infused the experience: Erik's finger painting a streak from her breast to her sternum as he worked on the front of her jeans, making the buildup as amazing as climbing onto him after using her mouth to get him ready, streaking his length with blood.

90

The edge is kind of intoxicating.

* * *

Of course, she's not going to start hitting clubs in search of new adventure. The edge is one thing, but she doesn't plan to plunge over it.

She chats up Kylie Belanger. She's new in the lower-cost grad residences, twenty-one, finished a degree and started right in on a master's, and she caught Gemma's eye on the stairs the second week of the semester. She's taller than Gemma with short clipped hair, bright red lipstick (sometimes black, suggesting a hint of the offbeat), and if Kylie means "graceful" as the baby name website suggests, it's appropriate. She carries herself well, must do yoga, maybe even some dance. If Gemma has a bi-curious streak, it's Kylie who piques it.

So she joins Kylie for a few meals, and yes, she does yoga to relieve stress even though the semester's just cranking up. Kylie has a grumpy advisor too, and she has two years of this ahead. So they find time to get together for some asanas.

It's easy enough to check for sidelong glances in the warrior pose, and Gemma notes Kylie checking her out with mutual curiosity that carries over to the showers and isn't hard to engineer into something more fairly quickly. Gemma understands marketing, consumer behavior and rewards. A convenient make-out session can be a great way to take your mind off a crusty advisor.

It's after a couple of those spontaneous sessions that she mentions the edge, and, as she suspected, it doesn't fail to intrigue the side of Kylie that's prone to that occasional and ever-so faint hint of kink that's complemented by piercings discovered in a friendly grope—navel, both nipples.

"I've heard of that," Kylie confides. "It's intriguing."

They try a little play with a knife from the cafeteria; almost no edge so it's the cold and the smoothness that's deployed. They start with nude yoga.

Nipples get a touch as Kylie strikes poses. Then Gemma teases her smooth-shaved lower stomach, flattening the blade on the labia. Kylie returns the favor, working the skin-warmed steel across Gemma's thighs once she's lying back on a pile of throw pillows.

"We should get something cool," Kylie suggests as she traces Gemma's belly button with the rounded tip of the blade.

"Like what?"

"I don't know, something *Game of Thrones*. I think they make all kinds of items like that, and knives for rituals and the like."

"On Saturday, we can go shopping," Gemma suggests, taking the implement gently from Kylie's grasp. She's been pressing it in a little too hard, creating discomfort.

Gemma puts it aside and pulls Kylie on top of her.

* * *

The first shop's a little utilitarian featuring some flashy numbers, but not what they're looking for. It's the third stop, a pawn shop, where Kylie latches onto something sexy: a stone-bladed job with a curved wooden handle. It's styled to look rustic, but it's obviously newer and crafted.

Gemma touches the rough black side of the blade—guy behind the counter describes it as obsidian. It's named the Eye of Sargas, possibly Sumerian.

"What's the provenance?" Gemma asks, half-joking.

"As I was told it," says the clerk, who's a big *Sons of Anarchy*-looking guy, "you don't want to give a knife to someone. Bad luck, so guy that brought it in didn't want to take any chances. Money changes hands this way."

"Why's it bad luck?" Gemma wonders.

"Severs the cord on a friendship."

Kylie takes it, touches it to her cheek and bats her eyes at Gemma. "This has gotta be the one. We'll buy it together. No danger there, right?"

"Sounds okay to me," the clerk says.

Gemma's puts up most of the cash. She didn't expect to part with so much of it, but the blade's a hand-crafted collector's item. Which means "sold on Etsy," she suspects, but it's putting a look of love-lust in Kylie's eyes, so okay.

Kylie's googling as soon as they get in the car. "Apparently Sargas is an older name for a star in the tail of Scorpius. It also means *arrowhead* in Persian. They're not sure of the name origin, but it's a binary star. Not what you think. One of two stars that orbit each other or a common object."

She holds up the knife and jiggles it. Giggles. "There you have it. This would be called an athamé." She's sounding it out. She corrects herself on the last syllable. "My. Ath-a-*my*. Used in Wicca but goes back to the Golden Dawn Society. Sometimes darker magic."

"Who knows where it's been?"

That prompts a sterilization search for stone, and they decide heating should take care in the unlikely event of anything lingering.

So: candles.

Also sexy.

* * *

Kylie accepts her bonds without resistance, extending her arms behind her as Gemma ties soft ribbon at her wrists, at the elbows.

She's wearing a black night dress. Sexy but expendable. She crouches on her knees near the edge of her bed, a silhouette in the candlelight. A glow edges her bare arms. Her breaths are audible, increasing as Gemma steps forward, the athamé raised.

Gemma lifts it into the air, clasped in both hands as someone performing a ritual might. Then she kneels in front of Kylie and places the blade against the fabric, pausing, letting anticipation build, just like Erik did. She makes the cut, parting a small *V* at the hemline. The stone's not the sharpest, but the lacy cloth offers little resistance, ripping readily, the slit widening as she moves the knife in a steady glide, watching the gown open over long, smooth, perfect thighs.

93

She pulls the fabric toward her to avoid danger over the abdomen, slowing above the sternum to look into Kylie's soft blue eyes. They're filled with adoration and submission.

She moves the blade on, feeling her knuckles brush against a soft breast. Then the lace is parted, and she rises higher on her knees, leaning in for a kiss.

Kylie's wearing the almost-black lipstick. Exotic.

She kisses hard, devouring her lips, finding Kylie's tongue for an entwining dance. Then, with the blade pressed into Kylie's stomach, she kisses down her chest, across her breasts, tongue teasing the piercings.

Kylie's spine arches as Gemma moves back to her neck. "Touch me with it," she demands. "Touch me with it there."

Gemma's careful, but she does.

Then she moves it back against the flat stomach. Up the abdomen. She makes the nick near a lower rib. Perhaps accidentally. Perhaps she intentionally presses a little too hard. She's not sure. Was Erik's accident on purpose?

A soft sigh-like expression issues from Kylie's throat, but then her head tilts back and she draws a slow, soft breath. "Kiss me."

Gemma leans in, flicks her tongue to the spot where the tiny round bead has appeared. When she moves back, another replaces the first. She touches that with a fingertip, flattening it, realizing what she's wanted. She presses until it smears, then draws a horizontal line below the rib cage. Kylie's abdomen rolls with the caress.

Kisses continue, and Gemma finds more crimson leaking from the pinprick. She grabs a shoulder, turning Kylie with a hint of roughness, cuts the ribbons and offers her the blade.

They trade off, with the drawing and smudging of blood. Kylie scrapes Gemma with the obsidian blade, the pressure deep enough to turn skin rosy, before doodling circles around her breasts and a line from breastbone to groin, like a gash.

They have to put on robes later for the shower down the hall. If anyone peeks in once they've closed the curtains, the swirl around the drain will look like the scene from *Psycho*.

*　*　*

"I read where there's power in blood," Kylie says. "Like supernatural power. I mean, it's what a lot of cultures believed. I found a PDF of a whole dissertation on it."

They're having lunch at a little bistro in town, sitting at an outdoor table. In the sunlight it doesn't seem as creepy.

"Some of it's anti-woman and anti-Semitic, of course, but you get past all the witch hammering, you can see that, to a less-enlightened mind than ours, there's a logic to a power being contained in the life force."

"I guess so, yeah."

"You have to wonder if there really is power to be harnessed," Kylie says. "A lot of it, philosophically, is about the will, your will, and kind of repetitive expression of it."

"I haven't pored over the details," Gemma says.

"Kind of exciting though, the possibilities." Kylie's eyes blaze. "You express your will, the blood shows the universe you're serious."

Just then, Gemma notices a drop of dark red Russian dressing dribbling from the corner of Kylie's mouth.

*　*　*

It's a day or so later when she sees more red. Head throbbing from efforts to express economic theory in English, lunch forgotten, she taps on Kylie's door for a break and conversation.

Since it's unlocked, she pokes her head in and sees streaks on the sheet, like the worst period on record set in during a nap.

Christ, looks like enough to lose consciousness.

She steps inside, closer to the crimson marks, black-red really, still wet and glistening under fluorescent bulbs. She notices what she thinks are thick bands causing a *Trompe-l'œil* effect. Then she realizes she's seeing thin tentacles, and her stomach turns.

No, not tentacles. She's seeing entrails, dull and pink-grey but striped with blood. She spouts more deific words mixed with profanities and stumbles backwards into Kylie, who's stepping into the room. She's in a robe, towel around her neck, hair wet.

"What the fuck happened?" Gemma asked.

"A bit of an experiment."

"What . . ."

"It's a rabbit. They have a million of them in the biology department."

It should be repulsive, but Gemma doesn't resist as Kylie rests a hand on her shoulder, moves in closer.

"I'm kidding. It's yarn and body paint. But it was kind of exhilarating. Thinking about blood and . . . everything." She presses a hard kiss onto Gemma's lips. "I thought about you being here. Not just smearing you with blood, but draping you with innards, snaking them across your belly . . ." Her eyes widen and imply more. "Can you imagine what's inside us?"

A scarlet tint blossoms on her cheeks, more than just aftereffects of the shower. She pokes a finger into Gemma's abdomen, the nail pressing through the fabric. It's hard enough to bring a slight pain to Gemma's flesh.

"That's a little more extreme than—"

Kylie kisses her again. "We can just imagine. Is there any way to be any closer to someone than . . . ?" Her head tilts back, eyes closed, features softening. "A total connection, to be wrapped in the other person's—"

"Let's hit the pause button," Gemma suggests, easing herself away. "I have to get back to my paper. Had only a few minutes for a break."

She caresses Kylie's cheek, smiles, slips out the door. When it closes behind her, she leans against the wall, taking in as much air as she can manage through the available avenues.

She can't stop thinking of Kylie pressing the stone blade into her side, piercing her abdominal wall, and of slipping fingers inside her.

She's a little wet.

How's this possible?

96

"Fucking insane." Connor's shocked when she catches him on a stroll across the quad. He's come by to walk with her to a class, but his pace slows. "If she's not joking, you better—pardon the pun or whatever it is—cut ties before this gets out of hand."

"She could be just pushing buttons."

"What do you even know about her other than that she's hot? You could have tapped into her inner—Jesus, everything has two meanings here—Dahmer."

"The serial killer?"

"Yeah, he came up in one of my abnormal psych classes. Jeffrey Dahmer was fascinated with the insides of his victims. They dubbed his condition a paraphilia." He pauses and pulls a Samsung tablet from his backpack, flipping with quick taps to his notes.

He shows her the word *splanchnophilia* and says: "Splank no filia."

* * *

In spite of those technical details, it's Erik's response that is more clinical.

"It was a little terrifying," she confides to him. "And a little creepy, but . . ."

The corners of his mouth tick up slightly. "You've inadvertently branched into fear play."

"When you're scared knife play is going to go too far?"

"Something like that."

He's sipping a mug of chai as he sits in an armchair in front of bookcases stuffed with psychology texts at his apartment. Dressed in a sweater with a shawl collar, rimless glasses on tonight, hair pulled into a ponytail, he's looking more like a Viking professor than the warrior she first met.

Well, let him instruct.

"Fear play, then—that's letting a scare turn you on?"

97

"Sex and fear produce some similar responses in the brain. And in the body. Maybe she's picked up on that and was pushing your buttons. Or maybe she's really kinky and wants to gut you and dance in your entrails."

"Thanks for that image. Is there a precedent for that?"

"Well, there are rituals involving just about everything historically, but in terms of play, you'd be passing SSC or even RACK."

"Alphabet soup."

"Risk-aware consensual kink. Pushes the envelope but with a handshake agreement it won't go too far. The risk here would be too extreme. No way the setting could be sterile enough. How would someone survive it? They'd have to be rushed to a hospital immediately, and the cops would have questions. It could go really wrong really fast, but it might be really exciting on the way."

* * *

A stripe appears across her abdomen as Kylie drags the blade. It's just a pink reaction, a tingle. They've agreed she won't break the skin, keeping it SSC to borrow Erik's term, or the official phrase. She's always had an inclination toward what's been dubbed novelty, so she's let the warnings slide, trusting the promises even as Kylie's lips touch and whisper into her ear.

"Your flesh spreads for me. You give yourself to me."

She closes her eyes, imagining the cold, jagged blade zippering skin, flesh giving way to the warm insides.

"My hand dips inside . . ."

The touch at her ear becomes a kiss, another.

"My fingers move in . . . out . . ."

Kylie's now wearing only a thin, black lace-up choker. Her lipstick is black tonight. She has ringed her eyes with dark liner, and Gemma imagines they are obsidian as well as the blade.

She feels the sting, the athamé biting too deeply. Grabs a wrist before it breaks flesh, pushes the arm away. "Too hard."

They've both allowed pinpricks before for the blood play, but with the imaginings, the mental movie show of penetration and entrails, the sting is frightening. She pulls closed the lace robe Kylie parted earlier, fumbles for the silk tie.

"You have to be careful."

"I wasn't going to go too far." The look in Kylie's eyes doesn't offer calm. It's too hungry. "I'm sorry." She puts an arm around Gemma's neck. Kisses hard.

Gemma allows it for a second then pulls away.

"I just want to be close to you."

"I know, I know. Close is fine, but . . ."

Fingertips spider-walk up Gemma's thigh. "You know how good it feels when my fingers are inside you. Think of the feel of even deeper. Erik said—"

She stops the move with a wrist grab. "You've been talking to Erik?"

"At the coffee shop. He recognized me, said he'd seen us together and that you were a friend." Her head tilts. Involuntarily quizzical. "I was a little hurt at first you'd told him, but he was intrigued, and we talked about blood and the power."

"Hmm. Could be clinical to him. He might be curious about what you believe or want."

His interest is clinical, but it smarts more than the blade's kiss. This has been about excitement, adventure, but now there's an emotional tug. A bit of jealousy? Or betrayal? From both of them?

It's casual, she reminds herself, even as she remembers trust is important when you're edging into RACK territory.

Kylie's mouth returns to her cheek, her ear, her neck, distracting. The sting shocks her out of a burgeoning ecstasy. The stone blade's slipped under the robe, is positioned beside her navel, pressing in too hard for comfort, the edge digging deep. It reminds her of that shot in *Psycho*, the one they filmed in reverse with the knife actually penetrating flesh.

She feels a rush, but she puts a hand on Kylie's wrist one more time. "Do we need a safe word? How about 'ouch'?"

"Sorry. Carried away."

The blade eases up but not completely as Kylie tries for more kisses that seem hungry and desperate.

Gemma pulls the wrist back again. "I think I'd better get some work done tonight," she says. "I only had time for an interlude."

It's the truth. She's been wrangling with her advisor on the virtues of a chapter on consumer behavior. She needs to revisit it. If she can concentrate. She slips off the bed, finds her jeans as Kylie rises onto her knees.

"Sorry, I didn't mean . . ."

"It's okay."

But the hungry look is almost carnivorous now. Coupled with the smeared black edges of her lipstick, it is more than unsettling.

"Talk to you soon."

She gets her robe off and a sweatshirt over her head in rush of fabric. Then she heads for the door, her last thought not of the hungry eyes but of the athamé and what it might feel like piercing flesh and muscle.

* * *

"I don't think this is safe any longer," Connor says on their morning walk across the quad. "You have been known to make some wrong decisions on impulse. That guy last summer . . ."

"This has just been a little refreshing, a diversion, but . . ."

"You need to be careful with her. She's looking a little stranger every time I see her."

"I may have inadvertently activated her inner goth."

"You might have awoken something worse, and I'm worried about what's up with you."

Gemma stops walking and grabs his arm, spinning him toward her. "What's that mean?"

He looks away, squinting into the sun. Then he shrugs. "I wasn't going to tell you, but I looked into her a bit."

"Did I ask you to do a background check?"

"I showed initiative. You're lucky she didn't have a real rabbit from the biology lab. Look—"

"I don't want to hear it." She takes a step. There haven't been any benefits in their friendship in a long while. He's as jealous as she was about Kylie mentioning Erik.

"Ask about her sister."

She stops. "What?"

"She had a sister die in an accident. I'm carrying books or I'd do air quotes."

Gemma feels her expression turn quizzical.

"It was a fall from a retaining wall behind their home."

"Christ, what did you do? Get a juvenile record unsealed?"

"I found news accounts."

She cocks her head and lifts an eyebrow.

"Then I talked to someone who was good with getting around roadblocks."

"So how do we know it wasn't an accident?"

"They were both on the wall. Sitting. The sister, who was younger, took a nasty spill. Went down on her head, and it opened up like a pumpkin."

"They think she pushed her?"

"She wasn't charged, but they found her standing over the body. Staring."

"That's kind of what you'd expect her to be doing, isn't it? Shock?"

"There was a quote in one of the articles from a neighbor. She talked about Kylie looking like she was in a trance—a fascinated trance, not one of shock and awe. Fascinated by her sister's pulped brains? That sounds like splanchnophilia."

He pulls out his phone, touches the screen a few times and finds something stored in his notes.

"She was like a kid looking at a bright, shiny balloon or the ice cream truck. It was beyond shock."

"All that was in a news article?"

"I said I got around some roadblocks. It was expressed for a police report. There were suspicions. Some reports of her talking about it to a neighbor."

101

"It's conjecture." Gemma is moving again. "I have to get to class. Watch the snooping, Connor. It's like you're a little obsessive."

They've never talked about his lingering crush on her, just kind of let it be unspoken and unrequited.

She leaves him to stand and stare after her.

* * *

Despite the privacy issues, the history lesson is unsettling, and she hasn't fully processed Erik-and-Kylie contact yet. She can't shake a feeling he connected with Kylie to push buttons, maybe offering suggestions to see where things might go whether it's out of curiosity or in some misguided stab at research.

Maybe there's a way to deal with both matters at once.

Following her morning session in a small group on tools to detect micro economic trends, she finds Erik teaching a course to a tiered lecture hall filled with undergrads. She waits on a hallway bench until he emerges following a round of the usual post-class questions, some from freshmen girls who seem infatuated as they tilt their faces to look up at him.

"Look, I know you've had some conversations with Kylie," she says after the preliminaries. "What's your take?"

"On her?"

"On her, on any convictions she's developing about blood and magic, anything like that."

One eyebrow ticks upward. "What's she saying?"

"What'd you tell her?"

His innocent look appears feigned.

"Come on, are you stoking anything? For your research? It can't be following protocol."

"That's a pretty severe accusation. If I were studying her or you, and I'm *not*, I couldn't do anything that would affect outcomes. It's just like you said: protocol. My involvement would poison the data. Is she concerning you? Still scaring you?"

It's a dodge, but she fills him in, and he nods as he listens.

102

"Yet you're drawn somehow? It's a little like adrenaline junky behavior. Especially with this info about her sister, you're terrified, but can you leave her alone? You know, some of novelty-quest behavior is thought to be in the genes. Do you have any background like that?"

"Maybe on my dad's side. He liked to climb things."

"Chances are restraint would prevail. It's a little different than anything I've come across so far."

"You weren't stoking things with talk of magick?"

"If anything, I answered a question. What do you think you should do?"

"Give it some time to cool, I guess."

He's playing the psychologist. Asking questions to make her search her feelings, and she knows that's true. Things have come close to getting out of hand, and she realizes that's what troubles her. She fears giving in to Kylie's impulses and her philia, what Kylie has a history and need for. It intersects Gemma's need for the new, different, odd.

"Cool is the best idea," she says. "Thanks for the chat."

She turns down an offer of getting coffee. Time to disentangle from everything for a while, focus on the thesis.

* * *

That works out fine for a week or so. She gets the chapter rewritten and turned in to her advisor for review, gets back to preparing for a rigorous discussion in a class and finds her energy again, and the curiosity that's fueled her work.

She answers Kylie's texts but keeps her at a distance. Just some space, she promises. Schoolwork's kicking her ass. Sad emoticons punctuate.

Kylie accepts it and all seems fine. Until Gemma staggers into her floor's bathroom one night, half dazed from REM sleep but compelled by a pressing bladder.

She's sitting down when she hears the rustle of vinyl and the rattle of rings of a shower curtain on its rod.

"Who's there?"

She regrets having relied solely on night-level lighting and not searching out the wall switch for the overheads. It's grey in here, shadows along the walls and in the corners.

"Hello."

Nothing.

Then a whimper.

She wipes quickly and rises. "Come on, who's there?" The suspicion's immediate. She knows deep down the acceptance of distance was reluctant, so of course her mind goes there: "Kylie?"

The sound's coming from the row of shower stalls at the opposite end of the room. She crosses the chilled tile, following the sound, ignoring the closed curtains that shroud empty units. Zeroing in midway along the row, she grasps the vinyl and rips it aside. She should have prepared herself.

It's Kylie, all right. She sits in the corner, floor around her smeared grey-black, her hands covered in a gleaming darkness, like oil in the dim light. Streaks stretch down her forearms, and her cheeks look like she's been crying black tears. Her white tee-shirt is spattered, her legs splashed almost like she's wearing shredded stockings, speckled like the otherwise stark tile walls around her, making the scene an alarming snapshot of gore and carnage in near black-and-white.

Gemma drops to her knees, checking wrists first then looking for wounds in other areas. She sighs relief when none are severe. Pricks and small slits have been made with the athamé that's at her side, and they've produced a lot of blood, but Kylie's been making the most of the lesions.

"Am I beautiful?" she asks.

"Lovely."

"Do you want me?"

Gemma kisses her forehead softly and mutters platitudes. Satisfied nothing's life-threatening, she slips hands under Kylie's arms and gets her upright, then peels off the tee-shirt and her panties. There's no resistance.

Gemma strips off her own gown before turning the water on, not waiting for it to get warm. Kylie cackles at the frozen blast, but it seems to steady her as well. She lets Gemma work with the spray, getting the blood off her skin. She turns and leans in, flattening palms on the wall as Gemma works to get blood of the stall so it won't look like a murder scene or a severe menstrual crisis.

"There's a blood moon coming up," Kylie says as a grey swirl circles the drain. "A lot of power. That would be an amazing time to be together. Think of it. The moon, red outside the window and . . ."

"Where did that come from?"

"Studying."

"Right." Gemma nudges Kylie's chin upward with a finger to look into her eyes. "Where?"

"Erik mentioned it."

"You talked to Erik again."

"We bumped into each other in the library. He showed me a book and some things on the internet."

After he'd increased the longing with separation.

"It's a good idea to stay away from Erik," she says.

"He's nice."

"Did he give you whatever you took tonight?"

A giggle.

Gemma finds her gown and slips back into it even though it looks like she's worn it to a homicide party.

"Wait here. I'm going to find something for you to put on and get you back down to your room."

* * *

She considers confronting Erik and decides against it. If he's playing a manipulative game or conducting a twisted research project, maybe knowing more about him is in order. Maybe she can take a page from Connor. It's not exactly observing market behavior, but similar principles apply.

She spends a little time doing research of her own. She tries on paper for a while, the web, old yearbooks at the school library. Seems average enough. She decides to follow him when she can, working to keep a safe distance.

He doesn't deviate from the mundane for a while. Research, meetings, coffee. No S&M clubs or arcane bookshops off the beaten path, and above all, no secret meetings with Kylie. Doesn't mean they're not talking or texting, but there's no direct contact.

She googles it and notes the blood moon's date. Just in case.

Erik's one divergence from routine comes on a chilly afternoon. He ducks down a side street unexpectedly, winds his way across a couple of blocks. It starts to look like rescheduling her workshop wasn't such a bad idea.

Gemma's first thought about the woman is: vintage. Her dress under a black overcoat looks somehow 19th century, a black-lace overlay, long, worn with high-heeled boots.

Erik talks to her briefly before she hands him an envelope, bulky, brown and sealed. After an exchange of only a bit longer, they smile and part ways.

Gemma's brain evokes a hundred possibilities. She tries to slow her thinking, focus on the rational. It, of course, can be research data. She looks like she could be the leader of a dark focus group.

She could be much more.

As the woman walks away, Gemma finds the presence of mind to pull her phone and snap pictures.

* * *

"Graphic artist?"

"Explains the garb," Connor says.

He's helped with the reverse image search and the other efforts online that have finally borne fruit. She goes by Annie Briar and has an Instagram featuring her work, selfies and portraits often with thorny borders. There's a definite goth leaning to her work.

"Doesn't tell us much."

"She'd be the person to go to if he needed diagrams for a dissertation," Connor says.

"That'd be an illustration you might put in a formal document. There could be other things in his work that needed a visual explanation."

"At least following him has kept you busy and helped enforce your separation from Kylie."

Touché. Good point. "I saw her heading to a class the other day. She looked a little pale, but she's hanging in."

"I could mention something to someone in Student Support Services," Connor said. "Give you a little distance."

"Maybe not a bad idea, just for her wellbeing."

* * *

And it's back to microeconomics for a while. She immerses enough to lose track of the passage of days. The chapter that's been in question gets a rewrite, and her advisor shows inklings of approval. The argument's "balanced and supported and furthers the concept set forth" in her outline.

She digs into another revision that should finalize it and let her move on to conclusions, fueling herself with caffeine and the occasional tablets a pre-med friend scores.

She leaves Kyliewatch up to Connor, trusting him to take notice when he sees her around campus. He's not to engage, just make sure she's not hurting herself (probably not a danger to others).

She worries less about Erik. If he was using them as some sort of experiment, he's probably tired of it and moved on to playing games with others if that's his kink. She doesn't worry about further contact with him. Karma will catch up with him if he's not as innocent as he professes. He'll push the wrong buttons, poison his data and find himself back at square one.

She's, of course, decided too soon that all is well. The blood moon is on the way and requests for personal space never really work.

Kylie texts her. It's not half-crazed and bloody in the shower room, so there's that.

Blood moon is almost here, and I have some new info on the energy. Can we get together?

Would love 2, but elbows deep in thesis. ☺ Maybe soon.

Can I show you the info?

They text-duel to a draw, a coffee date. Public, should be safe.

Gemma reaches the shop before Kylie the next afternoon. She hasn't had a break in a while so she indulges: a latte and a scone. She's relaxed and in the middle of those when Kylie pushes through the door like a microburst, looks around and spots her.

She's disheveled, hair looking untended. She hurries over and drops into a seat, eyes eager. A leather satchel dangles from her shoulder, bouncing against her hip as she moves. "It's good to see you."

"Nice to see you too. You want something? On me?"

She's not malnourished nor pale at least. No goth lipstick today, but there's a hint of desperation. "Just plain coffee is fine."

They wave over a barista and get that on its way.

"I got these pages," Kylie says, "on sex and blood magic—a segment of the *Infernus Facta*."

"That's supposed to be the, like, forbidden . . . what do you call them?"

"Grimoires. They were more common than the movies make it out, but the *Infernus Facta* is more like the *Grand Grimoire*, not the kind of novelty tomes that were passed around once upon a time. It's more the real deal."

She paws open the satchel, tugging out pages that look like parchment. Brown, stiff, jagged edges crumble with signs of age. "They're not in English, of course . . ." She leans across the table, pointing to symbols with bold dark lines that stand out amid rune-like characters in black and red.

She shuffles a bit, bringing out some photocopied pages, hand-scribbled documents. "These translate—"

108

"Hold on." Gemma catches her wrist. "Where'd you get these?"

"Don't be mad, but I was talking to Erik. He knew someone with contacts."

Kylie's coffee arrives, and they lean back so it can be placed in front of her.

"Listen to me," Gemma says once the barista is gone and Kylie's taking a gulp. Maybe she is malnourished a little. Gemma pushes the remains of her scone over to her. "I think . . . I know . . . It's a long story, but I saw Erik talking to an artist. This is exactly the kind of thing she'd specialize in."

Hurt and disappointment cross Kylie's features, then morph into an indignant mask. "It's not fake. We've always said there was something in the blood, power, energy. This says—look here—blood magic can be powerful. It can give you almost anything you want."

Gemma shuffles papers as Kylie gobbles the scone. "I'm not an expert on these things, but these pages are probably aged somehow, the symbols an artsy font. Can't you download those?"

She's poring over the markings and remembering Annie Briar's promotional materials as the pages rustle, startling her. Kylie's snatching them away, shuffling them into a smoother stack and stuffing them back into the satchel.

"Never mind, just get back to your thesis or whatever it is. Blood magic probably could've helped you with it."

"Sit down. We can talk about other things."

"I'm busy too. I have to study. I never thought we were in love, but I thought we had something and that we understood there *was* something."

She's out the door in a blink, leaving Gemma to deal with the check. That was as she'd intended.

She hadn't expected how much she'd wrangle with her sense of responsibility though.

* * *

Three days later, she takes note that it's blood moon day as she slips her jacket on before heading to her first class. She has to stay focused. Apology texts to Kylie have been ignored.

She tells herself it's not her problem. She sought a stress release and it got a little complicated. These things happen, and she couldn't have anticipated Erik and his manipulation. Kylie's an adult by any definition.

Gemma'll find a way to make it up to her later, but today's not a good day to make contact. Besides, a guest speaker on international trade is visiting her late-afternoon seminar. Gemma's watched his Ted Talk. Insights to benefit her thesis are likely. That's where her focus needs to be. Blood moon's ability to grant wishes or whatever aside.

* * *

Apparently, all is forgiven. The first text pops up as the guest is making a point on creation of demand. She mulls the irony as she looks at the picture Kylie's sent: a shot of her index finger with an almost perfectly round bead of blood. It catches a dot of white light that accents the black-red.

Gemma ignores it. Tries to listen to the speaker.

The phone purrs as it moves on the desktop beside her tablet. She forces herself not to respond, taps notes from the speaker's message. Looks at his Keynote.

But she can't leave it alone. Slides the phone to her lap so others won't see and touches the screen.

The new pic's Kylie's face. She's smeared the dab of blood from the corner of her mouth down to her chin. The look in her eyes can only be interpreted as hopeful.

"Shit."

She doesn't say it loud, but a couple of other students look at her. She flashes back a forced-smile apology and a nod. *Putting it away.*

The guest's making some of the same points from his Ted Talk. The familiarity is comforting. She nods a couple of times,

110

though he isn't looking her way and it is a sizable hall. Let everyone know she's paying attention. Her advisor's here.

She manages a while. Takes down a few points about subconscious consumer actions and fights the compulsion to look each time the phone purrs again in her bag.

She loses willpower when he elaborates on more material he mentioned in the Ted Talk. She bends sideways, looks at the phone's face without extracting it.

Kylie's sent a picture of the moon against a still-daylit sky. It's already visible? Reddish as promised and standing out against the darkening blue.

That's actually a later image. Below it is one she sent a few minutes ago.

Close-up. Wine-red lingerie. The lace peeled back on one breast as a fingertip applies blood to her already-hardened nipple.

Gemma's about to click off, even as the images tingle in her brain, but another image crops up. A building.

Another image before she can think: The Eye of Sargas in Kylie's hand.

Gemma almost swallows her next breath as her lungs freeze. That's Connor's building, a four-person unit, courtesy of his parents' largesse. What's Kylie suggesting?

Gemma nods back at the disapproving glances around her.

She'd better get over there.

* * *

The sky's darkening more as she exits the hall, a deeper, dimmer blue that makes the moon's reddish face stand out like a looming alien sun.

Gemma sets off at a jog, jacket belt flapping at her sides, almost-evening chill stinging her cheeks, bag and backpack rattling like a cloud of bats surrounding her. Connor's place is on the other side of campus.

She's never dreamed of anything like this, him being in danger. She's been feeling guilty about Kylie. Connor hurt is a never-forgive-herself scenario.

She picks up speed. She hasn't been for a run in a while, but she edges up to a sprint. It's close to the dinner hour. Campus isn't as crowded as midday, but no one's in a hurry. She abandons the sidewalks and people on strolls and thunders across the grass.

Don't let her be too late.

Maybe Kylie will just offer Connor an option to play.

Gemma yanks her phone out as calling in a warning finally occurs to her. Jesus, panic makes you stupid.

Straight to voicemail.

She tries Erik.

Voicemail.

Another picture pops in and she almost collides with someone while looking at it. Dodges, keeps up the sprint, looks at Connor's surprised face—a shot snapped just as he opened his door.

Does she dial 9-1-1?

She hesitates to think about the amount of explanation and potential embarrassment, and then Connor's unit is in sight. She heads up the stairs, finds his door once she's at the top, pounds.

No answer.

"Connor."

She has a key. They swapped long ago so they could check on each other if pressures and depression ever got too severe. She opens the door and pushes it inward. It's still at first, so the sight of Kylie makes her jump.

As Gemma takes her in, she feels instant ice inside her. Kylie looks like she's been flayed. In the dim light of the living area, the wet covering her flesh gleams. She's naked, not skinned but painted head to toe in blood, hair plastered to her skull, face masked, her tall, lean form and curves accented by the shine.

She's turned slightly away from the door, and a second's ticked as Gemma's been taking her in. She's late in noticing the

112

grey-red rope dangling from her hand in the next. Her gaze traces it to the floor.

The ice shoots through her limbs, her toes, chills her core in unison with what feels like an electric jolt.

More rope. A *lot* more. She can't estimate as her brain poses an old anatomy question.

The body just beyond Kylie's legs is opened, ripped by the stone blade in Kylie's other hand.

Ripped and—oh god.

Kylie sees her. "I can feel the power." She drops the rope and places a palm against her cheek, closing her eyes. "The universe knows I want you. It called you here."

The phone's still at Gemma's side. "I came," she whispers. She thumbs the Home button, lets it read her thumbprint as she keeps her gaze locked on Kylie's eyes, even as Kylie parts her arms and extends them.

"Here," she says.

Gemma goes over, accepts the embrace, feels the blood still warm as Kylie puts a palm on her cheek and leans in, kissing warm moisture onto her lips.

She kisses back, feeling the excitement melt some of the ice horror.

Kylie's kisses move to her throat. Blood soaks into her clothes.

She stretches the phone behind Kylie's back. Finds the icon, summoning the keypad.

Kylie rubs the handle of the knife against Gemma's abdomen. "I can feel your heartbeat, the pumping of the blood. I could open . . ."

Gemma folds an arm around her, drags her to her knees, kissing her neck, pressing into her. "I feel the power," she admits. She traces Kylie's slick hip curve. Her fingers glide on past. The intestines are slick too, oily. She presses a handful against Kylie's ribs, swirls the blood.

With her other thumb, she presses 9-1-1 and drops the phone as the dial tone issues.

Kylie's mouth drops open in shock.

113

The dial sound purrs.

Gemma deflects the knife hand and uses her weight to force Kylie backward. Despite the strength in her legs, she flops back onto the yards of viscera.

"Nine-one-one, can I help you?"

"Send help," Gemma screams. Please let the GPS work. A wish to the universe.

Questions come from the phone, but she stops talking. She's busy kissing Kylie . . . and snatching handfuls of the ropy coils, draping them around her.

She forces a loop around Kylie's neck, another, fighting the slippery gore, wrapping enough around her hands for purchase. She plops astride Kylie's ribs, uses her weight to keep her down even as arms slap at her sides and shoulders, trying to get the blade into her. Ignoring the resistance, she tightens. Will it hold? Be strong enough? What's that she read about sausage casings? A question for *Quora*.

She tightens more. Kylie's eyes bulge.

Maybe there's something extra in the guts. The power Kylie's talked about. Magick of some kind?

Regardless, the guts hold; they shut off oxygen as Kylie thrashes and thrashes. Gemma offers no relief. She tenses forearm muscles and biceps and keeps pulling, tighter and tighter until Kylie gets a glaze in her eyes nearing ecstasy. It lasts only seconds, and she stops moving.

Gemma's back arches involuntarily. She tilts her head, and her scream rips open the world around her, the fabric of the universe, as everything explodes inside her, energy bursting forth, her vagina pulsating, wracked with spasms. An expulsion of breath replaces the scream.

God, is she glowing? Is that new power?

Electricity jolts outward from her core along her thighs. She gets lost in something black and cosmic until the calling of her name snaps her back.

She looks up, closes her eyes with relief. Connor's standing over her. One cheek's slashed. Just one cheek?

"I locked myself in a closet," he says as Gemma stares at the cut. "When Kylie came in, she had . . ." He's looking down, taking it all in.

Gemma too gazes at the body on the carpet, past the ropes of gore. Erik's face is almost placid. Maybe he learned what he was hoping to learn about behavior or buttons and limits being pushed. He must've tried to stop what he'd touched off and become a fulfillment of Kylie's obsession, something far beyond edge play, beyond safe, sane, consensual, beyond RACK.

She hands him the Eye of Sargas. "Get ready to tell it all to the cops," she suggests. "Your life was threatened."

It's going to be like the conversations with her advisor. Who the hell can really explain human behavior?

She draws in a breath. At least with the energy that she's somehow absorbed, she feels equipped to keep trying. She feels the magick. Feels like she can do anything. Like Kylie promised.

Maybe Annie Briar wasn't a fraud.

Gemma leans over and kisses Connor's cut.

She tells herself it's to make it better.

ABOUT THE AUTHOR
SIDNEY WILLIAMS

Sidney Williams is the author of ten novels, a host of short stories, comic book scripts and more. He has worked as a newspaper reporter, reference librarian, corporate marketing writer and creative writing instructor with a focus on horror, mystery and suspense. His books include *Azarius*, *Night Brothers*, *Blood Hunter* and *When Darkness Falls*. He wrote three young adult novels under the name Michael August. Williams' newest works include *Midnight Eyes*, *Dark Hours* and *Disciples of the Serpent* for Crossroad Press, and his short stories have appeared in anthologies including *Quoth the Raven*, *Under the Fang*, *Hot Blood: Deadly After Dark* and *Demon Sex*.

Website: http://sidisalive.com

Twitter: @Sidney_Williams

THE HOUSE OF TEARS

BY JOHN PAUL FITCH

The woman's voice crackled with electricity, charging the very fabric of the room like static air before the breaking of a thunderstorm. "Are you prepared, Mr. de Leeuwin?"

Liam de Leeuwin flashed a row of yellow-brown teeth like a lizard. "Thirty years in the game, love. I'm yer Huckleberry." He shrugged off his tight silver suit jacket, dropping it on the floor and carefully folded back his white shirt sleeves to the elbows. He fished in his carry bag and hefted a palm-sized digital camera, holding it up proudly for his client to see.

She was shrouded in shadow, standing in the corner of the room and as such was mostly invisible on the camera's lens. Only part of her face was illuminated in the glowing embers of the cigarette she would occasionally raise to her lips. The sleek curl of her mouth, a sharp cheekbone, the glint of fire in her eye.

"So, what are we doing here? Straight, bi, gay? I've seen it all. Even done bestiality before. Filmed it in eastern Europe where it's not *technically* illegal." He nodded to the bed and the odd shape that lay concealed by the silk sheet there.

The woman remained silent and raised the cigarette to her lips again.

"I even done necrophilia once. Hell of a job. It was in the Indian subcontinent. This bird shagged the stiff cock of a hanged man. A criminal. His prick was rigid as Big Ben." Liam paused for a moment. "The noose still pinched around his neck. It must have kept his blood pressure up because his old member was puffed up like a balloon." He glanced at his camera, checking the lens and wiping it on his shirt. "I always have standards,

117

always use consenting adults, never any minors, or anything really illegal. And let me tell you, I always pay my performers well. It's why I charge the highest fees."

He gnawed on the end of a nicotine-brown fingernail. Liam spat the shard onto the floor and glanced around the room. Something about this place—the red door, the curtains, the shape beneath the sheet—made him nervous. None more than the silence and the anticipation.

He ran his hand back over his thinning, grey-black hair. "How did you find me anyway? Was it through Dotty? She's a great agent, best there is. I mean, this is a lot of money you're paying for what amounts to a home movie. Well, not a *home* movie. This place clearly ain't your home. You own this club, do you?"

The woman ignored him.

"What is it, some personal fantasy? Like to see your other half fucking someone else?"

"If we are ready to begin . . . ?" she said, exhaling a cloud of silver smoke like a dragon blowing fire and ash.

"Sure, um, whenever you're ready." Liam swallowed dryly.

There was a sharp click as the woman snapped her fingers. The shape on the bed writhed and undulated beneath the sheet. Liam wiped his forehead with his shirt sleeve and hit the Record button as the red door swung open. An overweight man in a blue suit entered the room. His shirt was soddened at the neck, his eyes wide, chest heaving.

The woman stepped from the shadows.

And it began.

* * *

The song changed tempo, slowing down. A trance track. Thomas Swinton grunted and clenched his jaw, his lips turning white.

Too loud. The Rope Room requires intimacy, privacy, intensity. You need silence to build the moment and the tension.

118

The girl's eager mouth opened, her lips curling into a smile, exposing her pristine white teeth. She gasped as Thomas tightened the cord around her neck. The rope bit into her flesh. It constricted her throat enough to limit her air, but not enough to strangle her.

The girl, blindfolded, strained against the ropes that bound her, her smooth stomach undulating as she inhaled. Her hips raised and lowered, raised and lowered, lifting her sex towards him. Thomas turned from her to the table behind him. He ran his hands over the assorted toys and implements on display before settling on a silver gauntlet. He held it up to the light. There was an image of a snake embossed into its surface and it glinted in the flash of red and white strobe lights. The finger joints were riveted, like a knight's gauntlet, and at the end of each finger the metal curved into a razor-sharp claw point. It was his own design and caught his breath.

Thomas slid his hand into the opening and wiggled his fingers till it fit tightly. A ripple of pleasure ran through him and he felt the familiar tingle of excitement in his crotch. *Freddy Krueger, eat your heart out.*

Thomas placed a claw tip on the girl's stomach and pressed gently. She quivered at the touch. Smiling, Thomas lifted his gaze and saw a man slouched in the open doorway to the Rope Room, naked and aroused, rubbing his foreskin between finger and thumb. Anger rose in Thomas's chest. "This is a private room. Don't you get it, dickhead?"

The man smiled and stroked his cock faster.

"I'm only going to tell you this once. Fuck off." Thomas shook his head. He hated voyeurs. They were parasites, feeding off other's sensations, stealing the experience from them. Thomas wanted to chase the man down and beat him senseless for invading the moment, but the rules of The Sanctuary stated voyeurs could watch if they so pleased. So, he gritted his teeth and turned his attention back to his sub.

He placed a claw-tip on the sole of her foot, gently but with enough force to threaten to puncture her tanned skin. He dragged it up, cresting the summit of her big toe with its glossy painted nail and down the front of her foot. She squirmed and giggled, her small, pert breasts jiggling. Thomas admired her taut, slim body as he ran his fingers up the inside of her thigh and orbited her hip. He slipped a claw under the fabric of her panties and with a quick stroke cut it free. The elastic snapped and fell loose. She gasped.

Thomas' ribcage beat in rhythm with the music's bass. His eyes were filled with the strobe of the lights. He grasped the snipped panties with his free hand and tore them away, dropping them to the floor.

The man in the doorway moaned loudly.

Thomas felt another flush of anger, the moment between him and the girl broken again. He shot a glance at the intrusion.

A woman stared at Thomas. She wore an all-in-one red gown that had the texture of velvet, secured with a black leather corset around her waist. She was thin as a reed, her complexion smooth as silk. Her hair was shaved into the skin on both sides and swept back from her forehead like a wave that ran down to the waist. Taut cheekbones sat beneath large dark eyes entirely without eyebrows. Rather than detracting from her allure, they emphasised it.

She stroked the voyeur's cock. The man leaned back against the frame of the door, his head tilted to the side and his eyes screwed shut, but the woman's attention remained on Thomas. Her gaze was magnetic, and Thomas felt like she was looking into his soul. The air thickened. Thomas's balls tightened.

Screaming broke the reverie, and then the woman was gone and the spent voyeur was slumped in the doorway.

Thomas looked down at the girl on the table. Blood pooled in the her naval. She screamed and thrashed as best she could. The blindfold slipped from her head and tears streamed down her cheeks, and Thomas realised that the needle-fingers of the gauntlet were plunged into her abdomen up to the knuckle. She was screaming, "Crimson. Crimson!" Her safeword.

Thomas pulled his hand free, tossed the gauntlet, and began to loosen the ropes. "I'm so sorry." He untied her and the girl sat up.

She looked down at her abdomen and clutched at the wounds there. "You fucking asshole." She began to cry.

"You'll be fine. They're just puncture marks," Thomas said, but his mind was not on the girl's welfare. His gaze wandered to the doorway. "Sometimes people get hurt when you play rough, you know. Part of the game." He left her to herself on the table.

The Sanctuary was almost empty tonight. With a cold breeze on the back of his neck, Thomas hustled towards the main entrance at the end of the lobby. Air seeped in, carrying the whiff of woody perfume amongst the other feral scents of the city. Thomas shouldered the ajar metal door aside and pushed out into the grimy alleyway beyond. The Sanctuary was in the industrial area of the city, and as such the neighbourhood was mostly unpopulated at night, making it the perfect place for an underground sex club.

Thomas noticed movement in the darkness and halted.

A figure stepped from the gloom and the exotic woman he'd seen earlier materialised, as if she'd come out of the wall. She stopped inches from him, too close yet not close enough. Thomas felt that ache in his balls again. She carried the scent of pheromones; he smelled her heat and it brought him to near climax. His head pounded, and his nose ran. He'd never known a woman so overtly sensual. She exuded sex. His mind reeled, giddy as a love-struck teenager.

Dizzy, Thomas came forcefully in his boxer-shorts.

"What are you looking for?" she asked with a soft, lilting European accent that he couldn't quite place.

"Who are you?"

She smiled coyly and ran her eyes down his chest. "I have been called many names in my lifetime, but you may address me by my original name . . . Magdalene." She placed her fingers on his face and ran the tips down his chin to his neck. He felt the ache in his loins again, deep, painful.

"You are searching for something more than this, aren't you? Something beyond flesh, beyond sensation. Transcendence? I can give you all of this." Magdalene pressed her hips against Thomas, slipping her wrists up under his armpits and clutching

121

his back. Her breasts pushed into his sternum. Her eyes were yellow and grey and flecked with green, and she glowed with an incandescence that throbbed from within.

Thomas' head swam and his legs wobbled. "What . . . what's happening?"

"You just have to accept my invitation. Say yes."

Thomas' lungs were screaming. The world began to feel slippery. "Y-yes," he whispered.

Magdalene's lips brushed his and he saw explosions of light in his head. Then she released him and the sensation of falling in warm inky blackness overtook him.

He awoke when it began to rain, coming to on his back as the night sky gave way to the creeping dawn, and he realised he was lying in an oily puddle of water. Thomas stood, his head still spinning, the taste of Magdalene's lips still sweet and fresh. His $4000 Tom Ford suit was ruined by the filth and the oil, but he didn't care.

He tipped his head to the rain, holding his arms out wide.

* * *

Towelling himself off after a hot shower, Thomas stood naked in the lounge of his apartment and surveyed the high rises and skyscrapers that penetrated the Manhattan skyline. Despite being a captain of industry, he hated the sprawl of the city, the monuments to mankind's ingenuity, the lines of staccato traffic that pumped along the roads and byways. He loathed the hustle and bustle of the crowds, toing and froing along the eddies and currents of the Big Apple, human flotsam and jetsam.

Thomas lived in a spectacular 14-room duplex apartment, situated high atop the prestigious Pierre Hotel on Fifth Avenue. He'd recently had it triple-mint renovated. Boasting extraordinary three-sixty-degree views of Central Park and the Manhattan landscape, it was the perfect trophy residence for a man of his worth. It had taken him twenty years of hard work in the predatory world of hedge fund management to afford a place like this. It was a nice space for a single man of forty who was in great shape despite the grey at his once-black temples and the wrinkles at the corner of his eyes and mouth. It was perfect for hosting dinner parties—he had impressed clients and theatre stars and politicians no end. But it didn't have what he *needed*.

Only The Sanctuary could give him that.

The chirp of a mobile interrupted Thomas' contemplation. He crossed to the coffee table, lifted the phone and looked at the number. It was the Singapore office again. They had rung three times as he'd been showering. Normally he'd have answered right away, business being the priority, but today he was preoccupied with his encounter with Magdalene. He had even masturbated for the first time in months. He couldn't escape the thought of her, her sheer sexual energy, her scent. His cock stiffened anew.

Putting her out of his head, Thomas called Marie, his PA, and informed her he wasn't feeling himself today. Despite her protestations and reminders that he had a very important meeting, he palmed her off.

"Reschedule it," he said and hung up before she could reply.

Thomas went to the kitchen and snatched up the half-empty bottle of scotch from the counter and poured himself a large measure. He carried the bottle back to the window, turned his attention to the cityscape and thought of Magdalene again.

* * *

"I'm looking for a woman who was here last night. Uh, unique-looking, red dress, corset. Is she here? Have you seen her?" Thomas shifted nervously in the hallway of The Sanctuary. It was early. The doors had opened only a few minutes ago.

The young blonde host shook her head. "She's not one of our girls. We don't get many other women in here, especially single women. The only ones who do come in are with husbands or boyfriends. If you like, I'd be happy to oblige you this evening, Mr. Swinton?" She cocked her head to the side and ran a finger down the lapel of her dress.

"Can you find out who she is?" he asked, biting his lip, already knowing the answer.

The girl lowered her gaze. "We don't keep records of visitors here, Mr. Swinton. We have some high-profile guests who don't like paper trails. I'm sure you understand."

Thomas sighed, waved her off and stalked down the hallway towards the sounds of yelping and leather meeting flesh at high speed.

The Sanctuary was practically empty; midweek was always quiet, the crowds congregating on weekends. Most of the rooms were unattended save for the dungeon, where a plump, redheaded dominatrix in a PVC cape and knee-high studded boots was servicing three naked middle-aged men. One lay on the floor on his back, his head encased in an iron mask, his chest reddened with whip marks. A second man was cleaning the dominatrix' boots with his tongue while she smacked his back with a riding crop. The third was on all fours inside one of the square steel cages and barked like a dog at his mistress' command.

Businessmen tended to pay to be humiliated like this, to be dominated by a woman. Thomas had seen CEOs, banking and Silicone Valley chiefs grovelling at the feet of leather-clad women. He'd even seen the (famous and apparently straight) owner of a rather large social media platform get fucked by a dozen women with battery-powered dildos. Thomas figured because powerful men wielded corporate authority by day that they craved subjugation by night. He'd seen their likes around the boardroom, trussed up in their three-piece suits and ties and their hair slickly parted, the snobbish way they regarded the world, the look of shame in their eyes. Behind their steely façade they were nothing more than nervous teenagers beholden to the fear that if someone, *anyone*, could see they had no self-esteem then their power would ebb away. They armoured themselves with expensive watches and pseudo-bravado personalities and bluster and locker-room talk.

Thomas knew better than anyone that almost all power was an illusion. You had to buy into the world for this to work; you had to give over your power to someone else, and that was something he could never do.

The dominatrix spotted Thomas and raised a finger, beckoning him to enter the dungeon. Thomas sneered and headed back to the reception desk. The corridor was empty, the receptionist gone, but on the desk lay a golden envelope embossed with a black circular symbol below which, in blood red letters, was written his name.

He could no longer hear the yelps of the men in the dungeon. All noise had stopped: the gasping and grunting, the thwack-thwack of the mistress's crop. The Sanctuary felt dead.

Uneasy, he slipped the envelope inside his jacket and hurried outside. He was out of breath when he reached the pavement of the main street and the light and noise of the real world.

* * *

The scotch bottle rattled against the glass. Try as he might, Thomas could not steady his hand. He took a mouthful of the oak-coloured whisky and savoured the liquor. It burned his throat as he swallowed before it mellowed and a sweet, peaty warmth filled his nostrils. Heat spread across his chest and tension melted from his shoulders.

He poured another large glass and regarded the envelope. Thomas traced patterns on it, his nerves jangling. He ran his index finger around the edge, savouring the roughness of the ivory paper. He placed the glass down and took it in both hands. It had been scented with a sweet perfume, that distinct aroma that had almost overpowered him at The Sanctuary last night. It was *her* scent—Magdalene's.

Thomas slipped his thumbnail under the flap and pulled the envelope open. A slip of parchment slid out onto the kitchen table. The material was something like vellum but had a somewhat velvety feel and was so thin that it was almost transparent. It had raised letters, emblazoned in red:

-The House of Tears-

125

An invitation. *The* invitation.

Thomas turned it over in his hands. On the back of the parchment, at the bottom in small print, was a phone number in golden type. Apart from the lettering there were no indentations on its surface; it bore no watermarks. Thomas placed the invitation back on the counter and reached for the landline on the wall. He punched in the numbers and waited, heart thumping in his chest, the thrum of rushing blood filling his ears.

It rang once. Twice. Then came a click, followed by the sound of soft breathing close to the receiver. The line was crackly, like Thomas had dialled some far-off country.

"Hello?" he said.

"Address please?" The voice was raspy, but feminine. Soft yet stern, a voice of quiet authority.

"I-I'm sorry?"

"Where are you calling from?"

"Seven-nine-five Fifth Avenue, Upper East Side. Apartment thirty."

"Six a.m. tomorrow." There was a click and the beeping of a disconnected line.

"Hello? Are you there?" Thomas looked at the phone. He pressed the disconnect button and dialled again but the call rang out. He hung up and drained his glass, shivering as the last of the scotch went down. His eyes fell on the invitation again.

Thomas studied the parchment, holding it up to the light. There must be some other clue. What the hell was The House of Tears anyway? Some exclusive club?

He moved to the bedroom, down a hallway beset with high priced art. Lying back on his king-sized bed, he reached for his tablet and opened the search engine. The House of Tears brought up several dozen hits, all of them on the same BDSM forum: The Pit, a board dedicated to extreme fetish and, peculiarly, the occult.

Thomas didn't care for the occult, likening it to religion and superstition, but his gnawing curiosity led him deeper into the forum, scrolling through the posts in search for a mention of the name, or for a clue as to its meaning. The only genuine hit mentioned a video clip titled "The Banker" that many of the members had seen. At the bottom of the page Thomas found a pinned link that carried the warning: "For extreme viewers only." Thomas double-checked he had enabled his VPN, and, satisfied, clicked the link.

The screen went black as the player loaded before a grainy amateur video rolled onscreen. An overweight man in a business suit was being led into a lavishly decorated room by a raven-haired woman in a red velvet gown.

Thomas gasped. "Magdalene."

She took the fat man by the hand and led him down several short steps into a sunken bedroom. The furnishings consisted of a single round bed and a plain table and chair. The room was swathed in heavy red curtains. The man, the banker of the title, ran a chubby hand over his clammy forehead. Magdalene spoke in her breathy voice and a shiver ran through Thomas' body.

"Are you prepared?"

The banker was fixated on the bed. He nodded and began to loosen his tie.

"What do you seek?" she asked.

The man swallowed hard before replying, "Transcendence."

Magdalene smiled and planted a soft kiss on his cheek. "Then this is where we part." She glided out of shot.

The banker stripped to the waist and crossed to the bed, dropping his shirt on the floor as he went. The camera followed him and over the man's shoulder Thomas could make out a shape concealed by a blanket. It writhed, and something about it set Thomas on edge. Its movement was unnatural. Worm-like.

Thomas held his breath. The banker was naked except for a pair of ludicrously long black socks that dug into the flesh of his calves. The bed listed to one side as he mounted it, his arse jiggling, knees sinking into the soft mattress. He remained motionless for a moment, surveying the sheet before him before grasping it and throwing it aside.

Thomas nearly dropped his tablet. "What the hell?"

127

The shape on the bed had no arms or legs. Its bald round head was entirely without the external features that make up a human face. This abomination had only a sucking *O*-shaped mouth that smacked open and closed with a kissing sound as it breathed and panted. Although covered in skin, the thing had the body shape of a man-sized slug. From its sides sprang thick black bristles like porcupine quills. Its only other features were a series of glistening orifices that ran up and down its body in an almost perfect line from front to back.

The banker ran his hands along the creature's sides, flicking the bristles, and the creature quivered. He trailed his fingers up to the sucker mouth, running circles around it, teasing it as it puckered. Then he mounted the creature by squatting over it and shoving his cock into the lowest orifice. He came after a few quick, hard thrusts and disengaged.

Within seconds he was ready to go again, moving up one orifice, then another. He hollered in excitement, his face scarlet with effort, eyes wide. The creature on the bed sighed with each thrust from the fat man. The banker, his cock dripping semen, finally placed both hands on either side of the thing's head and thrust into the pink sucker-mouth as deep as he could go, eyes screwed shut, spittle flying from his clenched teeth.

The bristles on the creature's sides extended outwards and downwards, piercing the bed and lifting its body. It looked less like a slug now and more like a centipede. The banker kept thrusting even as it began to curl around him. Then, with predatory speed, the thing whipped its body round and impaled the man's torso.

The man stopped thrusting and screamed. He clamped his hands around the creature's head and tried to pull his cock from the mouth, but he was stuck. The hole opened wider and wider, sucking harder with each movement until it covered the man's lower torso completely. There was a ripple of movement through the creature's body and the banker howled in agony. The creature's muscles contracted front to back, gaining strength as it fed upon its prey.

128

The man stopped screaming. His body deflated, his insides being slurped through his middle. All colour leeched from his face. He leaned so far backwards that he looked like he'd been folded in half.

The creature manoeuvred the near empty husk into its maw, and the video cut to black.

A wave of revulsion crawled over Thomas and he gagged. He slammed the tablet down onto the worktop. Blinking tears away and swallowing the rising bile in his throat, he downed the rest of the whisky straight. When it was done, he staggered to his cabinet and wrested the first bottle his fingers found from its place. He popped the cork and guzzled, trying to wash the shock from his mind with a shower of expensive wine.

Despite all of it—all the images he'd seen in the video—one face kept coming back to him: Magdalene's. And when he thought of her, he could think of nothing else. He had to have her.

Thomas kept drinking till he lost consciousness.

He dreamt of Emma. She smiled despite the noose around her neck, or perhaps she was grimacing. Her lips had turned black and peeled back from her teeth. Her terrible gaze burrowed into his flesh like hooks, or nails driven into his body. She lay back on the sheet-less mattress, her arms still bound to the headboard, ankles strapped to the bed posts. Her body was long cold, and her joints had taken on the colour of bruising as the blood pooled.

Emma's hips raised and lowered, working in a circle, her sex open to him. Thomas mounted her and shoved his cock in deep. He did not want to look into her dead eyes. He wanted to turn away but, in the dream, he had no control. The control was all hers.

She whispered for him to look at her and he did, meeting her accusing gaze full on. He thrusted into her cold body harder and harder and her hips raised to meet his thrusts with equal measure. Thomas could feel his climax coming.

"Kiss me," she whispered, her jaw set.

129

Thomas's lips pursed.

The telephone rang. It was still dark outside, the sun still slumbering under the blanket of velvet night. Woozy from the scotch and wine, Thomas rose and crossed the cold floor to the telephone, lifting the receiver mid-chirp.

"Sir, it's Paul, the night concierge."

Thomas glanced at the clock on the nightstand and sighed. "It's just after five in the morning. Is there some kind of emergency?" His stomach rumbled, and his head ached from clenching his jaw all night.

"Very sorry, sir. There's a . . . man . . . here for you. Says he's here to pick you up. I tried to get rid of him, but he is quite insistent and, well, *big*."

Thomas felt a surge of adrenaline. His headache seemingly evaporated. "Who is he, Paul? Did he give a name? What the hell does he want at this time in the morning?"

"No name, sir."

"What's his business?"

There was the sound of muffled voices before Paul answered, "Sir? He says he's to take you to the house?"

Thomas' eyes fell upon the invitation lying next to the phone, his destiny emblazoned on its surface in blood red letters. "Tell him I'll be down soon."

"Yes, sir."

Thomas quickly showered, sluicing away the grogginess while his stomach churned with nerves and his mind ran riot. *The House of Tears. Christ, they sent a limo for me at six a.m.! That was why they asked for my address.*

He shaved, put on a three-piece suit and wool overcoat, and checked himself in the mirror again, holding his own gaze, trying to calm himself. He ran his fingers through his hair. Despite the hangover and the dark circles under his eyes, he still looked every part the billionaire playboy.

Paul was waiting for Thomas when the elevator doors opened, muttering apologies. Thomas heard none and held out a

$50 note as a tip. Paul ushered him to the front door, holding it open to the morning. Thomas' breath clouded in the air.

A gleaming black limousine was parked at the kerb before the building. A huge, bald man in a tight grey overcoat, buttons straining to hold in his physique, stood at the rear door and opened it upon seeing him. As he approached, Thomas could make out a jagged scar that ran from the man's forehead over the apex of his dome. The man said nothing as Thomas clambered into the limousine and settled into the plush leather seat. The door slammed closed and soon they pulled off.

They turned north onto FDR Drive. Thomas looked out over the East River and, despite the early hour, there was still some traffic on the roads. They soon passed Upper Manhattan, crossed RFK Bridge and headed north, past the Botanical Gardens and out of the city.

"Hey, uh . . . where we headed?" asked Thomas.

The scarred man drove on, never once acknowledging Thomas's question or presence.

His headache reappeared with a vengeance, thudding into the space behind his eyeballs. The clink of the built-in mini-bar to his right drew his attention. He fingered the selection of small bottles and snatched up two vodkas, chilled orange juice and a glass. Mixing the drinks together with come crushed ice from a bucket, he downed the concoction and held his breath against the tidal wave of saliva that rushed into his mouth. He swallowed the spit tsunami back. Within minutes, he felt better, aglow with the warmth that alcohol generously brought.

The skyscrapers had long since disappeared and now even the terraced houses of the suburbs had yielded to the trees and frost-tipped fields of upstate New York. The rocking of the car and the thrum of the engine massaged Thomas and warm dreamless sleep overtook him.

* * *

The car was still. They had stopped moving. Thomas blinked and ran a hand over his face.

131

Are we there?

The passenger door lay open. A line of lights framed a gravel driveway beyond, illuminating a path between two thatches of trees which formed an arched canopy above it. He stretched as he stepped out, his legs and lower back stiff after having slept curled up in the back seat of the limo. Something popped and Thomas made a mental note to visit his chiropractor soon.

Gravel crunched under Thomas' feet as he marched up the path. Giant ferns crouched between the trees either side, lending the wood a prehistoric feel, like he was walking back in time, the plants growing the further he walked, and he half expected to glimpse some humungous reptile in the dark of the cover. He hurried onwards through ever-thickening foliage until he reached his destination.

A small squat building with a flat roof stood before him, concrete and square, like a keep or a small fortress set into the middle of a clearing. Pine trees encircled it. Its steel doors stood open for him.

Thomas pushed on into The House of Tears.

* * *

The long stone corridor was lit by flaming torches, walls draped in crimson velvet curtains either side of a black-and-white chequered floor.

"Welcome," came a breathy greeting.

She stood at the far end of the corridor yet her voice sounded closer, no more than a whisper. She sauntered towards him, her high heels clacking on the stone floor. She wore a red leather dress that barely seemed to fit. It was held by a pin at her waist, cinched around her hips and open from the neck down to her navel, its lapels falling open around her bare breasts. The bottom half of the dress was a mirror image of the top and flared open, her sex on display for him—or anyone—to see, framed by the tops of her thigh-high leather boots. Her vulva was pierced with rows of silver metal rings on both lips that clinked softly with each step she took.

132

He could practically smell her from where he stood. A shudder ran through Thomas' body, an animal surge he could barely contain. Magdalene's mere presence was intoxicating, overpowering.

She drew near and took his face in both hands and pulled him close. Her raven hair cascaded down around her porcelain face. Thomas gasped. She kissed his open mouth hard. He barely registered how cold her hands were, or that her mouth tasted like ash. His body charged with heat. He breathed in her scent, filling his chest till it felt like it was on fire and his heart might burst.

She broke from him, still maintaining the closeness. "You will see things here that you could never see anywhere else," she whispered. "This is a place of wonder and depravity, of angels or devils, whichever you choose them to be. You will see things you never knew you wanted until you see them. Things you never thought were possible or could possibly exist." She gestured towards the doorway. "Out there is the normal world full of ordinary people with ordinary desires. You've lived in that place your whole life, knowing full well that your desires go far beyond what that world can offer. But here"—she nodded over her shoulder—"beyond this corridor, you can fulfil your deepest fantasies and more. This is where you find yourself. This is a place of transcendence and the ultimate experience of the flesh."

"The House of Tears," he said.

She nodded. "You are here because you have gone beyond all normal human experience. You need something else, something more." She stroked his cheek. "You can enter here and see the sights we harbour, and you can have that which you cannot have elsewhere."

"You," he interrupted.

"Perhaps. If that is your ultimate desire, you can taste the forbidden fruit, but there is always a price. If you choose to accept my offer, you will be crossing a border from which there is no return. Do you understand?"

Thomas nodded. "I have nothing else I want."

She smiled. "Then come with me."

Magdalene took Thomas by the hand and led him along the corridor towards a set of stone steps that spiralled downwards. Together they descended.

* * *

They must have gone down a hundred steps in near total darkness. Thomas held onto Magdalene's soft hand like a child. He laced his fingers through hers, running his thumb over her sharpened nail. He could feel a low throbbing under his feet: a dance beat, drum and bass. A pulsing light from below grew stronger the further they descended. A repeating melody rose and fell, louder and louder.

The stairs levelled out and they stood on the threshold of a cavernous hall packed with heaving dancers, arms aloft, bouncing with the music. The hall was an amphitheatre hewn out of the very bedrock of the earth. Lights spun, multi-coloured and flashing. The too-loud music rattled Thomas' ribcage. Half-naked revellers ground on each other—less dancing, more humping—and the stink of sweat and other bodily fluids thickened the hot air.

The two people nearest Thomas bumped into him, a tangle of limbs slicking the arm of his suit with greasy sweat. They were wearing animal masks. Glancing around, he saw a menagerie of animal faces on the dancefloor: goats, owls, deer.

Magdalene let his hand slip from hers and pushed through the heaving crowd. The nearest couple were now shorn of all clothing and were no longer dancing but rutting. An orgy on a scale Thomas had never seen before— hundreds of people fucking together.

Magdalene slinked into the mob, which parted to let her pass. Thomas, meanwhile, was buffeted by the storm of bodies around him. He pushed his way through a ring of mostly naked men in goat masks, who stood in a circle around a girl. She lay on her back on the slick stone floor, her legs open and the fingers of one hand buried in her vulva up to the knuckles while the men jerked off above her. She wore a wolf head mask, grey, teeth

134

bared, and Thomas could have sworn that, just under the surface of the music, he could hear her growling in pleasure.

He had seen enough and turned away. Passing under the elevated stage where the DJ played his sermon to the congregation, Thomas staggered into the darkened passageway beyond, which was lit by neon blue strip lights at the base of the walls. She was waiting for him there. The music faded as they made their way down the tunnel.

When he reached a long glass window on the right, Thomas stopped. All around the room at the same height were other viewing windows, faces subtly lit by the glow of cigars behind the glass, hardened gazes watching. He turned his attention to the scene below.

Several feet down lay a well-lit operating theatre complete with chrome table and surgical lighting. A man in his early 20s was strapped on the table, bound at the wrists and ankles, arms and legs splayed like the Vitruvian Man.

Thomas stepped closer for a better view.

The man—a boy, really—glanced around in panic, eyes wide. Sweat slicked his hair to his forehead. He looked in Thomas's direction and they locked gazes for a brief second. Thomas gasped in shock: the boy's mouth was sewn shut with thick metal wire. Blood had crusted over the fresh-looking wounds, the skin surrounding them red and puffy.

"What the hell is this?" Thomas asked Magdalene.

She did not return his glare, instead avidly watching the room below.

There was the clank of a heavy lock being opened and three shapes lumbered into view. Their skin was the colour of pure snow and they wore white leather smocks, like surgical robes. Their heads were hairless, lacking even eyebrows. They juddered when they moved, and Thomas got the wild impression they were not men at all, but things taking the shape of men, things imitating human beings.

One of the three moved towards the boy's head, leant over him and drew its tongue across his sewn mouth. The boy panted heavily, thrashing in his restraints. The surgeons moved either

135

side and ran their fingers up and down his skin like lovers would. The one nearest the boy's head nodded to the other two, who turned and fetched their tools from the table behind them. They took a long thin scalpel each and then handed the leader a circular saw with a round serrated blade.

They began at the fingers, opening the skin and flesh and peeling it backwards, exposing the bone beneath. The scalpels cut with delicate ease. The boy tried to scream. The skin of his lips tore and the stitches popped one by one as the surgeons continued to fillet him alive.

They worked up his forearms, stripping back the meat. They separated skin, veins and nerves from flesh, cartilage from bone. The leader hadn't moved; he hovered over the boy's face, drinking in every moment of their victim's agony.

When the surgeons reached the upper arms, laying the skin to the sides, the leader placed the circular saw on the boy's sternum. With a quick, powerful thrust, he sliced through the bone, which gave way with a crack. The leader placed the saw aside and then plunged both hands into the wound, splitting open the chest cavity. Like vultures the triplets dived in, scalpel blades swishing. The boy stopped thrashing.

Thomas turned away, bile rising in his throat.

"This is what you agreed to—to navigate the waters of pure experience. Do not flinch."

"You never told me it would be like this."

"And yet, you knew." Magdalene turned back towards the spectacle.

Thomas swallowed and turned also.

While the surgeons finished stripping the boy of his skin, slicing it into neat ribbons, the leader sawed the boy's skeleton into pieces. He handed them to the other two as he went, and they expertly wrapped them in the strips of skin and placed them into a wheeled metal bin. After only a few minutes there was nothing left of the boy except puddles of blood, which drained down a small hole in the bottom of the chrome table. The three surgeons wheeled away the metal container and the lights went out.

Magdalene glanced at Thomas. "Shall we go on?"

"Fuck this," he spat.

He made his way back to the dance hall. The music still thrummed and banged, but the room was empty. Thomas stepped onto the floor, but where his foot should have met hard stone, it sank into the surface. He looked down—into a sea of undulating skin, of different mottled colours, rising and falling. Various limbs protruded from the carpet of flesh: a head here, a leg there. The revellers had come together in the most literal meaning, their skin running to goo and mixing into one visceral mass. The heads that remained still wore the animal masks, moaning and wailing for help.

Thomas fell away from the sight and turned. Magdalene stood serenely, her hands by her side, head tilted.

"There is nothing back there for you. You accepted the bargain. The only way is forward."

Thomas searched his mind for a solution. *There must be some way out. If there's a way in, there must be some other exit, somewhere?*

Magdalene raised her arms and held out a leather collar with a metal clasp. She moved towards him and placed the collar around his neck. It sat up around his ears at the side and a thick length of stiff leather ran up the back of his head, locking it in place. The clasp rested under Thomas' chin.

Magdalene clicked it closed, clipped a chain to the collar and turned, leading Thomas down the corridor.

* * *

She hung from two long iron chains, her feet dangling a few inches above the stone floor. Mascara ran down her face in tear-streaked sorrow. Her head had been shaved in brutal fashion: chunks of skin and flesh were missing, but a few strands of blonde hair still hung from her scalp, missed by the uncaring shearers. Her neck and shoulders were caked in a crust of dried blood.

They stood amidst a crowd which had gathered near the entrance to an arched stone tunnel. Magdalene had wrapped the chain attached to his collar around her hand several times. It held Thomas in such a way that he couldn't turn his head, the stiff leather not giving. Several suited men with expensive haircuts sat in front of them in a row of luxury chairs smoking large, acrid cigars.

The woman, spinning slowly in her shackles, saw the milling crowd and pleaded, "Help me! Please!"

Not one of them flinched. One or two even smiled, clearly enjoying the spectacle of seeing her beg. Perhaps they'd seen this kind of show before, already partaken of the sights of The House of Tears, returning regulars.

There was the ebbing sound of a low bell and the lights went down save a pair of spotlights, which illuminated the dangling naked girl and a round hole about the width of a man's arm in the wall behind her. Something glistened just inside the dark maw. Slowly, a featureless stump felt its way around the hole like a finger and began to probe, sensing its way down the wall. It raised itself from the surface and waved in the air, fumbling, looking for something, looking—

For the girl.

Thomas strained to turn away, but Magdalene yanked on the chain.

The thing in the wall extended further and further. It resembled a headless snake or a long, fat worm. It curled and flicked, blind yet sensing the proximity of its victim, until it bumped her on the side of the leg. She jumped at the touch and screamed. The worm wriggled side to side eagerly. It touched her again and this time it caught her, circling around her waist, holding her in place.

The girl wailed, her body wracked with heaving sobs. The tentacle released her and retracted. The stump slid back like a foreskin, revealing pink flesh underneath its tough hide. From a small hole in its end, a black claw emerged, sharp like an eagle's talon and curved. The tentacle rose stiffly, the spike held above and behind the girl.

With incredible speed, the limb flexed and swung down, and the spike gouged a deep wound into the girl's back. Her eyes widened, and her mouth formed a silent gasp. The worm rose, quivering, taut. It slashed at the girl again and her body jerked.

The men in the luxury chairs began to cheer, smoke billowing in the air.

The claw rose a third time, meat dangling from its tip, before slashing down. This time it hit the girl at an angle and she spun around, bouncing like a piñata. Her wounds were horrific and deep: ribs and spine exposed, lungs quivering beneath. The claw gouged into her face, raking down her neck and chest, taking the fatty flesh from her breasts. One of her shoulders dislocated with an audible pop.

The last slash tore her body from the arms.

The crowd stood and applauded, fat men with fat hands clapping at the ghastly show.

The arms bounced and swung in their chains as the tentacle slowly withdrew into the hole, leaving a trail of blood down the wall.

Thomas could help himself no longer. He sobbed.

Magdalene tugged on his chain and led him out as the crowd bristled and pushed past them.

Adjacent to the arched tunnel was a large hall with a domed roof. The place was thick with well-dressed clientele: men of all shapes and sizes, and several elegant women. The air was smoggy and humid and stank of stale smoke. A queue of patrons stripped off in a line along the grey concrete wall to the left. Shapes roughly the size of basketballs protruded from it as the men, some already excited from the previous display, hollered and joked like they were in a high school locker room.

Magdalene took his chain and pulled him with her in a circuit around the room. Men and women all bowed their heads as she passed, several of them falling to their knees—when their queen passed, her subjects fell to worship.

As they neared the murmuring queue, Thomas could make out the shapes in the grey wall he had seen from the entrance: Noses. Lips. Backsides.

People had been concreted into it.

Hips jutted out and where the leg bent at the knee they disappeared back into the cement. Toothless mouths and squashed noses stuck out at waist height. Drool and other fluids ran from them in long trails. Each patron took their turn, slipping their genitals into whichever orifices took their fancy and jackhammering away.

One ass stuck out of the wall, the flesh hanging from the bones as the muscle rotted away and collapsed. It was held only by a bag of grey-black skin. A fat bald man spat into his hand and ran it over his cock before jamming it into the asshole. He leaned back, sliding himself into it fully. He grasped the hips. As he thrust, the skin tore away and putrid flesh slipped from the bones, gliding down around his wrists. The man took no notice and kept on fucking.

Magdalene crossed the centre of the room and pulled Thomas along with her past a frenzied congregation of men grouped around a woman on a mattress, who reached out to people in the crowd, begging to be fucked. Thomas reeled at the sight of the surgeons' handiwork. Her skin had been flayed and laid open like the petals of a flower. Her abdomen resembled a massive vulva, where her nose and mouth should have been instead was an open wet red cavity, and yet she was very much alive—her eyes rolled around in their sockets with the lazy movement of an imbecile. Eventually, a skinny man and his friend took turns with her, swapping from her head to her body and back again.

There were three people engaged in copulation in the corner, a man at both ends of what appeared to be a woman sandwiched between them. The woman then turned, switching ends, and somehow Thomas was looking at a man. At first, he thought the person was dressed half like a man, half like a woman—part chanteuse, part gentleman—but a second look confirmed the reality. Here was a thing that was made up of both genders, sliced down the middle with the opposing parts sewn together.

When Magdalene had finished her circuit of the room and every living thing in there had bowed down in reverence to her, she pulled Thomas towards a door covered in red leather.

* * *

The chamber was bare except for a wooden chair, a lamp in each corner, and thick red curtains.

Magdalene chained Thomas to a hook on the wall and stepped behind him. When she came around to face him again, she brandished a thin, curved knife. She smiled coyly, placing the cold tip of the blade against his cheek. Thomas gasped as she ran it under his chin and poked at his neck with it hard enough to draw blood.

Her eyes lit with pleasure. "Are you afraid?" She drew the knife back, the tip red. "Or are you excited?"

"I don't know."

Magdalene curled an eyebrow. "I think I know the answer. And I think you do too." She leaned in and kissed him deeply. Thomas reeled from her scent and felt like he was floating in warm water. He never wanted it to stop.

Magdalene pulled away, placed the knife against his chest and ran it down his skin till it met the fabric of his clothes. She set to work slicing the buttons from his shirt and jacket one by one. They bounced on the stone floor and rolled away. Magdalene pulled Thomas' shirt from him and tossed it into the corner. Then she cut away his leather belt in one quick slice. Thomas stood naked as the day he was born.

Magdalene unclipped the chain and led him towards the wooden chair. "Sit."

He hadn't noticed the viewing windows until now. The panes were thick with the orange-red glow of cigar tips, the air like treacle, and a man in a white shirt stood behind the blinking red light of a camera in the corner, but Thomas was beyond caring now.

Magdalene stood before him. Magdalene, with her electric sexuality. His cock was rigid. His balls throbbed and ached. She fingered the pin on her robe and it snapped open, tumbling to the ground. Placing a hand on each of his shoulders, she straddled him and slid herself onto his penis. The chair creaked under their weight.

Magdalene dug her nails into the skin of his shoulder blades, drawing blood. Thomas groaned, relishing the warm silken touch of her body on his. He kissed her neck and along the line of her jaw, and ran his tongue up and into her open mouth. She lifted her hips and glided up the length of his cock, then slid down slowly. The chair creaked again, and again. She pulled her nails down his back, slicing into muscles, drawing skin from meat.

Thomas straightened and jerked, but Magdalene held him still. She slid her hands up and over his shoulders, down his pectorals, smearing blood on his chest. She bit his bottom lip. Thomas gasped and gripped Magdalene's buttocks. Her heels clacked on the stone floor as she rode him harder. She tore part of his lip away and blood cascaded down his chin. He felt the hot rush of semen and came loudly, burying his head between her breasts and panting.

For the longest while Thomas didn't breathe, could only see pulses of light behind his eyelids and hear the rush of blood in his ears. It was like he didn't exist; there was no Thomas, no ego, no consciousness. There was no business, no possessions, no fortune. He had never killed a man in a street fight as a teenager. He had never spied on his aunt as she changed at his house before a new year's party when he was ten. He had never watched his girlfriend choke to death with a noose around her neck. He had never been rich or poor, nor even a baby—he had never been born. It was bliss.

Thomas became aware that his lungs were burning. He inhaled and with the onrush of oxygen, so came the memories and baggage of his life. The regret, the shame, the horror of the things he had done. He saw Emma's face before him, tracks of mascara running over her cheeks, her lips black, eyes bloodshot. She was dead, and he had watched her die while he fucked her.

With his face pressed between Magdalene's breasts, he began to bawl. She held him firmly, arms locking behind his head, which pounded with the onslaught of images, people lost, of

142

death and miserable life. It was too much. Thomas screamed until his lungs were empty and he felt like he might vomit them onto the floor. And it was then that he understood why this place was called The House of Tears.

"It is too much, isn't it?" Magdalene purred into his ear.

Thomas could only nod.

"Do you wish me to take it all away? All the pain?"

He looked up into her face, eyes wet. "Yes."

"Then tell me what you want. Say the word."

"Forgiveness."

Magdalene uncoupled herself from him and stood. Thomas covered his face, ashamed of the tears, of his vulnerability. She lifted his chin with her finger, slipped the collar from him and let it fall to the floor.

Magdalene smiled and looked down. Thomas followed her gaze past her navel to her groin. The rings on her lips clinked as her vulva moved and her vagina opened like a flower. The slit extended as her skin parted up over her stomach, to her chest. She began to separate, layers upon layers of skin and flesh. Thomas looked to her face and watched as it too began to open like a slow-motion explosion.

"Forgiveness . . ." she whispered before her lips peeled back, her skull yawned wide and she fell on him. Her hands gripped the sides of his head, her nails puncturing through skin, penetrating down to the bone with preternatural strength.

He screamed in pain, but it was smothered as Magdalene brought herself down onto his face and his world turned scarlet.

* * *

Liam de Leeuwin turned off the camera, 100% certain he was going to vomit. Of all the things he'd recorded, of all the pieces of performance art, the queer sexual acts some people requested, he'd never seen anything as viscerally disturbing as what he'd just recorded.

Magdalene fixed the clasp on her robe and ran her fingers through her mane of dark, velvety hair. She wore the veneer of

143

a satiated lioness, content with her prey consumed, or perhaps it was the insectoid poise of a praying mantis having copulated and feasted upon her doomed lover. She spoke with a glacial tone. "I trust you captured the moment in full?"

Liam nodded, finding the conjuring of words one act too far. His shirt was stuck to his back with sweat, his mouth bone dry.

"Your payment is waiting for you at the front desk. Same amount as usual. I trust you'll uphold your end of the bargain."

Liam found his voice. "Yes, Miss Magdalene. I'll upload the video straight away."

She spun on her heels and strode to the door, hair bouncing with each step. "You're free to go. The limo will take you back to the city . . . unless there's something you desire?"

He slammed the camera shut and pushed it into his briefcase. He clasped it to his chest as he passed her, using it as a shield. Liam had no want or need of the pleasures Magdalene could offer. "No thanks, miss. I'll be on my way."

He sped through the House of Tears, his eyes on the floor to avoid looking at anything that might destroy his sanity. He ignored the spongey feel of the dancefloor and breathlessly flew up the hundred or so steps to the empty lobby, where a ziplocked satchel of cash awaited him on the reception desk.

The limousine weaved its way through the sparse freeway traffic towards the glittering lights of New York. Liam inserted the camera's SD card into the laptop and began uploading his latest video to the forum website. As he waited, he stared out at the magnificent city and wondered how on earth he would go about getting out of the pornography business once and for all. But he knew deep down that she would never let him leave. The Magdalene would find him wherever he went, however far he could run. It didn't matter if he lay low in a whorehouse in Alabama or squatted in a crack den in Indonesia—he had no place to hide.

Liam was a vain man, too, used to the finer tastes in life. He had expensive habits to maintain. The Magdalene paid well.

And besides, it was steady work at The House of Tears.

ABOUT THE AUTHOR
JOHN PAUL FITCH

John Paul Fitch writes and lives in Perth, Western Australia. He has written fiction, non-fiction, comics, television, and plays.

Twitter: @johnybhoy

Curious Fictions page: https://curiousfictions.com/authors/531-john-paul-fitch

Blog: https://johnpfitch.wordpress.com/

DANGEROUS BLOODLINES

BY W.T. PATERSON

"The most notorious serials killers of the '80s were the Wolfe Brothers," Ainslie said to a group of middle-aged tourists with cameras and fanny packs, "and this was their house."

She turned around and started leading the group into the living room when she heard a camera click. There was nothing in the hallways to take a picture of, except for her from behind. In these jeans, with the rips right below the folds of her ass cheeks showing just enough skin and black underwear, it was a common sound. Then came the all-too-familiar reprimand from the angry wife who whisper-scolded her husband for being *too damn obvious*.

"I was just seeing if the camera was on," the man protested.

"Then delete the photo!" his wife said through clenched teeth and a forced smile.

"When the tour is over," he said, starting to sweat.

Ainslie smiled wryly and walked with more sway in her steps. She knew what she could get away with and it was more than most girls. Her lips were always slightly pursed and her eyes were always half closed. She would only smile out of the corner of her mouth and somewhat raise an eyebrow. It was the "I want you" look, the "I don't want to know your name, I just want you inside me" face.

The other girls who gave tours often complained because Ainslie's groups would be full and she'd pull in two, sometimes three hundred dollars in tips per tour, with phone numbers written on the twenties. On a good night, she'd come home with close to two grand.

To be fair, the other girls were from the historical society and were passionate about having visitors get excited about history. They maybe walked away with twelve dollars on a good night and some random guy asking what type of crown molding was used around the doors.

Yet Ainslie drew the crowds, so she was the it girl. Every tour she gave was sold out, and sometimes people had to be turned away at the door to stay in compliance with the fire code. It nearly caused several fistfights in the parking lot among the rejected men. It helped that, if someone were to google "The Wolfe Brothers," they'd find just past the Wikipedia page and underneath a CNN documentary a site called Slasher-Sluts. There, hot girls stripped down to their underwear and took controversial photos recreating crime scenes, victim poses, and bedroom antics. Topping the list with a staggering gap between her and the rest was Ainslie. Half a million hits a week kept tours selling out and Historical Horrors, Inc. well off.

"Silas was the charmer, according to those who knew him, and it's rumored he could sweet-talk a vegetarian into eating a thick, juicy steak," she said, drawing out all the right words in all the right places. "Happy, which was his actual given name, was the more brooding one. Quiet, reserved, calculated, he was the brute force behind the two. Silas was the brains, Happy the muscle."

The living room had recreated crime scene tape and replicas of the furniture that had been found in the house when the brothers were killed during the three-day police standoff. The couches even had bullet holes and blood spatter designed by Hollywood special effects experts. They'd offered their services for free as long as "you know . . . Ainslie takes some pictures and posts them to her site for us . . ."

In the living room, the cameras clicked and the young girl stood by the window in her loose black tank top that showed both her black bra and tanned sides. It was reminiscent of the photo on Slasher-Sluts where she stood by the same window in only black panties holding a gun pointed at the window, her arms hiding her nipples. As long as they didn't show and she had bottoms on, it wasn't porn.

Now, tourists were getting almost the same photo for their home collections to brag to their friends that they were actually there and yeah, "don't let my wife hear, but that's the *same* girl."

"The FBI finally caved and called in SWAT snipers on the third day of the standoff when the brothers were fatally shot— bang bang—right through this window."

"Why didn't they just kick the door down?" a woman from the crowd asked. Someone always asked. It was a bit of knowledge that the FBI had tried to keep secret, but came out during the civil trial.

The house was booby-trapped.

"Only the brothers knew where to step," the vixen said, strutting over to the woman. "Any wrong move in any room and razor wire would slice open your neck." She pushed across the woman's throat with a gentle finger. "Or a spring-loaded blade would cut through your calf muscles, maybe sever your Achilles tendon." Ainslie bent at the waist and made two swiping motions against the woman's ankles. With the rips in her pants, the angle at which she was folded, and the sunlight becoming a spotlight, the room didn't dare breathe. "But my favorite was that they'd soak nails in rattlesnake venom and push them through slabs of meat. When the first cop broke the door down, he felt a wet slap against his face and only saw the meat. He didn't see the ends of the nails sticking out, which punctured tiny holes in the side of his cheek." She got right up to the woman's ear and brushed the back of a knuckle down her touristy sunburned face. "They say the brothers sat around eating popcorn and laughing while the officer went into paralysis and died in full view of the rest of the force. They had to rethink their entire raid." The last words were whispered like a seduction and the woman who'd asked let out a quivered sigh.

Ainslie smiled her miniature smile and turned around. "Any other questions?"

Every hand went up.

148

After the tour, Ainslie went home and into the master bath—stripped down to her underwear. She lived with her boyfriend Spike. His real name was Jamie, but that didn't sound dangerous so she'd first told him she wouldn't sleep with him unless he stepped it up. After that he'd come home with more visible tattoos and started calling himself Rust. When that didn't stick, it went to Spike. He now had tattoos up and down both arms, worked as a ship builder by the Savannah docks, and always wore a tight fisherman's cap except for when he slept and showered. Right then he was lying on her bed in his boxers and a gray V-neck jersey reading his Kindle.

When a girl like Ainslie wanted something, she got it and people like Spike were gladly willing to give it.

Most everything in the apartment belonged to the girl, the money coming from both the tours and the traffic on the site. They lived comfortably for their age, more so than many adults, but it was mostly Spike's doing. If it were up to Ainslie, she'd live in an unfurnished studio apartment with a single mattress on the floor, her thrift shop clothes that she could cut up, and the stack of books about the Wolfe Brothers. She was obsessed with them; it was all she ever thought about.

"Coming to bed?" Spike said.

Ainslie stared at herself in the mirror. "Come here," she said.

Spike got up and walked in, noticing her standing half-naked against the sink. "You okay?"

"You look so much like him," Ainslie said, opening the top drawer and pulling out a long butcher knife.

"Come on, not tonight," Spike protested, but Ainslie bent forward.

"Come on, big boy, I'm your victim. Make me feel like I have to fuck you to save my life," Ainslie teased, making Spike hold the knife.

"Ainslie . . ."

"Hold it to my throat and say you're going to kill me," she said, guiding his hand up to her neck so the blade touched the skin. "And this time, call me Lacey Moorish."

* * *

Spike gulped. "That was one of their victims, Ains."

"I know," the girl said, and Spike watched Ainslie slide her fingers down the front of her black panties. "Make me feel your power."

In the light of the bathroom, her body was flawless and smooth. With just enough of a tan, seductively sinister curves, and a body flaunting natural tightness, she was nearly irresistible. In Spike's able hands, the girl millions of people would literally kill to be with.

"Fine," he conceded. "Safe word?"

"No safe word tonight. No matter how hard I fight back, how much I cry and scream, you don't stop until you've come. Got it?"

"You need help, Ainslie," Spike said, running his finger around the back of her panties. Her soft skin was ready for him. The curve at the top of her backside was warm, her breasts perky and firm.

Ainslie grabbed Spike's hand with the knife and pushed it hard enough into her throat that it broke skin and drew blood.

"Please, sir," she said, voice trembling. "I don't know who you are or what you want but I'll do anything! Please don't hurt me!"

That got him hard. "Shut the fuck up!" Spike screamed, and he grabbed a fistful of her hair and rammed her violently toward the sink so she bent in half at the waist. He gripped the band of her underwear and yanked it so hard that it tore off, leaving her exposed and vulnerable. "Suck me," he said wrenching on her hair like reins as tears streamed down her face.

Ainslie got on her knees and quickly undid his pants. She wrapped her mouth around him and bobbed her head.

"Faster, bitch," Spike demanded in his best serial killer voice imitation.

She began making choking and gurgling noises, which made Spike thrust harder and deeper into her mouth—so firm that Ainslie kept hitting her head on the cabinets beneath the sink. Then he grabbed her by the top of the scalp and dragged her up to stand, pressing the tip of the blade into the fleshy underside of her jaw.

"Please, sir! Just don't hurt me again."

"Shut up, slut!" He spun her around, bending her at the waist again. This time he jammed himself inside her. She cried out in pain. "This is what happens, Lacey, when you become treasured!"

"Somebody, help me, please!" Ainslie cried, but Spike stabbed the knife into the wall and clamped his hand over her mouth. With his other, he violently squeezed her breasts over the bra. He could feel her heartbeat spiking beneath one set of fingers, hot breath on the other. He was on the verge of finishing. He was close. He was right there.

Pushing into her repeatedly from behind in an increasing intensity, he went even stiffer. He pulled out, finishing all over Ainslie's glistening back.

He paused for a moment to catch his breath. Then he pulled the knife from the wall and walked into the kitchen, throwing it into the stainless-steel sink. He didn't like that her blood was on it for real. Her role-play obsession was getting out of hand.

When he came back into the room, Ainslie was still standing naked by the mirror smiling a sick, fulfilled smile. She dabbed at the small slit on her neck with a cotton swab and put some lotion on it. Then she hit the lights, unclasped her bra to let it fall to the floor, and walked naked to the bed where Spike was already lying, staring at the ceiling, *through* the ceiling.

They were quiet for a moment. Then she turned into him and stroked his chest with a delicacy that could not have existed moments ago.

"I don't like it when you say that," he finally uttered.

"Say what?"

151

"That I look like him."

"Trust me, babe," she said, kissing him on the cheek and then biting his earlobe, "it's a good thing."

* * *

During Ainslie's next tour, another familiar question arose. The hordes of tourists trying to re-live a great American massacre always treated the Wolfe house as they would a Hollywood superstar. But that's how it went: the serial killers of history pulled more weight than the biggest action hero of the time.

"What made them do it?" a teen asked. He was with his parents and it was hard to tell who begged who to come along. Usually the teens on Ainslie's tours were dressed in all black and wore upside-down cross necklaces. They walked with a disenfranchised lurch and always seemed unimpressed. In truth, they loved every gruesome detail of every terrible story. Yet this kid looked like a first-year college student trying to test his new psychology major.

"The Wolfe Brothers were made out to be insane, but they weren't." She smiled at him. Her shoulders were pulled back as she walked with unbreakable eye contact. The group parted, giving her a pathway to the teen. "It's clear they had some disorder. Sociopaths, or paranoid schizophrenics, it seems like they thought of their victims as a disease. But it was quite the opposite, really. They operated on a near genius level and had immense respect for their victims."

"All the news reports said they killed at random though," the kid said, swallowing hard. Sweat beaded his forehead.

"Imagine you meet a man and he shakes your hand like you're old friends. The way he speaks, you start to think you *are* friends. Then your guard drops and he's extracting information from you. Though really, you give it up freely. Things like where you live, if you're married, have kids, have roommates, have a job. But here's the kicker: *you* wouldn't be the target. Whoever you talked the most about—your wife, your husband, your kid, your sister, your best friend—they are the target."

152

The crowd went silent. Ainslie was smirking and the college student had lost his smugness. She was so far into his personal space that her breasts were brushing against his chest every time she inhaled.

"That doesn't make sense," he managed to choke out.

"No? They take away the thing that is the second most important part of your life and what happens?" She dipped her hands into her back pockets and rocked between tiptoes and heel. With each pass, she lifted her chin and teased his lips with hers.

The kid struggled to find words at first. "If y-you take away the second most important thing, it will feel like the most important? And therefore you crumble?"

"Two for the price of one," Ainslie jested.

"Well, what's the first most important thing?!" a guy with a fanny pack asked.

Ainslie put her hand on the back of the kid's neck and pulled him down to her face. "Tell them, college boy," she whispered, tracing her finger across his throat.

"Your . . . your own life is the most important thing," he said and shoved his hands into his pockets in a vain attempt to hide the growing bulge in the crotch of his pants.

She blew him a kiss and moved the tour upstairs.

"Happy Wolfe wrote in his journal, 'True beauty is *the* flaw of our species. It has no place amongst the violent and ugly world of men.' He also carved a Ouija board into his bedroom floor," Ainslie said.

There was a hushed rumble in the crowd. People were hesitant to follow her up the stairs, which sometimes happened because good people—people without the urge to set fire to the world—realized the gravity of death.

"How many people did they kill again?" a woman asked. She clutched her necklace; inside her palm, the charm of a cross.

"Forty-two that we know of," Ainslie said, "but those were just the ones they wanted police to find."

Slowly, the crowd ascended the creaky wooden stairs to see the rooms where the brothers had slept and devised ways to

153

eradicate beauty from the world. This was always the part of the tour where someone fainted and, sure enough, ten minutes later, a guy went down.

Though he ultimately blamed the heat, he claimed he'd seen something that no one else had: when he'd looked into a mirror in Silas' bedroom, darkness had glared back.

Ainslie didn't let on but knew all about the *eyes of darkness*, as she called them.

* * *

Spike got home and walked into the bedroom. Ainslie was sprawled out on the bed, slash wounds across her throat and wrists, blood soaking into the sheets.

"Ains, we just bought these," he said softly, tossing his jacket onto the chair. He was teetering on exhaustion and looking to catch a quick nap before dinner but now had to do laundry.

"Can you imagine?" the girl asked, fake blood turning her white shirt into a crimson see-through. Her nipples were hard with excitement. "What if you came home and the Wolfe Brothers got to me first? What if you actually found me like this?" She pursed her lips and arched her back.

"Honestly, I'd think it was a joke until you shit yourself," he said, walking into the kitchen and cracking open a soda. Spike took a big frustrated sip.

"There are no more great men anymore."

"Are you high? Ainslie, I know you love researching the brothers and have a fascination with them, but any normal person wouldn't come home to this and think it was okay. Whatever happened to dinner and a movie? Nice sex, you know, without the threats of violence and getting slapped around? Maybe for one night we can live out my fantasy?"

Ainslie curled her lips and sat up. "What's *your* fantasy?"

"A functional household," he said without hesitation. "You play happy wife, I play husband. We watch the ballgame, have some beers, then we have sex, slow sex, and hold each other afterwards."

"I know your mother was a drunk and you never knew your father, and your childhood was fucked up with that whole *gun* thing," she said, glossing over some less than savory details, "but why would you want to pretend to be the image of something you aren't?"

"Says the girl who fakes her own death on a daily basis." He laughed condescendingly. "And I don't know, maybe it's because if sometimes you fake it, you actually start to feel it. Maybe I want some comfort."

"Come here." Instead of motioning with one curling finger, she used her whole arm.

It looked welcoming, more than any other time before, and so Spike went and sat on the edge of the bed. Ainslie massaged his thick shoulders, the fake blood smoothing out over his skin. She kissed him on the cheek, leaving a big blood-stained lip mark.

They stared at each other in the mirror by the door.

"That feels good," he said.

"You have me," she told him, gazing into his eyes through the reflection, "and I won't let masked men come into your home and threaten to murder you while you sleep."

Spike started to tremble. That night, the darkest of nights, was scorched into his memory. Hearing his mother beg for her life in the next room, being threatened by *good people*—it was a nightmare that he never woke up from. The masked intruders had wanted vigilante justice, unlawful revenge, and they'd gotten it.

"Ever since that day, I've had this thing inside me that just wants to . . ." Spike paused, hating the words that were coming out of his mouth and the thoughts he was having.

"Kill them?" Ainslie finished.

"Yeah," he said, feeling ashamed.

"Like father, like son," she whispered, moving her hands from his shoulders to under his shirt and across his chest. "They were scared of you, of your bloodline."

"I'm the bastard son of the worst killer in US history," he said.

"That's a rare power, an almost unheard-of legacy, Jamie."

Ainslie had used his real name and it took a moment for it to register. "And that's the only reason you're with me, I know. I'm just trying to fool myself into thinking that I'm not the son of Silas Wolfe, and you're attracted to me because I'm a good person and I take care of you."

"That *is* the reason," Ainslie said. "I've also never come so hard as I do when I'm with you."

"I guess it doesn't matter why you're with me," Spike said, slowly quashing his doubts. "You're with me. I'll chalk it up to having lucky stars."

"You sit on the couch and flip on the game. Take a load off tonight. I'll take care of dinner."

"Yeah?"

"And I'll wash the sheets."

Ainslie kissed him again and then wiped the fake blood off. Spike stood to change and then went into the living room to flip through the channels.

* * *

Ainslie stripped the sheets, showered, re-sheeted the bed, and cooked dinner with her hair in a ponytail. She sat next to Spike with her feet tucked underneath her and ate while they watched football.

That night they had slow, passionate sex. Their bodies went black, blue and white from the glow of the moon, and their skin sparkled with sweat. For the first time, Ainslie felt Spike, really *felt* his body and affection for her.

Yet even amidst his restrained lovemaking, his hand stroking her hair, their midsections slick with lust, she felt in him an insatiable darkness. It was a madness that harbored evil, a lifestyle that begged to be set free.

It was in that moment that she wondered whether to tell him that she had missed her period for the second month in a row.

* * *

Ainslie waited until Spike was asleep before she dug herself out from under the covers and slipped on her shoes. Wearing tiny white gym shorts and a plain white tee-shirt that hugged her curves like skin, she walked through the night to the Wolfe Brothers' house.

She had made keys for herself during the second week of the job. Since she gave the most tours, the managers of Historical Horrors, Inc. had also given her the passwords for the alarm system.

This wasn't an uncommon occurrence. Ainslie often wandered into the house in the early hours of the morning to sit and revel in the atrocities. It was there that she had stumbled upon the most curious feature of the house . . .

The Brothers were still there.

The Ouija board that had been carved into the floor often pulled the glasses off tourists, which then acted as makeshift planchettes. When Ainslie had first noticed this, she came back that night with one made from a chunk of broken glass used on one of the Brothers' victims. She'd had it sent to her by one of the Slasher-Slut fans who'd paid an enormous amount of money for it on eBay. (All he'd asked for in return was a date. Ainslie had accepted the gift but never went on the date.)

Using this glass, she could communicate with Happy Wolfe.

The *eyes of darkness*, she'd found, was really the apparition of Silas Wolfe. In the mirror, two dark spots would appear on the wall behind the looker that only existed in the reflection. When the looker connected gazes with the spots, they would see into Silas' soul and become deeply frightened. This led to the fainting spells, but the tour wasn't a haunted tour and Ainslie had wanted to keep the information to herself.

On that night, she felt particularly excited. Using the hand-etched board to summon Happy and then calling forth Silas from the mirror, she stood ready to receive the praise of the men she admired.

The air became cool and ambient voices echoed like a wind about the room.

"Hello, boys," she said with a smirk as an invisible hand pushed through her hair and a foul stench like hot, dry breath hit her shoulders. There were faint scents of pomade and cedar too.

"To what do we owe the pleasure?" the first disembodied voice echoed. It was Silas. She knew this because of his smooth and articulate cadence. Happy had a slower, more lumbering speech.

"I want to feel your touch again," she said as a ghostly hand cupped her breasts with steady, sophisticated fingers. Ainslie craned her head backwards and let herself be felt up. "Yes," she whispered.

Ghostly fingers ran up her legs like an electric tingle and slowly back down. Though she couldn't be certain, the touch felt like it was coming from callused, hair-on-the-knuckles hands.

"You remind me of Lacey Moorish," said Happy's floating voice. It sounded like he was saying it through a snarled smile.

"I love it when you say that," Ainslie whispered. She loved being compared to their first known victim.

"Wait," Silas' voice said. The unseen hands cupping her breasts moved away. "You're different." The pomade scent gave way to the metallic, iron aroma of freshly spilled blood. Then it soured into beer-soaked sweat.

Ainslie took off her shirt and sat on the ground as if the words hadn't affected her. "Let me feel your power," she said through closed eyes and pinched vocals.

"No," Silas said, and suddenly she couldn't feel them near her anymore. This made her suddenly concerned. The tension in the air grew thick. She no longer felt safe, and worse . . . wanted.

"What?" she asked, trying not to sound desperate or rejected.

"You carry our bloodline," Silas said.

"A boy," Happy echoed.

"Yes, so you can live on forever!" she triumphantly exclaimed. She squirmed on the floor and ended up on her hands and knees with legs spread apart.

A haunting, menacing laughter filled the dark room, bouncing off the wooden walls.

"They should have killed him that night," a whisper said, and she couldn't tell which brother was speaking. Ainslie sat back on her heels and looked around the room.

"Beauty has no place in the world of men," another voice echoed, and it sounded like Happy, but she couldn't be sure.

"Am I beautiful?" the girl asked, slowly gripping the bunched-up tee-shirt next to her. She brought it to her bare chest, now coarse with goosebumps.

"My child, you are no such thing. You confuse carnal lust with beauty; you confuse loyalty for love. You think power is the ability to give or take life, but this is not true. Power is the ability to maintain it. Dying is easy, and this is your flaw." It was Silas speaking. "My son will never be normal. You have taken that from him because you make him relive the shame of his father. It's your obsession with fantasy. Now another will soon come into this world and our theory will prove true."

"There is no hope, only suffering and rejection." Happy. "Everything else is a thin veil."

"Why do you tell me this?" Ainslie said, her eyes welling up.

"Because we also take from you the things that made you cling to hope. You will never have us, only in your fantasies. You will never fully have my son, only his body. You will never have a functional family because of these choices, all of which have led to us, and all of which will one day leave you unglued," Silas said.

There was a rumble against the windows and the floorboards creaked. Ainslie felt breath on her throat, hot with decay and madness. An unseen chest pushed at her, firm but not muscular.

"This is the price of having your dreams come true," Happy grunted. "It opens your eyes to the disappointments that came before and will surely come after."

Ainslie put a quivering hand on her belly as hot tears poured down her cheeks. In the darkness, she sat almost naked as the room felt like a window had been opened. The pressure changed. The air grew thin and stale. The familiar smells vanished.

Whatever had existed before was gone. In every sense of the word, she was alone. She was shivering. She had been abandoned yet again by the men she looked up to the most.

At that moment, something inside her belly moved, and for the first time in her adult life, Ainslie felt the unfamiliar grip of fear find a home inside her mind.

And it wouldn't be the last.

ABOUT THE AUTHOR
W. T. PATERSON

W. T. Paterson is the author of the novels *Dark Satellites* and *WOTNA*. A Pushcart Prize nominee and graduate of Second City Chicago, his work has appeared in over 40 publications worldwide include *Fiction Magazine*, *The Gateway Review*, and a number of anthologies. He is a current MFA candidate at the University of New Hampshire.

Send him a tweet @WTPaterson.

SEX EDUCATION

BY ANNIE KNOX

Sex.

They tell you so many things about sex. Sex is for sluts. Sex is for marriage. Sex is dangerous. Sex is disease. Sex is a sin. Sex is something special, to be treasured. Sex is what boys want.

When I was younger, I was set off by the word. Seeing 'sexual education' on my timetable had my twelve-year-old cheeks flushing a bright pink and my heart racing, a strange sensation in my stomach that I would later understand to be a sickening desire.

I watched our biology teacher explain awkwardly what a dick was, what balls are for—pumping us girls full of sperm, impregnating us, population growth. All so scientific considering the act we were discussing. We looked at awkward pictures of men lying rectangular on top of women who were on their backs, arms outstretched, staring up at the sky above their cartoon male companions. Later in life I'd realise that the picture was the perfect example of "lie back, think of England." Even at a young age, girls are shown these shitty, boring pictures depicting future versions of themselves lying in submission with men on top of them. There was no discussion of orgasm, exploration, fun. Just lie back, let them stick it in, jack in back and forth until they spout sperm into you. Not something to enjoy.

I lay in bed at night, every night for months on end, touching myself, imagining someone in me, on top of me. It scared me, made my stomach tight, made me hot. I wriggled under the covers, trying to stay silent, terrified someone would walk in.

My parents moved around the house, zombies with heartbeats interacting with me only when they couldn't find the television remote. They spoke to each other in muffled tones, matching the muted colours of our pastel house and bland foods and quiet, unexciting lives. I watched them avoid touching each other, saw how they lay rigid and apart at night, and it matched the pictures in the book.

Romance entered my life at age thirteen, when I watched a romcom with my friend and recognized, for the first time, what it meant when two characters vanish backstage together like that. Laughing, happy, teeth glinting, fingers interlaced, lips sliding against each other. It looked sweet, too sweet to be related to the perfunctory act of sex I'd learnt about. Watching it made my gut burn, my vagina throb.

"It means they're in love," my friend told me. "That's what you do when you're in love."

I had never seen my parents act like that before.

Love. Another level. Sex for reproduction, sex for love.

When I was fourteen I got on my knees for the first time and felt nothing. I was at a house party drunk off two rum and Cokes, and I didn't know the boy above me. Love was nowhere. Love didn't matter. My head was tipsy and he wanted me to touch him, so I did. He told me to put it in my mouth and I asked why. That wasn't for reproduction. That didn't make sense for love.

The sight of a dick repulsed me, and putting it in my mouth didn't help. Above me he grunted and groaned, and it slipped back and forth, hit the back of my throat and made me choke. The pulse of desire that thrummed through my veins when I touched myself at night was gone. The heat in my skin and blood and the dizzying sense of euphoria was nowhere. I was cold, my knees ached, my jaw needed to be clicked. I left before he was done and he called me a bitch.

As I walked back to the party, pissed off at the discomfort in my knees, I passed a boy called Danny from my class. He looked down at my scratched knees and a dark grin crossed his face. His pupils met mine and he raised his eyebrows. I told him to fuck off.

163

My friends were shocked at my behaviour. They called me slag, slut, whore, but giggled and clasped their hands together and asked me for the details. I told them to try it, that it was amazing. I told them what they wanted to hear.

I let another boy lie on top of me when I was fourteen, a few weeks later. He chewed at my thighs and licked drunkenly, disgustingly at the lips of my vagina whilst I put him in my mouth again. This boy I knew, from maths class. He smiled at me a lot. I thought he had seemed nice, but at that moment I'd felt sick. I wanted to throw up at the taste, the texture. I lay and let him do what he wanted, bored and uncomfortable. I remembered the cartoon girl in the biology book and wondered if whoever had drawn her had based her on a similar experience as mine: lying, waiting for it to be done. I wondered why it was made to look so good in the films when it was so crappy in real life.

When he was done, he got off and gasped for air. I went to hug him, knowing that when you were with someone, that's what you were supposed to do. He turned away, feigning as though he was reaching for his drink. I sat up and pulled my knickers back up to my waist, let the hem of my dress return to mid-thigh. I got up and went to leave the room.

"Hey," he said breathlessly. "Cheers for that."

I accepted his thanks. I needed thanking, as it wasn't like I'd got anything out of it. I waited to see if perhaps he would ask something else. It wasn't for reproduction, so perhaps it could be for love. But he stayed quiet, so I left the room.

Danny was outside, waiting to use the bathroom. The same twist of a smile lighted his face, eyes flickering over me.

"Find what you were looking for?" he asked, like he already knew the answer.

I told him to fuck off again.

* * *

The first time I had sex, it still didn't do anything for me. I went through the mechanics like a robot, letting myself be kissed,

164

tongue invading my throat like a tentacle, slimy and obtrusive. The boy was a stranger from a club where the music had been too loud for us to talk and the drink had been cheap if you bought the dirty stuff. I had been drunk enough that I barely realised it was happening until it was almost over: a mess of sheets around me, a pair of hairy legs on mine, frantic rutting against me, a stomach scraping over my own. I lay back and thought not of England but of my own bed, my own hand, as he slumped on top of me, hairy chest against my boobs. He pulled out and threw the condom to the side and fell into a deep sleep next to me without a word. With my head buzzing and my body awake but unsatisfied, I went home.

Still in the same dress, feeling cheap and dirty and used and not at all like a girl is told they should after their first time, I got on top of my bed and found Danny on Facebook. Maybe he'd recognised something in me that I hadn't yet. I shut his Facebook page and tried to touch myself but it made me want to puke, so instead I sat in the shower and let hot tears trickle down my cheeks, thinking of all the girls in films who got rose-covered beds on their first time, who got to enjoy sex. Was there something wrong with me?

I slept with many men over the next few months, hunting for something I couldn't find. Every time I went to class after another unsatisfying night, I caught Danny's eye and he would smirk at me like he knew. Like he could read what happened from just looking at me. It made me feel shame and yet it lit that part of my stomach in a way that nothing else could. Even my own hand didn't do the job anymore.

I watched porn and heard the way the girls moaned and groaned, studied how they curled their hands into fists, bit their lips and gasped. I wanted desperately to feel the level of pleasure they experienced. But I came across a lot of other videos, videos of girls moaning and groaning and biting their lips but their hands were slack, their eyes filled with the same dead, fed-up, sickened gaze that left my own when I was letting someone screw me.

165

When I was sixteen I got into my first fistfight after school, after detention. I was walking through the trees nearby, the shortcut to home, and was roughly shoved. I fell to the floor and scraped my hands, and my heartrate picked up in anticipation of a scuffle.

I got to my feet. Danny stood behind me grinning like he'd been handed the crown jewels. I pushed him back. He hit me and I punched him in the stomach, blood warm and honey-like dripping from my nose. He caught me in a headlock and we wrestled, me pulling him to the ground and hitting him until his lip split. He rolled me over and settled on top of me, heavy and pressing me into the ground with his weight, and his dick hardened against my thigh.

He grinned at me in the light, teeth shining white and crimson, and I suddenly felt he knew what I felt too. My stomach throbbed with desire so strong it was smothering and musky, and I lifted my head and kissed him hard, blood metallic and salty between us. I reached down and yanked his top off, right there, halfway between the school and my house.

We fucked. I didn't come. But it felt like nothing had before. It felt like something . . . *important*. He pulled out and came over my chest, rubbing the substance onto my skin. Light was falling; birds sang as the leaves darkened to black against fading grey above my head. He got dressed, helped me back into my clothes. I had rough bruises on my hips, scratches on my back from where the skin of my spine and shoulder blades had been scraped raw by the ground. It felt amazing. He ran a hand over my back and I shuddered into it.

When he offered to walk me home, softer than I'd ever seen him before, I gave him a rough shove that made him laugh and walked on by myself.

When I got home, I looked in the mirror and mechanically prodded my swollen nose, my bruised eye, the marks on my sides from where his fingers had gripped me tight. I thought of the blood trickling from his cut and the desire that hadn't died down rose in my gut anew, steady and sure, and I lay down on my bathroom floor, the tiles cool against my sore back and skull.

I rubbed and rubbed until I had to bite my lip to stop sound from escaping, and I came so hard I juddered on the floor like a fish out of water. I trembled afterwards, feeling like my skin wasn't even my own. I climbed into the bath, the water gentle and warm, and soaked in the steam until I was in my own body again.

My bed was softer than it had ever been before, my sleep deeper than I'd ever experienced.

I sat at breakfast with my pastel-coloured parents in their pale turtlenecks and drawn faces and waited for them to notice the clash of bright hurting purple and yellow beneath my eye. They didn't look at me. They said nothing. Our house remained a void, a place where colour and noise and personality died.

Danny came to speak to me in school. A direct contrast, with the slit of red in his pink lips, his sharp cheekbones decorated with rosy life, his sparkling, dark, dangerous eyes.

"Sleep well?" he asked, that same knowing smile in place. We shared a secret now and I liked that sense; that it was something to keep quiet, something just for us.

"Yes," I said and turned into my classroom, leaving him alone in the corridor.

* * *

I had detention that night. Danny did not.

The school was quiet, and the room was filled with silence that buzzed with what I was thinking. I was aware of my knee-length socks sliding down my calves as I looked at the man marking papers like a robot at the desk across from me, was aware of the blood in my wrists and neck. I closed my eyes. He was my *teacher*.

I got up, anxiety under my cheeks and tongue like flies, and moved towards Mr. Clerkenwell.

"Detention isn't over yet," he said.

"I know."

The sound of my voice must have told him what was coming. He lifted his head slowly, warily. "Then why are you in front of me?"

167

I moved with overconfidence, fuelled by the idea of telling Danny what I'd done. I sat on Mr. Clerkenwell's lap, legs on either side of his. He didn't even try to turn me away, just ran his hands up my back. He grew hard in seconds.

I felt nothing, just like with the men before Danny—nothing special, nothing exciting. My insides were dead, my mind clear, my heartrate steady. He hoisted me onto the desk behind him, and the door suddenly opened. He leapt back like he had been burnt, and I turned my head to see Danny in the doorway. He moved quicker than I could have expected, grabbing Mr. Clerkenwell and flinging him away from me. A flash of movement and the man was falling with a hand over his nose, blood pouring through his fingers.

I tightened and got hot again, suddenly burning for it. Danny turned to look at me and I leapt up, shoved him. He pushed me back so hard I tumbled over the desk to the floor. By the time I sat up again, he and Mr. Clerkenwell were fighting, punching each other hard enough that each fist made a thudding sound that resonated in my gut like a wave of arousal. I joined them—a fist to my stomach, an elbow to my face. I hit Mr. Clerkenwell; felt his nose crack under my knuckles, and gasped at how it affected the rest of my body. Wet smeared across my cheek as he slapped me hard enough to split skin. Then he gurgled at me. Coughed. Stepped away.

Danny looked at me, a knife in his hand gleaming bright crimson in the light, as Mr. Clerkenwell crumpled to the floor. Fearless, I stepped over the choking man and wrapped my arms around Danny's shoulders. I slammed my blood-slickened lips into his, groaning at how alive I felt: every pore of my skin was open and breathing, every brush of his lips against mine set off a fire in my stomach, and my breath was hardly getting into my lungs before it was getting out.

He tossed the knife aside and we slid to the ground, not bothering to undress beyond tugging my panties to my knees and him yanking his trousers down far enough to release his dick. I was so wet, wetter than I'd ever been, and I realised there was dampness beneath my legs and back too, as warm, wet blood had oozed from Mr. Clerkenwell's lifeless body, soaking into the ground around me and my skin. Danny grabbed my thighs and pulled me beneath him and pressed down, down, down.

It ended with harsh breathing, both of us coming at the same time. I pushed him off, wanting the ecstasy for myself. Air rushed against where sticky blood dried on my skin, my hair matted with it. I tasted it in my mouth still, and the throb of the hits I'd taken echoed with the pulsing in my clit. The fire slowly died down, and I breathed and breathed and listened to Danny doing the same next to—

"Come on, get moving. I want to get out of here too, you know."

I blinked. Mr. Clerkenwell stood at the front of the room, packing his books away. He raised an eyebrow and I stared back, wondering what he would say if he knew what I had been imagining. If he knew I was wet beneath my skirt from thinking about murdering him. I was shocked at my own mind, having taken my girlish fantasies about my teacher and turning them into a bloodbath. But arousal still panged in my stomach.

I left the room with my bags on my back and my skin seeming out of place, thrumming with desire and nothing to do with it.

I moved throughout the empty school, aware of Mr. Clerkenwell walking behind me, the sound of every footfall. I was mindful that we were the only ones in the building, that I could probably kill him if I wanted to. He'd be hard to fight, sure, and I'd get a few bruises, but I was starting to understand that my brain took pain for pleasure.

Mr. Clerkenwell bade me a pleasant evening as he locked the doors behind us and strolled to his car and got in, driving away. The night around me was pink, the building behind me a huge, cold shadow looming over my head. I scurried across the parking lot, afraid of myself but stronger, more empowered. I rushed through the trees, weaving my way towards home, pumped through with placebo-adrenaline as though my fantasy had actually happened and I were fleeing a murder scene.

A body collided with mine and I was pushed roughly against a tree. Danny's dark eyes gleamed at me, his teeth bared as he smiled, and I thought of a wolf about to eat its prey.

I wasn't prey though. I surged back and pushed him away with such force that he fell over his own feet and crashed to the ground. I moved to straddle him, hold him down with my body, and his eyes widened in surprise.

"What, you expected me to stop fighting?"

"Never," he replied, for once that stupid smirk nowhere to be seen. "You're a fighter. Like me."

I told him what I'd dreamt of while in detention. Of him killing for me and us fucking in the blood next to the body.

"You're insane," he breathed out, and then he was sitting up to kiss me, running his hands through my hair until he was tugging it, hard, harder. I gritted my teeth against the pain and dug my fingernails into his back. He gasped and then grinned, but not that sly, sneaky grin—a beautiful, wild smile unlike anything I'd seen a boy or man wear before.

When we were done, I pushed him off like I had in the dream and lay in the dirt breathing. Every pull of air was new and exciting, not stale. A breeze made me cold, so cold, but I didn't care. As the chill rushed over my chest, I massaged where he had come, the sperm seeping through the red lace of my bra to graze bare skin. A leaf rustled and was blown across into my ear. I was able to be on my own, to appreciate the way my body felt, and yet be aware of Danny a few inches away.

After minutes, I heard him move about. I wasn't ready to get up yet but his hands, gentle and soft like they hadn't been earlier, wrapped around my arms and guided me up. I sat and let him dress me in his jumper, didn't protest when he shoved my blouse inside my bag. I wasn't stupid; I knew what wearing a boy's jacket meant after you had slept with them. Claiming. Belonging to someone.

If any of those other men—the ones with the disgusting, sweaty bodies and the grunting and the mindless, careless, selfish rutting and their come inside of me that made me feel sick and dirty—had ever tried to give me something to wear to claim me, I would have vomited. But it was different with Danny. It didn't seem like claiming, or belonging, or restriction or false affection. It felt right, like it was a symbol of care.

He was looking at me with expectation in his gaze, so I flipped my hair out of the way, removed the necklace I had worn around my neck since I was 7—a simple, green gemstone on a black lace—and held it out until he took it. He looked down at it and smiled. Another new smile for me to catalogue and remember. A warmer smile, still knowing but not smug. He put the necklace on, nodded at the jumper, and told me it was to keep me warm. I told him the necklace was to touch when he was wanking, to remind him of me, and he laughed, a sudden explosion of sound in our quiet bubble among the trees.

He walked me to the edge of the woods but no further, turning right when we reached the path where I turned left. He did something odd then: he leaned over and placed his lips on the side of my head, into my hair. A short second of a kiss. Then he was gone into the night, which had turned heavy and black.

It began to rain and I walked home, the weighted drops of water slowly soaking through the jumper.

* * *

We had the same cover teacher a few weeks later, and Danny turned in his seat to look at me with hot, burning eyes. I sat throughout the lesson sensing something approaching. Something different. My thighs tingled with anticipation. I ran my hands along my legs under the desk, wanting desperately to tease myself.

I went into the woods at lunchtime, hoping Danny would be there—I couldn't wait the rest of the day—and wandered our usual path. I heard someone following me: heavy footfalls, leaves crunching underfoot. My shoulders tensed against my will even as a smile, the first in days, split my cheeks.

The world around me went black as a heavy material landed over my eyes and my heartrate tripled. I thought of calling Danny's name but the lack of sound had me trembling, and

171

something about the void of the blindfold kept me quiet. Hands removed my clothes, lay me down, gentler than Danny usually was. The thought it might be someone else made me crazy, terrified; aroused, alive. I wasn't sure if it was too much or too little but I was already damp down there. A body settled onto mine, and something dug into my collarbone, something I recognised instinctively from years of sleeping on it: my little gemstone necklace, the one I had gifted him. A strange warmth settled in my chest as relief caressed me.

I bit my lip as he moved over me, gasped as he entered me, and realised I was more turned on than I had ever been before.

Something sat at my throat, something that bit cold into the skin, and I suddenly gasped for air.

"Careful," a familiar voice whispered in my ear, hot and heavy and sounding just as turned on as I was. "My hand might slip," he said, wicked teasing in his tone.

After what could have been five minutes or an eternity, I was lying alone again, spread out on the ground, letting the nature beneath me permeate my skin and enjoying the sensation of sticky liquid on my chest. My breaths were long and soothing despite lying out in the open, naked, in full daylight, with the sound of schoolchildren not far away. Everything smelt fresh. I hadn't noticed scents in a long time.

The cloth was eased away with soft hands. I opened my eyes slowly. The light burned, made them water, but the sky—it had never been so blue, the grass and leaves never so full of greens and browns. Danny's face appeared above me and although I'd always noticed his colours, they stood out even more: the gleam and shine to his dark, dark eyes; his pale skin; the slash of pink of his mouth; the flop of hair, the colour of a hazelnut. He smiled down at me and held out the object that had pressed into my throat: a knife. A large, dangerous knife that reflected the stunning blue of the sky and fire of the sun on its straight, sharp blade.

I stroked at my neck with the tips of my fingers, settled and content in a way I'd never experienced before. Had I always been this fucked up, I wondered? Or had it happened slowly, over a period, without me noticing?

I sat up sluggardly, like I was in a dream, and Danny dressed me. I helped him pull his blazer on and was surprised when he drew me into his arms, against his chest. His muscles and warmth rejuvenated my sensitive body, grounding me.

"Was it like in your fantasy?" he asked. "Did it feel as good?"

"Yes."

* * *

I wore his jumper in the house, in front of my parents.

Mum spotted it after several days and asked in an emotionless voice, "Do you have a boyfriend?"

"Not really. I'm just having sex in the woods with someone I barely know."

She nodded, eyes glazed, fixed on something far away, something in her brain. She'd stopped listening right after she'd asked the question. "I'm thinking of divorcing your father," she said, as if he wasn't washing dishes at the sink next to us.

Dad didn't respond beyond a nod and a toneless, agreeable hum. They'd had the same conversation for several years now.

I went back to my room to look at myself in the mirror, a habit I couldn't seem to break since I'd started having sex with Danny. I traced the marks he'd made on my body and thought of him doing the same in his room. I looked at the pictures of myself as a child displayed around my space, smiling politely into the camera like a good little girl. I wondered if anyone else had an inkling that the same polite child would grow to be me, or if no one had realised.

* * *

I was invited to a party a few weeks later, and my friends told me to come.

"You haven't got any in a while," one said, laughing. "Maybe you'll find someone."

I wondered if she realised every time I'd told her of someone I'd slept with in the past, she'd called me a slut.

I poked a particularly deep bruise on my hip bone underneath my clothes and smiled at Danny sitting across the room, pretending he wasn't listening. "Maybe," I said. "Maybe you're right. I might find someone."

I got ready for the party with the same group of girls and sipped at fizzy sickly champagne while they gulped at it, watching them all get steadily more and more drunk before we even left the house. They giggled hysterically and put on layers of make-up and perfume that made me want to gag. I put on my dress, the one in which I'd lost my virginity (whatever that even is). I glanced in the mirror. I didn't look like me in the gown anymore. Instead, I looked like that lost girl stumbling home, drunk and in tears.

I took it off again and put on a newer one, one I hadn't yet worn with the intention of enticing someone into fucking with it. I waited a moment, then put on Danny's jumper too.

The girls told me I looked like I was ready for a night in and that I should change. I laughed it off, the laugh feeling as fake as it sounded, but they were already too intoxicated to notice.

We left and sat in the taxi and it was like I was with my parents: overwhelmingly boring and separated and empty. I wanted to cry, quite suddenly, in the back of the stupid cab on the way to a party with girls I secretly despised. I wanted to be as alone as I felt, to lock myself in my room away from everybody, my parents, Danny.

He was there as soon as we got through the door, standing off to the side, talking quietly to someone. He caught my eye, saw the jumper, smiled. Without returning the kindness, I walked away from my friends and into the kitchen, where I poured myself a vodka and Coke with more spirit than mixer. It tasted disgusting but I didn't care; I wanted it to blanket me like it did my first, disappointing time.

I fell further into despair as I downed the drink, desperate for any measure of comfort, of being taken out of my body. I was sick of my body, fed up with it. I'd let too many people at it and

174

now I was standing in this kitchen, drinking, wearing a boy's jumper like I thought it would fix the issues in my head.

Danny came into the room and watched me drink with a raised eyebrow but didn't try to stop me. "You okay?"

I poured another drink, determined to get rid of the hideous misery that had invaded me. He went to place a hand on my shoulder and I told him with more fury than needed, "Do not touch me."

"What's wrong?" he asked.

"I'm not sure," I said. "But I don't want to have sex today."

"We don't have to." He frowned. "That's not what this has to always be about."

"Then what *is* it about?" Tears slipped from my eyes. "I'm wearing your stupid fucking jumper. You never come in me. I don't understand!"

"I . . . I didn't think you wanted me to."

I wasn't ready for this conversation yet. The drink was finally hitting and I downed my second, holding in the urge to gag and shoot it right back up out my throat. "I'm going to the toilet," I said.

Danny nodded, eyes clouded. He moved back to let me pass. "I don't know what's going on either," he said, making me pause. "I'm wearing your stupid fucking necklace. I . . . You said you might meet someone else tonight and it made me want to kill them, even though it's wrong to feel like that."

The beginnings of arousal racked my body, dimmed by alcohol. "I like it when you talk like that," I said, and went up the stairs, past couples kissing in a way that made me even iller, tongues sliding and spreading saliva over cheeks and chins. I passed a bedroom where I heard retching and leant in, asking if whomever was in there was okay. There was a groan and I moved in a little further to find a large, older boy—a man— beside a desk, in the dark, sounding like he was sick.

"Do you want some water?" I asked, moving towards him.

He stood, towering over me, and the lower half of his face cracked into a jagged leer. I backed away.

"Have you been sick?" I asked. "I can find someone to help you if you want me to."

He followed me to the door, pinned it shut behind me, and twisted my hand away from the knob.

The dim arousal that Danny had set off inside of me was slapped away by a palm against my cheek.

He hit me and it didn't feel right. When Danny hit me, it set off something in my skin. When Danny hit me, he got off on it just as much as I did. We got off on seeing *each other* get high on pain.

This man didn't want me to hit back, and he wasn't striking me to set something off in my skin. I could see it in his eyes. He was hitting me because he could, to show me he was stronger, superior. Not to make me feel alive; to make me afraid. To make me cry.

A fist to my ribs caused fuzzy whiteness to blur my sight. Hot, unwanted tears slid down my face in response before I could blink them away.

"Yes," he whispered in my ear. "God, that makes me hot."

I told him to stop and I meant it. He groaned in pleasure at the word and I was hauled from the door like a rag, slammed into the centre of the bed by meaty hands.

I tried to yank free and my wrists creaked beneath his fingers. He was huge, too big to get away from. I wished desperately I hadn't got mad at Danny. I wished he was there. I wished *I* was stronger. I knew what was going to happen and I wasn't scared of the fucking; I was scared of the end, when he would let loose that hideous groan men emit and release his spunk into my body, and then the pain would start when he would slither out and leave me sticky and disgusting in a manner that couldn't be washed away no matter how much I showered and scrubbed. It would always be in there, inside my body where fingers and shower gel couldn't reach, seeping into the walls and creases and crannies of my vagina forever.

I uttered a single scream for help before he managed to clamp a hand over my mouth. His sausage-fingers, digging and intrusive, raked down my thigh, over the sensitive skin, the

176

roughness so unwanted and foreign, and he was panting dog-like breaths into the top of my head, into my hair—

The door smashed open in the background and slammed shut again. Someone crossed the room. My assailant's weight lifted from my body, and as his sweaty hand left my lips, I could gasp in air again. I sat up.

Danny stood next to the bed, the knife we'd used together in the woods in one hand. The man stood with his back against the wall, terrified, arms up in surrender, in a mockery of the position he'd held me down in. Danny glanced at me and I realised he was waiting. I nodded, the movement hardly significant despite being the most important thing in the world.

Danny crossed the room. The knife glinted as he drew his hand back and then carved it down towards my attacker. The man opened his mouth but all that came out was a whistle of air as the blade punctured his throat like a fist into fragile, whittled, aged bone; punctured him like he had been planning to puncture me.

"Stop," I rasped as Danny primed the knife to slice again. The man was sinking down the wall, blood spurting from the wound.

Danny turned to me and beamed at the expression on my face, the dark grin—*my* grin. He held the handle out towards me without question and I climbed off the bed, snatching it from him. The man tried to plea as I approached him, but he could only gurgle. Strength flooded me at the look on his face. I felt powerful, vengeful.

I swooped and sliced through the side of his throat. Blood jettisoned and I yanked the knife out, twisting it towards me as I stared into his eyes.

Blood landed hot on my cheek and forehead and into my mouth. I gasped at the taste, at the sickness beating in my stomach unbearably. I turned and, like in my fantasy, flung my arms around Danny and clamped our blood-slicked mouths together. My lips glided along his as the dying man let out a final gasp behind us.

Danny was hard in his trousers, a line against my inner thigh. It was hot through his jeans, pressing into my skin. My heart

177

raced, my stomach tightened and my clit pounded in anticipation.

I felt alive again. Like myself. And like a lock sliding into place, I accepted it.

ABOUT THE AUTHOR
ANNIE KNOX

Annie is an actress and writer based in London, currently residing in an attic referred to as 'The Batcave'. A keen horror fan, she's always up for a good time with some fake blood!

TOUCH OF DEATH

BY C L RAVEN

I met the love of my life today.
Shame he died yesterday.

* * *

I applied pale pink lipstick to Mrs. Williams' wrinkled lips. Petunia Passion was her shade, her husband said. The funeral was tomorrow, so he was paying her one last visit. I wanted her to look her best. Just because you're dead doesn't mean you can't look nice.

The door opened and my business partner, Victoria, wheeled a stretcher in. "New arrival. I hate it when they die young. It's such a tragedy. Especially when it's an accident." She parked the stretcher in the corner, then came to check on my progress. "You always make them look . . . alive."

"We all have a secret superpower. Mine's a weird Midas Touch, though it's not a useful superpower outside of work and I can't use it to fight crime. My red leather catsuit was a waste of money." I finished up and returned Mrs. Williams to her coffin.

Victoria made notes on her clipboard. She was tall, in her early forties with greying blonde hair. After Life Funeral Directors had been in her family for generations. She had taken me on as a partner two years ago after it became clear she wouldn't have kids to pass the business on to. I preferred the dead to the living anyway. They were less disappointing.

180

"I'll get started on the new one." I rose and removed my gloves, plucking a new pair from the box.

Victoria wheeled Mrs. Williams out. She was better at dealing with the families and I was better with the dead. We made a great team.

I headed over to the stretcher and unzipped the body bag, revealing the most beautiful man I had ever seen. Dark hair cut short, three days of beard growth and deep green eyes that were only slightly cloudy. The type of face that appeared on posters selling anything from fragrances to haemorrhoid cream. I unzipped the bag, further revealing a perfectly sculpted body marred only by the purple noose imprint that had brought him here and the ugly *Y* incision the pathologist had made. I shook my head at the Frankenstein stitches they'd used to sew him up. They had no finesse.

The police had taken his clothes for evidence. Pity. I would have enjoyed undressing him.

Wait, no. That was not a good thought to have right now.

I glanced at his hand. No wedding ring. I frowned. Why should I care about a wedding ring? I was doing repairs, not asking him out for a drink. He was way past his 'use by' date.

I picked up Victoria's clipboard. According to her notes, his name was Nate Morgan, he was twenty-eight and had been a circus acrobat. Young, fit, strong, good-looking and flexible, with a love of danger and adventure. He was my perfect man.

He was also dead.

My heart pounded as I unzipped the bag the rest of the way. I stopped and stared. Nate had died with what funeral directors term 'Angel Lust'. In layman's terms, an erection. This occurred in hangings or violent deaths where the man died upright or lying face down and was left there. Funeral directors usually tucked the erection under the man's waistband. Like living men do. But I could find a much better place to put it.

I pinched my arm. That was *not* a thought I wanted plaguing me. But I couldn't stop staring at it and then feeling appalled when I started to throb in inappropriate places.

This was stupid. I'd worked in funeral homes all my adult life. I'd seen hundreds of bodies, some with good looks or great bodies and sometimes both. But none had made my stomach flutter, my hands shake and my libido awaken like Nate did. No living guy had ever made me feel that way.

Oh no. I was starting to sound like a Mills and Boon heroine.

My hands slid over his smooth skin as I freed him from the bag. He had excellent muscle definition. I discarded the carrier and moved him to my workstation, taking my time covering his post-mortem stitches in a layer of putty. Mixing his skin tone took the longest but after I'd painted the noose imprint, it was completely invisible.

I wheeled the embalming machine over.

Before I could stop myself, I yanked off my gloves and stroked his arm. I glanced at the door, worried Victoria would suddenly walk in. As I bit my lip, my trembling fingers explored his chest, skimming over every muscular curve. Nerves and fear of getting caught heightened my desire. My fingers glided over his stomach, inching lower. I became wet as I imagined playing with his erection.

No. This was wrong. What the hell was I *doing*? He was a client. A *dead* client. It had been a while, but I wasn't *that* desperate. Maybe plugging his holes would kill my romantic mood. It would be difficult to fancy someone once you've shoved cotton wool up their rectum.

I forced myself to focus on my job, making an incision in the carotid artery and inserting the tube. I switched the machine on, listening to it suck out blood and liquids before I pumped him full of embalming fluid. I then inserted a trocar through his belly button to inject his organs with the fluid too, before screwing a trocar button in place.

Victoria poked her head around the door. "I'm heading off, Isla. I'll see you tomorrow."

"I'm just finishing here, then I'll lock up."

"You should be out enjoying life, not staying here 'til ten every night."

"Better to stay here working than go home to leftovers and trashy TV."

"Join a dating site. Find a hobby. You won't meet Mr. Right hiding away down here."

I already had.

* * *

As soon as I got home, I googled Nate Morgan. The first result was a news article about his death. He'd been performing a routine on aerial silks, but something had gone wrong and the fabric wrapped around his neck. As he rolled out of the move, the material strangled him and he hanged in full view of the audience.

I logged on to Facebook and tracked down his profile. Most photos were of him with his dog. Hot, brave, he loved animals and was single—why did I have to come into his life when it ended? Why couldn't I have met him in the supermarket rather than the morgue? Life really wasn't fair.

His Instagram page had more photos of his dog and pictures of him climbing mountains, doing circus tricks and surfing. My lust awakened as I spied his topless photos. The leggings he wore for acrobatics showed off every muscle, every bulge, his pert peachy posterior. He was perfect.

And he was colder than a snowman's carrot.

When I finally fell asleep, I was tormented by erotic dreams of Nate. My love life was clearly in need of CPR if I was fantasising about a dead man. Yes, Nate was exactly my type, but my type had a pulse. Only perverts fantasised about corpses. I definitely wasn't a pervert: I didn't own a mac, or have a creepy moustache, and I'd never stolen women's knickers in my life.

I woke aroused, so I pleasured myself to one of his photos. It felt wrong, but that made it better. I imagined my fingers were his and when I came, it was more satisfying than usual. Imagined sex with him was better than real sex with my exes.

Maybe I did need to join a dating site. Or stop dating terrible men who thought the clitoris was some kind of exotic plant.

Victoria was in when I arrived. She smiled when she saw me. "I hope you didn't stay too late."

"I was a good girl. Home by eleven."

"I need you to do make-up on Mr. Morgan first thing. His brother's coming in for a viewing at twelve o'clock."

Brother? I perked up. Maybe he'd be equally as hot. It was probably against company policy to date a client's grieving relative, but it was likely a violation to masturbate to photos of your dead client too. But if Victoria didn't know, she couldn't fire me. Nate's brother had the advantage of being alive. Dating him wouldn't lead to me appearing on a weird attractions documentary with people who married roller coasters and had sex with their vehicles. I didn't want that to be my legacy. People would think I couldn't get a living man.

"I'll get started straight away."

My heart beat faster at the thought of seeing Nate again. I shook my head. What was wrong with me? I wasn't seeing him again, I was going to apply make-up to make him look alive. That love spell I'd bought off eBay was clearly defective.

I headed downstairs to the morgue and took my stuff to my locker. I fetched my make-up kit, then tied up my long raven hair and donned a disposable apron and rubber gloves. My stomach fluttered and my hands shook as I opened the fridge door and pulled out the drawer.

He was just as beautiful as he was the day before. He still didn't look dead. Heat spread between my legs as I gazed at him, the urge to kiss him growing stronger. I forced myself to focus and transferred him to a stretcher.

Victoria entered, wheeling a coffin. "His clothes are in here when you're done."

I nodded, rolling the stretcher to my workstation. "It's such a shame. He was so young and handsome."

"Killed for a stunt. What a waste."

"He died doing what he loved. How many can claim that?"

"You googled him too?"

184

Inexplicable jealousy surged through me. Victoria had plenty of men chasing her. She didn't need to steal mine.

"Stalking our client, huh, Victoria?" I tried to sound like I was teasing.

"I needed to know if it was an open investigation so I could be prepared to deal with the police."

Oh. So she wasn't masturbating to his photos like I was.

I opened my make-up kit and gently sponged foundation onto Nate's face as Victoria left. He'd maintained his colour and only needed a light shading. Same with his Cupid's bow lips. I was loath to glue his eyes shut, but no one wanted to be watched by the milky eyes of the dead, so I placed caps over his eyeballs, smeared glue onto his lids and lashes and held them shut. Sometimes tiny stitches were needed to hold them in place but the glue worked well.

Crossing to the coffin, I fetched his clothes: a charcoal suit. I slid his shorts up his legs, fighting the sudden urge to trace my fingers up his penis and feel it throb in my hand. What the hell was wrong with me? My Midas Touch couldn't bring him or his penis back to life no matter how good my handjob skills were. I licked my lips, longing to run my tongue up his length and circle the tip before sliding it into my mouth and hearing his gasps of pleasure.

No. The only gasps I'd hear would be Victoria's ones of horror if I were caught. I couldn't suck Nate back to life. Death wasn't venom.

I yanked his shorts up and put his trousers on him, rolling him towards me to pull his light grey shirt on. I couldn't resist hugging him, the feeling of his firm body pressed against mine arousing me further. His hand flopped onto my back and I imagined him undoing my bra strap. I rested my head against his chest, wishing I could hear his heartbeat.

I had to stop. I wrestled his jacket on him then lay him down and buttoned his shirt before putting on his socks and shoes. I tucked his erection under his waistband but my willpower betrayed me and I gently squeezed it. That felt so wrong. But so

185

right. I wanted to feel it sliding through my grip, hear his heavy breath as I pumped it faster until he exploded into my hand.

I called Victoria before all my sense deserted me and we manoeuvred him into the coffin. It wasn't easy acting professional when I was more turned on than the Blackpool illuminations. Victoria wheeled the coffin to the lift while I discarded my gloves and apron then joined her in the chapel. It was painted crimson, with a black carpet and red seats. The coffin stood on a table in front of the chairs, like it was on a stage. Soft lighting gave the bodies a healthy glow.

Time dragged. I amused myself by picturing Nate's brother. By the time he arrived half an hour later, I'd convinced myself he'd be his identical twin. I've never been so disappointed in my life, not even when I discovered my Smarties Easter Egg was missing the Smarties a few years ago. Where Nate was tall, dark-haired, beautiful and sculpted, his brother was shorter, with floppy blond hair and a body more suited to pie-eating than weightlifting. So much for me being able to live out my erotic fantasies on him! Why couldn't *he* be the one lying in the coffin, while Nate stood there, tears making his green eyes sparkle?

I pinched my leg. Wow. That was a nasty thought. I was turning into a horrible, depraved monster. I couldn't wish death upon someone because I didn't find them attractive!

"Good afternoon, Mr. Morgan. Your brother is through here, if you'd like to follow me." Victoria shook his hand and led him to the chapel, where Nate's coffin lay.

I slunk off downstairs to prepare the embalming machine for my next client and to deal with the raging disappointment.

"Talk about opposites," Victoria said, walking in an hour later with Nate's coffin. "I'd never have guessed they were brothers."

"Nate clearly absorbed the looks from their gene pool," I replied. Did my voice sound bitter to her? It did to me.

"The funeral is next week, after the inquest."

"Looks like you'll be with us a little longer, Mr. Morgan." I smiled at Nate's corpse. "Let's get you back into your room. I know it's small but at least you're not paying for it, and the air con is great."

Victoria helped me lift him out of the coffin and return him to the stretcher.

The bell rang, indicating there was a customer upstairs.

"I'll leave you to return Mr. Morgan to his room." Victoria headed for the door. "There's a car fatality arriving at three. Family wants a viewing but it was a head-on collision so the client will need lots of work."

"I like a challenge."

Victoria smiled and left.

Unlike most dead people, Nate looked like he was sleeping, his lips slightly parted as though waiting for a kiss to rouse him. I couldn't believe we only had a week left together. The heat between my legs grew as I imagined leaning down and tasting him. Though not with that morning breath of his. I fetched my breath-freshening spray and made him minty fresh.

I watched the entrance, expecting Victoria to walk in because she'd left her phone again. She didn't return. I wheeled the stretcher to the fridge and opened the door. I slid Nate across onto the drawer and covered him with a sheet.

"Goodbye, Mr. Morgan."

I leaned over and kissed his soft, cold lips. His arm flopped down, stroking my thigh as it fell. My nerves tingled. I whimpered and grasped it to place it back beside him. I hesitated. It wasn't like he was unconscious and I was taking advantage. He was dead.

And yet, my body wouldn't listen.

I guided his hand between my legs and stroked myself. I gasped and kissed him hard, grasping his erection. My heart thudded at the pleasure, at the fear of getting caught. This wasn't enough though. I had to feel his touch on my skin. Maybe working with the dead had unhinged me. I never did anything bad: I obeyed the speed limit even when I was the only driver on the road, I never parked on double yellow lines, never dropped litter. But craving a dead man's touch aroused me in ways reading erotica never could.

I pulled away and undid my jeans. As I was about to push them down, the door opened.

"Forgot my phone."

I swallowed a scream and swiftly put Nate's hand in the drawer beside him, facing the fridge so Victoria couldn't see my open jeans and guilty expression.

"I'm going to surgically attach that thing to you," I joked, hoping she didn't notice my voice quivering, or that I was probably sending lust signals to any man in a twelve-mile radius.

She laughed. "See you at three."

That was close. I yanked the sheet over Nate and shoved him in the drawer, slamming the door shut. I hurried to the toilets, locked the cubicle and pulled my jeans down. My satin knickers were wet. My fingers eased my torment, stroking me through the cloth. I imagined they were his fingers, then I pictured him smiling at me as he knelt down, his lips and tongue bringing me unimaginable pleasure. I cried out as I came, bracing myself against the wall.

I just had to get through the next week and then Nate would be buried and this whole thing would become a shameful memory that I could laugh and cringe about, the way I did when I thought about my first boyfriend and his '90s boyband dress sense.

My phone buzzed. Victoria.

Car crash victim is here.

Maybe working on a mangled body was what I needed to remind myself the dead were truly dead.

* * *

The following week was the longest week of my life. I chatted to Nate every day as I worked, and it was nice not to get the usual reaction of revulsion that living men gave when I mentioned my job. I told him everything about me, and through his Facebook page I learned loads about him. I guess his brother couldn't bear to delete his social media. I'd downloaded my favourite photos, printed them out and stuck them to my

188

bedroom wall so they could keep me company at night. In a moment of madness, I considered getting his face put on a sex doll, but that would've been creepy. I'd already established I wasn't a pervert; I was going through a bad attraction. Everyone has those 'what was I thinking?' moments. This was mine. (My period was probably due. Hormones had a lot to answer for.)

I lay in bed, thinking about Nate. It was his funeral tomorrow. I'd never see him again. The thought made me feel sick. He was alone in the morgue. I should keep him company. Say goodbye properly.

I dressed in a long black satin skirt, a black blouse and jacket, and fishnet stockings. They were for Nate, as was my red lacy lingerie. I dressed slowly, allowing his photographic gaze to linger. The thought of him watching me turned me on. Nate's surfing photo helped me climax.

I ran to the funeral directors' and let myself in. In my head, I imagined this to be like one of those scenes in romantic movies where the hero runs through a crowded train station to tell the woman he loves her before she disappears from his life forever. (Okay, so my scene was slightly different, but my life wasn't exactly a romcom.) I kept the lights off and opened Nate's drawer.

"I'm sorry, Nate. I need to see you once last time."

This was crazy. But I couldn't stop thinking about him. One look and I could say goodbye properly and move on with my life. Find a lovely, handsome man who had a great sense of humour and a beating heart.

I hesitated before removing the sheet. What if he had rapidly decomposed? Would I still love him with marbled skin and a body full of gas? Could I see past his seeping juices and unpleasant fragrance?

Well, love wasn't just about looks.

I wrenched off the sheet before my courage failed me. He was every bit as beautiful as the day Victoria wheeled him into the morgue.

I sprayed breath freshener between his lips and kissed him hard.

189

"Oh, God, I love you."

I couldn't wait any longer. This was going to be our last moment together and I didn't want it spent in this cold, clinical place. I manoeuvred his coffin over and positioned it beside the drawer. I carefully lifted him into it and pushed it towards the lift. The lift opened and I steered him into the chapel. I dragged the coffin onto the table, then lit the candles in the aisles. I fetched more candles and placed them around the coffin. Deep down, I was a romantic.

I climbed onto the table and straddled him. I slowly unbuttoned my blouse, teasing him. Raising his hand, I held it to a breast as they were bared. I slid my top off then stood and unzipped my skirt. It tumbled, revealing my red knickers and fishnet stockings.

"Do you like them? I bought them for you."

I straddled him anew and lifted his hands. His touch sent sparks of electricity shooting through me. I kissed him as I unbuttoned his shirt. My fingers danced along his pecs, skimming over his autopsy scars. They only made him more beautiful. I ran my tongue up his chest and slipped it between his lips, breaking one of the stitches.

I knew it was wrong, but if Mary Shelley could lose her virginity on her mother's grave and still be considered an influential woman, I could have one night of passion with the man of my dreams and not be vilified.

I sat him up, his cold lips caressing my breasts. I imagined his tongue licking the tender skin between them. I ran his fingers down my back and onto my arse, spanking myself with his hand. Bad girls deserved a spanking and having sex with a corpse was definitely not something good girls did. I moved my hips, rubbing against his lap, his bulge exciting me.

"Mmm, someone's ready to play. You naughty boy," I whispered in his ear before nipping it.

I wriggled down, taking my time undoing his trousers and stroking him through his shorts, my fingers sliding under his balls and gently squeezing them. Biting my lip, I lay him down then eased his shorts off. I slid a condom and a cock ring onto him and switched it on. I leaned down, kissing him, my tongue probing the tiny stitches on the inside of his lips as I slid my knickers down my legs.

This was the moment I'd been fantasising about. I hoped he wasn't a disappointment.

I lowered myself onto him, gasping at his coldness. I should've brought heat pads to warm him up, but the cold made my heat warmer. Vibrations from the cock ring only heightened the pleasure. I guided his hands over my body and breasts as I rode him gently, wanting this moment to last. I gasped, my head tilting back. It had never felt this good before. I didn't know if it was his cold penis, the daring of doing something society wouldn't approve of, or the fact we were in love. I cried out as two orgasms surged through me.

I lay in his arms, his hand stroking my back and arse, my fingers idly playing with his buzzing, vibrating erection. I would never get bored of him.

I pulled him from the coffin and we made love in different positions. Doggystyle was a bit awkward. I had to prop him up against the wall, then manoeuvre onto my hands and knees and shimmy back onto him. But God was it worth it. His upper body flopped onto me so I guided one hand to my breast and the other to my clitoris as I rode him like a champion. My orgasm was worthy of an award. We collapsed face first, the cock ring buzzing against me, coaxing more pleasure from me.

"You're insatiable."

I was tempted to take him home with me so we could make love every night, but I didn't want to wake one day to find he'd rotted whilst I slept and ruined my bedsheets. I had the skills to keep him looking good, and Lenin's perfectly preserved corpse proved it was possible, but Nate deserved to rest in peace. One night was all we could ever have.

I reluctantly dressed us both and kissed him goodbye before grabbing my cock ring and placing him back in his coffin. I returned him to his drawer and left, a smile playing on my lips as I recalled our scandalous night of passion.

* * *

I donned my top hat and walked outside to the hearse. Victoria usually led it, but she was at a funeral directors convention and had asked me to stand in. If anyone should lead Nate's cortege, it should be me. She didn't know him like I did. She didn't love him like I did. (Okay, so the dead weren't ideal romantic partners, but neither were serial killers, and people married *them*.)

I got out as we reached Nate's parents' house and knocked on the door. Eventually, his family and friends walked out, their faces stony, eyes wet. None of them were as handsome as Nate.

I dug my fingernails into my hand. This was one of the hardest days of their lives. I shouldn't be comparing them to the man they were about to bury. It wasn't their fault they were inferior.

I stood in front of the hearse and waited for them to fill up the limos. They'd ordered two: one for family, one for friends. Nate's dog jumped in with the family. I nearly cried.

I walked in front of the hearse as it meandered to the cemetery. Traffic stopped to let us through. When we were partway there, I got back in the vehicle and we drove at twenty miles an hour the rest of the way.

Nate's brother and friends carried the coffin into the cemetery's chapel. Usually, I stayed in the hearse, but this time I sneaked into the building and sat at the back. I should've been at the front with the rest of his family, not skulking like a secret mistress. I loved him too.

My throat burned as silent tears trickled down my cheeks. I was going to miss our talks. Miss seeing his handsome face every day. Miss giving him a good morning and goodnight kiss. Miss the way he felt beneath me as we made love in his coffin.

I slipped out before the other mourners and waited beside the hearse. They slid the coffin in and we drove to the grave site. I was glad they were burying him and not cremating him. I couldn't bear the thought of such perfection being reduced to ash.

192

I stood at the back of the crowd while the reverend said a few words and passed around the box of earth. I couldn't believe I was never going to see him again.

The mourners moved away and I stepped closer to the grave. "Goodbye, Nate. I love you."

* * *

I visited Nate's grave every Friday, leaving a red rose by his headstone. The memory of our lovemaking kept me fulfilled. I tried dating other guys but none excited me like Nate had. I'd even tried sex in a graveyard for the risky buzz but I couldn't orgasm. They didn't know how to satisfy me like he had. I missed him terribly and regretted not taking him home.

One night, I went to his graveside armed with a spade, but I stopped myself. It wasn't fair to disturb his eternal sleep because I couldn't get over him. Digging up a body for sex would make me president of the perverts' club and that wasn't a promotion I was comfortable with.

"New client," Victoria announced, wheeling a stretcher in. "Easy one."

I took her clipboard and scanned her notes. Trystan Willows. Thirty. Died of a brain aneurysm while doing gymnastics.

Victoria left me alone. I unzipped the bag to be greeted by a well-toned body and a handsome face. I moved him to a stretcher. His hand brushed my backside. My dormant lust stirred.

No. This couldn't be happening again. Nate was special. I was aroused by him because, had we met when he was alive, we would've fallen in love. It seemed only the touch of the dead could bring me to life. That definitely made me president of the pervert parade. I always had been ambitious.

My fingers danced up his leg, pausing at his waistband. No Angel Lust. Unfortunately, the dead didn't rise. It wasn't fair. Men were able to have sex with corpses. It shouldn't be difficult for women.

"Goodnight!" Victoria called. The front door shut.

193

Tutankhamun had been embalmed with a ninety-degree erection. It wasn't something I'd attempted; I'd never considered using corpses as sex toys. I fetched the embalming machine. It was always good to learn new skills.

I swiftly made the incision and inserted the tube, adding a smaller one to his penis. As the machine pumped fluid around his body, acting like a heartbeat, his member stood erect. Biting my lip, I listened for Victoria's car, then grabbed the vibrating ring and a condom from my bag. I tugged his trousers down, used my stool to climb up and straddled him. I kissed him.

"Cold and hard. Just my type."

ABOUT THE AUTHOR
C L RAVEN

C L Raven are identical twins and mistresses of the macabre. They're horror writers because 'bringers of nightmares' isn't a recognised job title. They write novels, short stories, comics and film scripts. Their work has been published in magazines and anthologies in the UK, USA and Australia. A story of theirs was published in *The Mammoth Book of Jack the Ripper*, which makes their fascination with him seem less creepy. They've worked on several indie horror films as crew and reluctant actors and have somehow ended up with lead roles in the forthcoming indie horror film *School Hall Slaughter*. In their spare time, they hunt ghosts, host a horror radio show, look after their animal army, and try to look impressive with polefit. Their attempts at gymnastics should never be spoken about.

Webpage: http://www.clraven.wordpress.com

Twitter: http://www.twitter.com/clraven

LEAVE ME BREATHLESS

BY SUZANNE FOX

"What the fuck!"

I rolled off the bed and bounced to the floor in a twist of sheets. Pain crunched through my hip in a flare of delight that warmed my insides and brought a smile to my face. I looked up at the naked guy who had just pushed me off him and onto the floor. "You said you were up for something a little … different."

"Different? That was fucking, stupid. You crazy bitch." He rubbed a hand over his bare chest, smearing the blood from a partially severed nipple across his pale skin.

I pushed myself up and knelt by the bed, watching him grab a handful of tissues from the bedside table and dab at the blood. Holding the reddening wad in place, he struggled one-handed into his jeans, grabbed his remaining clothes, and shuffled to the door.

"Hey! Where are you going?" I yelled at him. How could he think of leaving? His torn nipple had to be hurting. Surely he wanted some retribution for the little mutilation job I had done to his chest? Maybe a slap to the face, a twist of my arm or—what I really craved—his long fingers tightening around my throat as I came on his cock.

"I'm putting as much distance as possible between you and me, you weird freak!" He lifted the tissue and studied the damage. A slow trickle of blood travelled down his torso.

"Wait," I said, realising he was serious about abandoning me even though we hadn't fucked yet. "Don't go."

196

"Fuck you, Jess." He pulled on his tee-shirt. Immediately, a dark stain blossomed through the cotton fabric. "I've had as much as I can take of your . . . your"—he rubbed a hand through his mussed hair—"*weirdness*. You are not normal. Get it? Sort yourself out. Get some fucking help before the next guy you try this shit on with does something bad to you."

Before I could crawl across the floor to reach him, he finished dressing and stormed out, slamming the door behind him.

I pulled myself up, climbed onto the bed, and curled into a ball. Tears dissolved my mascara, stinging my eyes and creating warm, black trickles as they coursed down my cheeks to stain the bed sheets. This wasn't the first guy who had dumped me for the same reason. Maybe I *was* crazy. Perhaps it would be for the best if I got professional help. But I didn't want to. Instead, I wanted the thrill that came from living dangerously and enjoying the darker side of sex. There had to be others out there who were like me, who wanted to take it to the edge of the darkness. I hoped there were.

* * *

I guess, if anyone cared to ask me, I would say my unusual appetites probably began at St. Philomena's Catholic School for Girls.

I remember the first day I walked through the tall, wrought-iron gates to that renowned institute of learning. It was a grey September morning. The gothic building loomed dark and oppressive at the head of a curved drive lined with overgrown rhododendrons. The damp air gave the leaves a dark gloss that showcased shadows and secret hiding places.

I was pissed off. Mum and Dad had chosen this dump to be the place where I finished my education after being kicked out of Middleton High for doing the same things that my friends did. The only difference was that I had been caught. Several times.

So, I smoked. It wasn't the end of the world. Most of the kids at my previous school did. Okay, some of them drew the line at a pack of Silk Cut, or a pouch of Drum for the connoisseurs who preferred to roll their own. I rolled my own too, but I liked to add a little extra oomph to my roll-ups. It helped to take the edge off a crappy day at school. It wasn't that which got me expelled though. It was the batch of brownies that I baked as an afternoon treat for my teachers. My God, what an afternoon that was. Old Miss Watson, the most prudish crone in the world, was trying to get it on with the lesbian PE teacher. Mr. Fenwick, the geography master, was running around the hockey field with his tie wrapped around his head yelling that he was Rambo and going to save all the prisoners while several other teachers lounged on the grass giggling at him. It was fucking hilarious, though none of *them* thought so afterwards.

The next day I stood in the headmaster's office while Mum bawled and blew her nose into a sodden handkerchief, and Dad glared at me with a stare that said if there hadn't been any witnesses present he might have murdered me. Eventually I was frogmarched from the office to Dad's car and driven home while he ranted and promised to ground me until I was eighteen.

My behaviour didn't improve during my time at St. Philomena's. I still smoked, I supplied a little weed to my new friends, and I was cheeky with the nuns. The difference at St. Philomena's, though, was how they dealt with me. My parents thought I had seen the light. No more did they receive phone calls from irate teachers about my latest escapade and, as far as they were concerned, no calls meant that I was behaving in school.

They were wrong.

I remember the first time I was caught smoking behind one of the overgrown rhododendrons with a boy from a neighbouring school.

"Devil's whore!" Sister Magdalene's fingers sank into the flesh of my upper arm as she dragged me to her office. (I swear that woman had talons for fingers because the following day, five purple bruises decorated my tender bicep.) The stares of the *good* girls burned through me during that walk of shame through the school's corridors, but I didn't give a shit.

We reached her office and she shut the door behind us.

At the sound of the clicking of the lock and seeing her deposit the key in a pocket concealed in the folds of her voluminous habit, a niggle of trepidation wormed its way into my mind. What was the old cunt planning? I'd been hauled into teachers' offices many times, but never had anyone bolted the door before.

"You can't lock me in," I said, my voice cocky and presenting a bravado I didn't feel.

"Be quiet, girl." Sister Magdalene stepped forward until she was almost nose to nose with me. The stench of old fried onions invaded my nostrils. Our faces were so close I could see every wrinkle and blackhead that mapped her sallow skin. "I know that you were trouble at your previous school, but here at Saint Philomena's we do not tolerate such behaviour. Do you understand?"

So, it was to be another lecture. The anxiety that was rising in my chest began to settle. I'd been lectured to by far more intimidating figures than this shrivelled old nun.

"Stand in front of the desk," she commanded.

Emitting a long sigh, I shuffled towards the mahogany monstrosity and waited for her rant to begin.

She said nothing.

Puzzled, I turned to see what she was doing. Sister Magdalene walked to a large cupboard, unlocked the door and drew it open.

The interior of the dark-wood case was lined with an array of long thin sticks. Some were pale rattan with curved handles. Others had straight stems, bound with leather grips.

My breath caught in my throat and—

I stared like an imbecile for several seconds as her intention dawned on me. "What do you think you're going to—?"

"Shut up!" Sister Magdalene selected a straight cane with a handle bound in tan leather and strode towards me. "Bend over the desk and lift your skirt."

"No chance. You can't lay a finger on me." I smirked at the bitch, smug in the knowledge that her threat was nothing but an empty promise. A feeble effort to make me scared. It had probably worked on countless other girls in the past, but there was no way I was going to cow to her tyranny. I folded my arms and stared her down.

I heard the swish before feeling the flare of pain across my thigh. I yelped and jumped. Thrown off balance by her subversive strike, I didn't see her move closer to grab my wrist until it was too late, and I was forced face-down across the scarred desk. The nun's bony but strong hand held me in place despite my frantic struggles. "Let me go," I squealed.

"Not until you've received your punishment," she hissed. "Six strokes of the cane. You can accept them willingly, or I can hold you down like the dirty, little animal you are."

Humiliation, anger, fear, shame all battled for control of my mind and body. I didn't want to give in but the thought of being held down while she caned my backside was unbearable. The more I struggled, the tighter her grip got. The woman had superhuman strength. I stilled, figuring the humiliation of being seized in place whilst being caned would be far worse than accepting it without a struggle. Better to get it over with and try to keep some modicum of dignity during the process, I thought.

"Wise move, Jessica." The nun released her grip on me and lifted my skirt. The heat rose in my face like a fever and I braced myself for the first stroke.

I heard the whoosh of displaced air as the switch cut through the stuffy atmosphere a split second before pain erupted across my flesh. I gasped, but not from the soreness that was spreading from the point of impact. Hell, it hurt—of course it did—but there was something else that underscored the discomfort.

The cane struck a second time. This time my gasp for air almost sounded like a moan and I twisted my body in response.

"Keep still, girl!"

I steadied myself in preparation for the remaining four lashes. The fucker increased the intensity with each swing. I didn't care. After the final welt I was floating in a different dimension. Euphoria deadened the pain and I felt incredible.

Standing, I turned to face the nun and thanked her. I had to bite my lip to stop myself from bursting into laughter at the sight of her wrinkled face crumpling even more with disappointment. No doubt she'd caned others before me who had bolted from the room in floods of tears. That wasn't happening today, and Sister Magdalene's miserable face betrayed her vindictive nature.

"Get out," she yelled, pointing towards the door.

I re-arranged my skirt and followed her direction.

With each step I embraced the warm glow that radiated from my backside, but there was something else—something that was a whole new sensation for me, and it felt *delicious*. The secret area between my legs burned with a wet warmth that tingled. I felt swollen, tender and incredibly sensitive. Each step created a friction that excited and teased. I loved it.

I loved it so much that I became Sister Magdalene's worst nightmare. I stumbled from one infraction to another, living for the moments when I was bent over that ancient desk stinging, burning, and dripping wet from each stroke of her rattan canes.

* * *

Eventually I had to leave school. University life was much more liberal than a convent school. Smoking dope was the norm. Nobody was going to punish me for that, and I was at a loss for how to get my kicks. Thank God for Melanie.

I shared a small flat with Melanie. A small flat with thin walls. Walls that couldn't drown out the sounds of moaning, buzzing or screaming that emanated from her bedroom most nights. I envied her freedom, her lack of conventional standards, and her libertine lifestyle. Even when alone at night she still indulged in raucous, solitary pleasure. Meanwhile, I tried to get through the day-to-day grind without any outlet for my frustrations. Until one night.

"Fancy a night out, Jess?" Melanie peered around my bedroom door, a smirk appearing across her heavily made-up face.

"Oh, I don't know," I said, pointing to the mountain of books that threatened to bury me alive under an avalanche if another huge lorry thundered past the building.

Melanie rounded the door and came closer. "One night won't hurt. There's a new club in town. I know the doorman. It sounds . . . interesting."

Would one night off do me any harm? I decided that it wouldn't and, an hour later, with help from Melanie, I was dressed to thrill and on my way to The Vault.

Melanie had not elaborated on the nature of the club and even if she had, nothing could have prepared me for what lay behind its industrial exterior. The bar was filled with the most fascinating and glorious people I had ever seen. I had never encountered so much latex outside of a hospital before. Bodies clad in reflective, skin-tight rubber mingled and chatted with others in various stages of dress or undress. Chains, cuffs and collars were as ubiquitous as the plethora of nuns in my old school. I felt like Alice when she fell into Wonderland.

I was pulled from my enchantment by her hand grabbing mine. "I've got to see the dungeon," said Melanie. "I've heard it's amazing."

At the word *dungeon*, a twinge of hot excitement returned to my cunt, bringing back memories of being bent over Sister Magdalene's desk. Is this what had been missing from my life? Passing through the tall double doors was like stepping into another world. I felt like I had opened the biggest box of delicious chocolates in the world, and each one was tempting me to take a bite.

The air was electrified. Screams and moans fused to produce a harmony of tormented pleasure. I breathed in, savouring the aroma of warm bodies and musk, and my cunt contracted in excitement. These people were doing things that I had been unknowingly craving. Different scenes battled for my attention, but one couple's activities drew me closer.

I let go of Melanie's hand, my feet finding their own path across the floor and coming to a stop before a naked, blindfolded woman, her wrists pulled high above her head and secured to the wall with chains. Similar chains bound her ankles, fastening them to iron rings fixed into the floor and restraining her body in an *X* shape. A metal stand before her held a vibrator against

202

her pussy. As I drew closer, I could hear the buzzing of the vibe as it played against her clit, forcing her towards orgasm. I could smell and taste her arousal and, as the vibrator worked its magic, her partner flayed her breasts and body with a leather flogger. Sweat sheened her whip-marked figure as the first throes of her climax took control of her body. Her lips parted and her chest heaved as a shrill scream of pleasure escaped her throat.

The flogger plummeted to the floor and her partner's hand shot forwards to clutch her throat, cutting off her squeal. Her body twisted within the confines of her restraints and her face contorted as she tried to draw breath past the garrotting grip of the hand around her neck. A dusky tinge bloomed across her cheeks and lips, and tears seeped from beneath her blindfold.

My instincts screamed for me to run forwards and break his hold, allowing his victim to suck in life-giving air, but I was transfixed. The image of this helpless woman, desperate for breath and yet unable to stop the orgasm that ripped through her like a tornado, imprinted itself in my brain. She convulsed as though she was having a seizure. Sweat drenched her skin, reflecting the dim lights of the dungeon. Time froze. Nothing else existed as far as I was concerned. The other moans and screams that filled the cavernous room faded to nothing. All I could hear were choking gasps as she battled to remain conscious. A battle she appeared to be losing.

Eventually her writhing slowed, and she slumped forwards, held upright only by her chains. Her partner released his grip, tugged the blindfold from her eyes and lifted her chin with a tenderness that belied his previous brutality. The woman's eyes fluttered open and she sucked in rasping gulps of air. Her chest rose and fell with each lungful, drawing my gaze to her trembling breasts. Her nipples were as hard as stone. I lowered my stare. Her climax dripped from her cunt and drenched her thighs, and I heard a faint whisper slip from her lips: "Thank you, sir."

Within seconds the man released her from her bondage, lowered her to the floor, wrapped her in a blanket, and held her close as she came back to life in his arms. As soon as she had recovered enough, he lifted her and carried her to a nearby recovery area. It was beautiful.

A hand grabbed my arm and I jumped.

"Are you okay?" said Melanie. "You were staring like a zombie."

"What did I just see?" I asked. "Who was that?"

Melanie followed my gaze. "The tall guy with dark hair? I know him. His name's Adam." She looked at me. "Did you get turned on watching them?"

"It … it was fucking amazing. I thought she was going to die from an orgasm overdose."

She smiled. "Breath-play. It's Adam's thing. If you like, I can introduce you to him."

My heart stalled. I wanted to but … "What's the point? He has a girlfriend."

I wasn't prepared for Melanie's outburst of laughter. "Adam doesn't have a partner. He plays with lots of different people. Men as well as women. Give him some time to take care of her and then I'll take you over to meet him."

Thirty minutes later, I was introduced to Adam, and Melanie had wandered off to pursue her own fun with a tattooed girl she had met at the bar. For the first time in my life I felt tongue-tied. I wanted to submerge myself in the ecstasy I had seen on the face of Adam's play partner, but I wasn't sure how to ask, or even if I would be able to endure it. Plus, I was not prepared to be forced to come in front of a club full of people.

He sensed my unease.

"I never play with someone I've just met," he said. "Why don't we get to know each other better and, if you still want to play with me, we'll arrange some private time together."

* * *

A few weeks later, after many hours of discussion and negotiation, I caught the bus across town to Adam's flat for my first experience of breath-play.

"You don't have to go through with this, you know," Adam said.

I nodded. I had never been so sure of anything. The past few weeks had been an epiphany for me. Experiencing a flogging from a man for the first time, getting used to the restriction of heavy bondage, and being forced to come again and again— under Adam's tutelage, I felt ready to embrace the next step in my journey.

"If you feel it's too much to take, just safeword or tap out. I promise I'll stop immediately and release you."

"I will," I lied. I had no intention of breaking the spell once it had begun.

I followed Adam into his bedroom. His iron bedstead was to be my prison while he worked his magic on my body. At his bidding I removed my clothes and lay down on the bed, breathing in the dark aromas of previous fucks that scented his sheets. Soft rope was looped around my wrists, drawing both hands above my head before being pulled tight and secured to the headboard. Already my cunt was wet with anticipation.

Two more pieces of rope soon had my ankles bound to the foot of the bed with my legs spread wide. A stroke of Adam's fingers along the length of my slit turned my body into a quivering mass of expectation.

"I'm not going to blindfold you," he said. "I need to see your reactions if I'm to keep you safe."

"But I want the blindfold." I hated the whine that rose in my voice, but I was looking forward to the full experience. I wanted a personal replay of his scene in The Vault.

Adam shook his head. "I only do that if I know someone well. This is our first time and I need to see how you react at every stage."

My chest felt hollow with disappointment. I craved the scene I had witnessed. I was about to say more when I saw his hesitation. I was so close to experiencing the thrill of asphyxiation that I had to be careful I didn't blow it. "Of course. I understand." Except I didn't. I wanted the whole fucking experience and I wanted it *now*. I needed the restraint, I wanted the sensory deprivation to heighten everything I felt, and I knew that Adam was a pro. He knew what he was doing. Everything would be fine, but I had to go along with his wishes if I was to get anything, and I was so horny my cunt ached.

I gave Adam a big smile of encouragement. "I'll follow your lead."

His shoulders dropped and he relaxed once more, picking up the wand from the nightstand.

His fingers stroked against my clit until he got the reaction he was looking for and then he pressed the wand against my sensitive spot, securing it in place with duct tape around my thigh. "Are you ready?"

I nodded. Seconds later, an intense vibration shuddered between my legs as Adam flicked the On switch. Arching my back, I groaned and let the electrical stimulation work its enchantment, bringing my flesh alive.

A stinging lash across my abdomen drew a yelp from my throat. Adam swung the leather flogger again and again in a constant rhythm, warming my skin in a sequence of throbbing strikes. I trembled as a series of sensations, simultaneously painful and gratifying, engulfed my body. Each stroke of the whip formed an unholy union with the pulsation of the wand to push me onwards to the climax I craved. Layers of sensation wrapped me in a cocoon where nothing mattered other than feeling, and it wasn't long before I felt the familiarity of a building orgasm. Through gasping breaths, I whimpered. "I'm going to come. Oh, fu—"

My throat contracted under his iron grip. Long fingers squeezing, stopping the oxygen from filling my lungs. Panic flowed through my veins as I tried to gulp in air. A scream died on my lips as I failed to exhale through a constricted larynx. Seconds felt like minutes, minutes grew into hours, and darkness began to fall before my closing eyes. Wrenching my wrists against the ropes, I fought to free myself but it was futile, and my exhausted body grew weaker until . . .

The orgasm ripped through me like an explosion, electrifying my muscles in a dance of ecstasy. My pussy gushed a waterfall that drenched the sheets, and conscious thought abandoned me. My only focus was the ultimate orgasm that tore me apart and reduced my form to a quivering mess.

Adam released my neck and an assault of noise and light bombarded my senses. I was reborn to a world of excess wonder.

As my orgasm dissolved, I sank into the bed exhausted beyond anything I'd ever experienced before. My limbs and body felt leaden, but my mind was soaring. This intense high beat any drugs that I had ever sampled. I was drowning in a sea of bliss and I didn't care if I never returned to reality.

* * *

Reality returned a few months later.

"Jesus, Jess." Adam ran his hands through his hair. "You're becoming obsessed. Can't we spend some time together as friends? I swear you only care about getting off. There's much more to me than that, if you only took the time to actually talk to me."

"We are friends, but I need this." I grabbed his hand and pulled it towards my neck. "I want more. I want you to keep choking me for longer. Please." I hated that I was begging, but our playtime was getting less and less satisfying. For me, at least. The thrill no longer matched the first time Adam had stolen my breath. That time I was scared as well as excited. I guess I had lost the fear and that was taking the edge off the experience. I wanted him to inject it back into our play.

"For longer? No chance. I've pushed my limits for your crazy demands already. It's me who takes responsibility for you and I'm not prepared to take you any further. People die doing what we do when they're not careful."

"But, I'm fine," I pleaded. "Nothing's ever gone wrong."

"That doesn't mean that it won't. I'm not comfortable doing this with you anymore. You're too dangerous. If you're going to keep pushing yourself, find some other mug to play with. Someone who doesn't care what happens to you."

The bastard left after his outburst, leaving me aching with need. Every breath was a painful reminder of the ecstasy I craved. I needed someone to take my breath and lead me into Nirvana, but I wasn't stupid enough to try it alone using a belt. I knew how that shit could wind up. I had to return to The Vault where there would be others willing to help me.

Week after week I dragged myself back to the club. I played like a desperate woman, taking on anyone who had the slightest interest in breath-play, but no one took anything any further than mild choking. I was going crazy. My whole body craved the ultimate climax that grew out of near death. Endless nights with lightweight players did nothing to satisfy the primal need that grew daily inside me and screamed for satisfaction. I even tried baiting my partners: bites to draw blood, a deliberate fist to the balls, pinching, and on one memorable night, I used my teeth to tear foreskin. All that got me was a black eye, but my neck remained unscathed.

Eventually, the local community shunned me, and I was haunted by muttered "red flag" accusations. I was no longer welcomed in The Vault.

I didn't need them anymore. They set themselves on pedestals as edge players, but they were as vanilla as ice cream. I had glimpsed the edge, and I wasn't going to stop until I met it head on. And if I couldn't find what I needed locally then it was time to explore what the online world had to offer.

My fingers danced across the keyboard of my laptop. Why hadn't I tried this before? Had there always been this many kink sites waiting for me to discover them? For the first time in months I felt a glimmer of hope. I wasn't alone in my desires.

One profile stood out among the many and, as luck would have it, he didn't live too far away and was happy to meet up.

* * *

Pulling my coat around me against the wind, I walked the short distance from the railway station to the address I had scribbled on a piece of paper. I was shivering, although whether that was

208

from the evening chill or the anticipation of the night's promised event was impossible to tell.

It wasn't the most salubrious of neighbourhoods. A rusting washing machine littered an overgrown driveway, music blasted from a house fronted by a garden of weeds and a group of teenagers gathered on the street corner, plumes of smoke rising from their shared cigarette to be dispersed by the easterly wind.

Pushing my shoulders back, feigning a confidence I didn't feel, I walked past the group of teens, ignoring their crude catcalls. The locality didn't matter so much as what had been promised to me this evening: the *ultimate* in breath-play.

I stopped outside a boxy semi-detached house with paint peeling from its rotted window frames and checked the address. I had reached my destination. I had hoped for a nicer place, but what did it matter if he gave me what I craved? My finger hovered over the doorbell, a last-minute attack of nerves holding me back. I had two choices: turn around and catch the next train home, or step into the unknown and experience the supreme act of sexual pleasure.

I took a deep breath and pressed the doorbell half expecting it to be defunct, but there was a faint musicality emanating from behind the closed door. I waited an eternity, or so it seemed, before the door opened.

The guy before me looked normal, which went a long way to settling my anxiety. His hair fell to his shoulders and appeared freshly washed, and his clothes were clean too, emitting a soft aroma of a floral, fabric conditioner. From what I could see of the interior of the house behind him, it seemed equally clean and tidy. I relaxed.

"Jess?" His eyebrows raised in a query.

"That's me." I smiled and held out my hand, which he gazed at in amusement.

"That's a little formal, don't you think? Considering what you want me to do to you."

Heat burned my cheeks. I wanted him to take me seriously. I needed this outlet. I had waited far too long. "Um, sorry. You're right. It's Shaun, isn't it?"

209

He nodded and stepped aside. "Are you coming in?"

I stepped into the hallway. He closed the door and locked it with a loud click. I jumped.

"Don't worry. It's not a great neighbourhood. If I don't lock it anyone could wander in."

He led me into a small sitting room that was shabby but clean. A tabby cat lounged on a cushion, staring at me with inquisitive eyes. It was a normal home.

"Can I get you a drink? Tea? Coffee? I don't recommend alcohol before doing this."

"No, thanks." I didn't give a shit for social niceties. It wasn't what I was here for. I was as comfortable with the setting as I could be, so why waste any more time? "You seem nice and all," I said. "You don't need to try and make me feel at home. I'm ready whenever you are."

"Don't you want to talk it through first? It's not without risk. I mean, I'm pretty experienced, but this is extreme and . . . shit happens sometimes."

Oh, fuck. He was sounding like all the others before: *It's too dangerous. You might get hurt.* In other words, *I'm not man enough to give you what you need.*

Hands on hips, I squared up to him. "Are you saying I travelled all this way for nothing?" I felt the anger growing. "Did you lead me on, making promises you don't intend to keep? If it's a *vanilla* fuck you're after, you're on the wrong website, Shaun."

A bruise-inducing grip on my arm caught my attention. Finally, he was showing me a sample of what I was expecting.

"I'm deadly serious." Shaun released my arm, leaving a delightful ache in its place. "You're not the first woman to turn up eager to play on the edge, but very few have the stamina or the nerve to take it all the way. In your messages you said you'd been let down by men who couldn't fulfil your needs. Well, I've been let down by women who promised they could go all the way. It turned out they didn't have what it takes. They panicked and ran."

"Not me." I stared him in the eyes, noticing how much darker they seemed after his outburst. "Hands around my throat don't cut it anymore. I need to be taken to the brink. I want you to steal my breath until there's nothing left in my lungs and I'm fighting you for my survival. I want to feel the darkness come down. I know there are risks involved. I'm not naïve. Take me there. Please. No one else has been able to."

I could see him considering his options. I knew Shaun wanted his release as much as I needed mine. I held my breath and prayed.

"Okay, if you're sure?"

A smile split my face. "I've been ready for a long time."

Shaun led me upstairs to a bedroom he had already prepared for my arrival. "Did you bring it?"

I pulled the battery-operated wand from my bag and handed it over. "I put new batteries in it today. It'll last as long as you do."

"Hopefully." He put the wand on the top of a plastic-sheeted nightstand. "Take off your clothes and get on the bed."

It was finally going to happen. I fumbled the buttons of my blouse in my haste to remove it. Nervous anticipation stole my co-ordination and I stumbled while pulling off my jeans. Finally, I removed my underwear and stood before him in all my naked glory. From the look on his face he seemed more than happy with what he saw.

"Lie on top of the board on the bed, with your head at the bottom."

Shaun had laid a piece of wooden board along the length of the rubber-sheeted bed. It was roughly two feet wide and six feet long, with four long leather straps attached to it at regular intervals. Pillows had been stacked underneath it, at the top of the bed so that it was inclined.

I inched my way onto the board expecting it to wobble and overturn, but it was surprisingly stable. I reminded myself that Shaun had done this many times before. He was practiced. He had perfected his technique and now I was going to reap the benefits of his experience. I settled into position with my feet at the raised end. "Like this?"

"Almost," he said. "Shuffle down slightly so that your head is further down."

I did as he instructed.

"That's better. Now spread your legs slightly while I put this in place."

I opened my legs and felt his rough fingers against my cunt.

"You're wet already." He smirked, positioned the battery-operated wand against my clit and pushed my legs together to hold it in place.

Even though the wand hadn't been switched on, the mere pressure of it against that sensitive nub of flesh was already turning me on.

Cold leather wrapped around my ankles as Shaun tightened the straps, securing my feet to the board. He did the same with the remaining three straps. When he had finished, I was restrained at my ankles, my thighs, my waist (which also secured my arms to my side) and my chest. I was completely immobile, held fast with my feet raised and my head down. I flexed my arms against the straps, savouring the pinch of the leather on my skin. For the first time since my early days with Adam, I began to feel the old excitement rising in my soul.

"I'm going to ask you one more time," said Shaun. "Are you sure you want to go through with this?"

I nodded, banging the back of my head against the wooden board. "I'm one hundred percent sure."

"Okay, let's begin." Shaun crossed the room and picked up a piece of folded material from the nightstand. He flicked it open. It was a pillowcase. He returned to my side. "Raise your head."

I did as he said and my view of the cracked ceiling disappeared as Shaun placed the pillowcase over my head. The cotton fabric had the same laundered aroma as his clothes, and I took a deep breath.

"I'm not going to speak again other than to check in with you. You need to be prepared for me to begin at any time. Do you understand?"

"Yes." My voice was a hoarse whisper and my whole body tensed in readiness. My skin goose-bumped as Shaun's fingers brushed against my thighs when he reached for the wand and turned it on. Oh, God. The instant vibration against my clit set my nerves alight. It was finally going to happen.

The cold water shocked me, and I sucked in a mouthful of air. Or rather I didn't. The water soaked into the fabric of the pillowcase, moulding it across my nose and mouth and creating a barrier to my breath. No matter how hard my lungs fought to inhale, nothing happened. This was unlike anything I had ever experienced before, and my body fought against it. Blood thundered through my veins trying to carry the life-giving oxygen to all parts of my body, but there was nothing to give. Instinctively, my limbs railed against the straps in panic.

The water stopped and a thin stream of air seeped through the wet fabric and into my lungs. My panic subsided and I became aware of a rising heat between my legs as the wand wove its magic. Tingling travelled from my cunt through my body, teasing me with the promise of a climax that would shatter all my previous experiences. I began to pant.

A voice next to my ear spoke. "Are you all right? Do you want me to stop?"

I shook my head. "Don't you dare." My words were muffled by the cloth, but I heard Shaun's acknowledgment.

The cold water hit my face in another breath-stopping torrent, and I tensed against the restraints. The taut leather bit into my flesh, mocking my bid to escape. Burning erupted in my chest as my lungs battled to draw air through the sodden cloth, but it was hopeless. The wet fabric had created a perfect seal across my nose and mouth. Flashes of colour exploded beneath the blindfold as I bucked and writhed against the drowning sensations, whilst the wand continued to torment my pussy.

As darkness began to descend, taking away any conscious thoughts I had, the flow ceased and once more I was able to breathe. The sodden pillowcase moulded against the contours of my face made each breath a feat of endurance, and yet each tiny inhalation fed the orgasm that was building deep inside my trembling body. Fear and pleasure were conspiring to propel me to the greatest climax of my life.

Again, Shaun's voice filtered through the cacophony of sensations bombarding me. "Are you okay? I think we're done."

"No, no. Please don't stop." The words scraped my throat as I forced them out. "Longer this time."

I felt him move away, and the sound of running taps from the nearby bathroom broke through the pounding of my heart and the whoosh of blood as it gushed past my ears. Thank God Shaun was prepared to push further.

I opened my mouth against the soaked fabric trying to take as deep a breath as possible and was flooded with a fresh gush of water. My lungs burned as they tried in vain to expand. It felt like my nose and mouth had been pinched closed. Nothing could breach the wet barrier. My chest heaved as I kept trying to breathe, and the burning evolved into a deep, nagging pain that contrasted with the building pleasure between my thighs. My cunt was as wet and dripping as my face. Then the darkness began to fall once more.

Simultaneously, colour exploded through the darkness and a fire erupted in an orgasmic burst of pleasure that I had never achieved before. Fireworks danced, blinding me even beneath the confines of the pillowcase, and a discordance of noise filled my ears. The orgasm tore through my soul and sent bolts of electricity through every shredded nerve of my body. I shook within the leather restraints and tried to scream but there was nothing left in my lungs to make any sound.

The pressure of the wand against my clit continued to build, forcing one orgasm after another from my weakening body, but now terror was advancing, usurping the throne that pleasure had held. My body was still coming despite my rising panic. I needed to breathe.

My mouth opened to call a halt to the waterboarding, but only silence slipped from my lips. Shaun continued to pour the water onto my face, oblivious to my panic. Pain ripped through my lungs and my fingers danced against the wooden board in a futile attempt to tap out.

214

The leather restraints constricted. I wanted to scream when I realised that Shaun hadn't tightened them. There was no longer any control over my limbs. My muscles spasmed and jerked, fighting the bonds. Something snapped. Did I hear it or only feel it? I couldn't tell through the fog that was drowning my brain, but an agonising pain shattered my left arm.

I pleaded with Shaun to stop but he couldn't hear my silence.

The pain spread from my lungs to my head. A terrible pounding surged through my brain with each frantic beat of my heart and still my body orgasmed relentlessly. It was too much. I wanted it to stop. I needed to breathe again.

The pressure inside my skull grew until the agony was unbearable. Every cell in my body was shrieking but no one could hear. Then, the pressure detonated.

The hood was ripped from my head and through a blood-filtered haze I watched Shaun trying to undo the leather straps. His mouth moved, but no sounds reached me. He faced me and I felt the breath of his words against my cheek as he silently shouted. He lifted my arm and I felt nothing. It slumped onto the bed as he released it.

What was happening? I felt like a prisoner inside my body and the world had turned crimson.

Shaun snatched his phone from the nightstand and jabbed the screen with a finger while he paced. Turning towards me with fear in his face I watched his lips mouth the words, "*Ambulance, urgently!*"

I closed my eyes and sobbed in silence.

ABOUT THE AUTHOR
SUZANNE FOX

Suzanne Fox grew up in Staffordshire and now lives in the far west of Cornwall with her husband and three crazy cats. Suzanne writes both horror and erotica, occasionally combining both genres, and has had short stories published in magazines and multiple anthologies. She has an affection for the darker aspects of sex and BDSM, and loves to incorporate this into her writing. She hopes that you enjoy reading her contribution to this exciting collection and invites you to follow her on Facebook and on her Amazon author page.

Facebook: https://www.facebook.com/suzannefoxerotica/

Amazon: https://www.amazon.co.uk/Suzanne-Fox/e/B073SJX746

ABOUT THE EDITOR
DAVID OWAIN HUGHES

David Owain Hughes is a word-slinger of horror and crime fiction, who grew up on trashy B-movies from the age of five which helped rapidly instil in him a vivid imagination. He's had multiple short stories published in various online magazines and anthologies, along with articles, reviews and interviews. He's written for *This Is Horror*, *Blood Magazine*, and *Horror Geeks Magazine*.

Hughes is the author of six horror novels, four short story collections and a plethora of novellas. Although he predominately writes within the bracket of horror and its multiple sub-genres, he's recently branched out into crime fiction and is slowly carving out a superb series of crime/noir thrillers under the umbrella title of *South Wales*.

Facebook: https://www.facebook.com/DOHughesAuthor

Amazon: http://www.amazon.co.uk/David-Owain-Hughes/e/B00L708P2M

Webpage: http://david-owain-hughes.wix.com/horrorwriter

Goodreads: https://www.goodreads.com/author/show/4877205.David_Owain_Hughes

Twitter: https://twitter.com/DOHUGHES32

ABOUT THE EDITOR
JONATHAN EDWARD ONDRASHEK

Jonathan Edward Ondrashek is a horror/dark fantasy writer and editor who hisses and screeches at sunlight. He's the author of The Human-Undead War trilogy (*Dark Intentions*, *Patriarch*, and *A Kingdom's Fall*). His short stories have appeared in numerous anthologies, including the highly acclaimed *VS: US vs UK Horror* series, *Nothing's Sacred Volume 5*, and *It Came From the Garage*!, which featured Stephen King and Guy N. Smith, among others. He also co-edited *Deranged*, *F*ck the Rules*, *What Goes Around,* and *Man Behind the Mask*, boundary-pushing anthologies featuring work from established and new voices in the horror genre. If he isn't reading, editing, or writing, he's probably drinking beer and making his wife regret marrying a lunatic. Feel free to stalk him on social media.

Facebook: https://www.facebook.com/JondrashekAuthor

Website: https://www.jondrashek.com